Order this book online at www.trafford.com
or email orders@trafford.com

Most Trafford titles are also available at major online book retailers.

Printed in the United States of America.

ISBN: 978-1-4907-0584-2 (sc)
ISBN: 978-1-4907-0586-6 (hc)
ISBN: 978-1-4907-0585-9 (e)

Library of Congress Control Number: 2013911441

Trafford rev. 07/31/2013

www.trafford.com

North America & international
toll-free: 1 888 232 4444 (USA & Canada)
fax: 812 355 4082

JOEY WILLIS

TO ANOTHER WORLD

A.J. Kenyon

Illustrations by
Tom Kenyon

For my beloved children,
Tom, Peter, and Jonita.
May all your wishes come true.

About the Author

Anita Kenyon lives in a seaside suburb of Melbourne. This is her first novel, which has been inspired by her love of telling stories to her three children. Anita believes that fantasy lives in all of us.

CONTENTS

CHAPTER 1

Entering Another World

Joey Willis gazed at the seagulls and the deep-blue waves of the ocean. His thin, long bare feet quickly walked along the beach. The noisy sea gushed on the shore, the glary sun shined, and the wind blew against his face. He smelled the scent of sea salt and dead sea creatures. He decided to get his feet wet, and without warning, the cold waves quickly splashed against his body.

Olivia ran behind him. He enjoyed his sister's company, and she followed him wherever he went. Joey recently turned eleven; he was two and a half years older than his sister, and he was very protective of her. They both enjoyed the beach and playing games together.

With his plastic toy shovel, Joey dug in the sand. "Olivia, do you want to make a sand castle with me? We could make our castle look like medieval time and play fantasy games." Joey had a *th* whistling sound with nearly every word he pronounced; his front right tooth was slightly chipped.

Olivia had been occupying herself with a large seashell, using it to dig in the soft, smooth sand. She turned around and looked up at her brother, who was now standing directly in front of her. With the sun glaring on her clear, smooth face, her brown eyes squinted. She sheltered her eyes with her hand. "Yeah, why not, it would be fun." She glanced at Joey's shovel. "Give me your shovel, I need it more than you do," she demanded.

Joey, disappointed with her, moved his head from side to side. "No way, this is my shovel, you can use your hands. Anyway, I'll be doing most of the work." He slammed his shovel down and dug his way through the sand.

Olivia stood up and crossed her arms. "Then I'm not going to help you build your stupid sand castle, you can do it yourself." She turned away from her brother and wandered off towards the other end of the beach.

Joey did not pay much attention to his little sister. He was used to her demands and tantrums. All he wanted to do was to enjoy the beach and build a sand castle. So he continued to dig, mould, and pat the sand. In his mind, he pictured a spectacular castle.

After a few hours, he finally finished the castle. He also found seashells and pretended they were armoured men with horses and swords. Joey was sure Olivia would love the castle. He looked around the beach for her, but there was no sign of her. He searched in every direction, but she was nowhere to be seen. Joey was getting worried. He continued to look around the beach.

"Olivia, Olivia, where are you?" he yelled. Joey feared something horrible might have happened to her. He had been so occupied with his sand castle he had not noticed where she had wandered. He ran to the other end of the beach. "Olivia, Olivia, where are you?"

Joey watched the water, but the waves had washed off all traces of footsteps. *Where could she be? What could have happened to her?* He quickly turned around and looked behind him, to his right and then his left, but still there was no sign of Olivia.

In the not-so-far distance, he noticed a cave and ran towards it. "Olivia, Olivia, I'm sorry, I didn't mean to upset you! You can have the shovel. Olivia, where are you?"

Without hesitation, he entered the cave. *Maybe she had wandered inside?* Farther inside the cave, he stumbled on some sharp rocks. "Ouch!" The rocks slightly grazed his bare feet. He wished he had had time to put on his runners. "Olivia, Olivia, where are you?" he cried.

The cave was cool and musty, and the smell was like the dead fish at the seafood markets. The farther Joey walked into the cave, the darker it became. He desperately needed a torch. He could barely see.

Along the side of the cave, Joey stumbled across a few burning sticks and matches to give light. It was clear to him other people had been here. He quickly grabbed a burning stick and lit it up. "Olivia."

With the burning stick held tightly in his hand, he continued his search inside the cave. He heard water running and little noises. It sounded like crabs or some sea creatures scuffling. He walked farther into the cave until he came across something on the ground. He quickly realized it was Olivia's favourite red jumper. He picked it up and held it close to himself. Now he was sure Olivia had passed through here. *Where could she have gone with no torch?* Joey was very determined to find her.

Finally, the rocks cleared and the ground became smooth. He could easily run on the hard, cold sand. "Olivia, Olivia, it's me, Joey, where are you? Olivia!" he yelled.

At last, Joey came to the end of the cave; there was still no Olivia. With the burning stick he noticed pictures on the cave walls. Pictures of hands and footprints painted yellow, red, and purple. It looked as if peoples' feet had walked on the walls with paint. He touched the cave walls to feel the drawings. The artwork was incredible, and the drawings were smooth—all except one yellow left hand. He touched the palm of the hand with his fingers. It felt like a real hand had wedged itself through the rock. He looked to his right and noticed another hand similar to the yellow wedged hand, but it was a right hand and red in colour. Joey was amazed and wondered how a cave wall could have prints of hands and feet so clearly moulded into it.

He searched around the cave for a position to hold his burning torch. He found a pile of rocks near the cave paintings. He carefully placed the torch between the rocks, making sure the torch would not fall, and then he tied Olivia's jumper around his waist.

The cave paintings made him feel drawn to press his hands against the grooved yellow—and red-painted handprints. Once he placed his hands on the paintings, he felt himself being pulled toward the wall. He could not understand what was happening to him. He was frightened. He tried to pull his hands off, but the force was too strong. His hands were stuck on the cave wall.

Before Joey had a chance to call for help, the cave started to spin around him until he could no longer see the cave. All he could see was a coil of colours. It was like being in another world or another dimension. Out of fear, he tightly closed his eyes, hoping that by not seeing anything, things might get back to normal. Joey was terrified.

Finally, his hands became free. He tried to open his eyes, but a strong wind made him feel like he was inside a hurricane. He scrunched himself into a ball like a fearful creature trying to hide from danger. Then everything went black.

* * *

Gradually Joey regained consciousness. He was no longer scrunched into a ball; instead, he was lying flat on his back. He opened his eyelids and saw bright red above him. He was not inside the cave but outside somewhere else. It was odd because the sky was bright red with yellow stars. He turned his head while still lying flat on the ground and noticed the ground was purple, the dirt and all. He tried to sit up, but relented because he almost lost his balance.

Joey took a really good look around him and realized he was on a cliff. *I'm trapped, and there's no way of getting down from here. How will I be able to get out of this?* He was afraid. He was stuck on a purple ledge on the verge of falling down a cliff. As far as he was concerned, if Olivia went through the same ordeal, she could have already fallen. She could be dead.

This was a very weird-looking place. There was no sign of the cave, which meant Joey could not get back to the beach or his home near the beach for help. "Help, someone, anyone, helppp!" he called out, his voice echoing.

Joey carefully peeped down the cliff and noticed funny-coloured trees. Some were bright orange, some were bright blue and others were red. *What is this place? It could not be Earth. Am I in heaven? Could I have died in that cave?* Joey knew people could not go through walls.

He slowly tried to sit up, but the ledge was crumbling around him. This was no ordinary ground. It was fragile and crumbly. He turned to his side, but the ledge moved, and before Joey could say or do anything, suddenly it collapsed. He was falling down the cliff. He quickly grabbed a branch from a small bright-orange tree beside him.

Joey's heart was pounding; sweat poured down his face. The branch was hurting his hands. If he did not get help soon, he would fall and die. His legs were dangling in the air, and the branch was not going to hold him much longer. "Help, help, someone, anyone, please help me. I'm going to fall, I can't hold on much longer!" he screamed.

He heard the branch crack, and then it suddenly broke. Joey was falling through the air. "Arghhhhhhhhh!" He knew this was the end for him. He was going to die.

Swoosh. His back landed on something soft. He opened his eyes and noticed he was still in the air. Beside him, he could see red wings flapping, and it was not an ordinary feathered wing; it was scaly. He had no idea what it was, but whatever it was, it had saved him. All Joey could do was hold on to the scales with both of his hands. *Phew! What a relief.*

Whatever it was that saved him suddenly landed on a flat surface below the cliff. Its wings lowered so he could jump off. He was so shocked he did not want to see what had just saved him. Without looking back, he frantically ran in the opposite direction. His heart was pounding and pounding. *Banggg!* A large yellow tail dropped right in front of him. This was it; he was trapped, and there was no way he could escape.

Joey slowly turned around and lifted his head to look at what it was. What he could see standing only metres away from him terrified him. He screamed again, "Arrrrgghhh!" The scaly creature was a monster. It was twice the size of an elephant. The creature had a long yellow scaly tail, red scaly wings, huge sharp teeth, a long nose, and four large stumpy feet with claws almost bigger than its head.

Joey was horrified. Even though this creature had saved his life, he was sure it had only saved him for lunch. Joey looked around and tried to run in the other direction, but the creature blazed fire from its mouth. He stayed glued to the spot.

"Who a-are y-y-you? Please don't eat m-me!" cried Joey. His whole body was shaking, and suddenly, he accidentally wet his pants.

The creature stood still. His huge round black mirrored eyes stared at Joey. "I do not want to eat you," he answered in a sweet, soft tone. A very long tongue poked out as he spoke. "My name is Alcon, I am a good-luck dragon. In your case, you were very lucky I came along. I mean you no harm, I am here only to help you. What is your name? And why are you here?"

Joey let out a huge sigh of relief and tried to regain himself. He stood still and looked at Alcon with pure amazement. Seeing a real dragon and one who could speak to him was incredible. He knew many stories about dragons, but this one was for real.

"Well, Alcon, or whoever you are, my name is Joey Willis. I was trying to look for my sister, Olivia. Have you seen a small girl? She has straight, long brown hair. She was wearing purple shorts and a white T-shirt. Well, she looks just like me, but in a female version." For the first time, Joey smiled.

Alcon stared at Joey as if he were studying him. With his long tongue still poking out, he replied, "I don't think I've seen your sister. Maybe the druggons have taken her. Are you from Earth?"

"Yes, I'm from Earth. Who are druggons? And what is this place? Where am I, if I'm not on Earth . . . and what have they done with Olivia?" asked Joey.

"Druggons are bad dragons. Their bodies are black with red wings. If they have your sister, they'd probably try and use her to return to Earth. You are on Magical World. Here, the good and bad could happen to you. That depends on what you or your sister has done on Earth."

"What do you mean by what my sister and I have done on Earth?"

Alcon stood up, stomping his four legs to pass behind Joey towards the red river. He drank with his long slithery tongue like a giant puppy. After a good ten minutes of drinking, he stopped and moved closer towards Joey. "If you have done bad things on Earth, you would have created a bad energy force around you. This would give you problems here. You see, the bad energy would come back to you and your sister ten times stronger. If, on the other hand, you or Olivia did good and wonderful things on Earth, only wonderful things would come your way. Can you remember the last incidences between you and your sister?"

Joey's legs were getting tired. He sat on a purple rock, his elbows on his knees and his head between his hands. He was silent for a few minutes. "Well, we were both on the beach, and I asked Olivia if she would build a sand castle with me. She wanted my shovel, but I didn't let her have it, and I told her that I needed it more than she did. She became very upset with me and ran off to the other side of the beach."

Alcon raised his head. "The druggons may have been disguised as humans and persuaded her to go with them. She was angry with you, which would have created bad energies. The druggons love bad energies. It's like feeding a lamb to a tiger."

Joey glanced up at Alcon. He threw a purple rock into the red river and shook his head. "No, she is not a bad person. If what you are saying is true, then why didn't they get me? I was mean to her. I told her she couldn't have the shovel."

"What did you do after you found out Olivia was not on the beach?" asked Alcon.

Joey stood up, gazed around, and walked closer to Alcon. "I went to look for Olivia. I felt bad for not letting her use my shovel."

Alcon looked sad for Joey. "That is why the druggons were not attracted to you, because of your good thoughts towards your sister and your wonderful idea to build a sand castle together."

"My sister didn't do anything wrong. She wouldn't have had bad thoughts about me. We've had plenty of disagreements before, but nothing like this has ever happened to her."

Alcon stomped loudly towards an orange tree. With his sharp white teeth, he swiftly broke off a fruit. He swallowed the fruit in one big gulp and then turned towards Joey. "I cannot explain why this happened now with your sister. There is no use worrying about what happened. That is not going to get your sister back. You need to focus on finding her and, hopefully, saving her."

Joey came closer to Alcon. "How can I save my sister? Could you help me? Could you help me find these druggons and bring my sister back to me?"

"I don't know if I can help you. Druggons are very mean dragons. They are twice my size, and their magical powers are very powerful. I don't think any good-luck dragon like me has ever beaten their powers."

"Then what is powerful enough to beat them? How much time do we have?" asked Joey.

"The unicorns have great powers over the druggons. They live near the cowchees. The cowchees worship them, and they are very friendly towards earth-people. Well, you could call them angels."

Joey could not believe what he had just seen and heard: Alcon, cowchees, druggons, unicorns, Magical World, purple ground, red rivers and sky, bright-coloured trees and plants with edible fruits. He looked all around him. This place was so different from Earth; it seemed much more beautiful. The air was very still. The weather was not too cold or too hot, and the atmosphere was so calm and peaceful.

Joey's stomach was loud with hunger noises. He climbed the same orange tree Alcon ate from and picked the same fruit. "Alcon," Joey said, jumping down from the tree with the orange fruit still in his hand, "can you take me to the cowchees? Please say yes. I have to find out as much as I can about these druggons. There must be a way to get Olivia back." He took a bite from the fruit.

Alcon stared at Joey with his huge mirrored eyes and blinked slowly. He sat on an old tree stump with his long scaly tail wrapped around a branch. "Okay, I will take you to the cowchees, but we will have to walk, just in case the druggons see me flying and follow me to their home."

"Great, let's go. By the way, this fruit is very nice, what's it called?

"That, my friend, is called a sario fruit."

"Mmmmm, very delicious. It's very sweet, and it tastes like sponge cake. I have never seen this type of fruit before."

"That's because Earth never grows such a fruit. The food grown here is perfect. We have no junk food in Magical World—all our food is very healthy and nutritious."

"Wow, so I can eat as much as I want and never get sick or fat or have tooth decay?"

"That's true," Alcon answered, nodding.

CHAPTER 2

Encounter with a Druggon

Joey and Alcon started their journey walking through Magical World's forest. The ground was soft and comfortable under Joey's feet. Wearing only his black shorts and red short-sleeved shirt, and Olivia's sweater still around his waist, he was not cold or hot; the weather was just perfect.

"Alcon, this place, it's like a dream come true. I mean, apart from my sister missing, everything here is what any kid would dream of having on Earth. Tell me, is there anything else I can eat here?"

Alcon leapt from one huge rock to another, almost stumbling and losing his balance. He jumped off a rock and continued to stomp through the blue grass and bright-coloured tree shrubs. "You can eat anything you want. The trees and plants provide all the food you need, including the leaves and branches. You don't have to worry—none of the plants are poisonous to eat. You never have to go hungry here. You should try and drink from the red river."

Joey turned towards Alcon. "What does it taste like?"

Alcon pointed his long nose in front of him. Before he could say anything, Joey ran towards the red river.

It was the most beautiful view Joey had ever seen in his entire life. The red river flowed down between purple rocks like a waterfall. All the trees of different colours surrounded the river. To Joey, this was a banquet. He scooped some liquid in his hands and drank it. "Mmmmm, this tastes like strawberry soda." Above his head he saw a huge black tree with black sticks. He picked one and chewed it. "Mmmmm, this tastes like liquorice, my favourite." He tried every fruit tree and small shrub he could see, and to his delight, he enjoyed everything. His stomach was so full. He felt completely energized, and none of the food made him feel ill.

Alcon also helped himself to a good meal. "We're going to need every bit of energy for our trip, Joey, so eat up," said Alcon, munching a blueberry pie.

The trip was long. Joey's legs were tired. "When is it going to get dark around here? We must have been walking for hours," Joey questioned.

Alcon was ahead of him. He stopped and turned to face Joey. When he turned, his long tail swished through the shrubs and accidentally toppled a few small trees. "Oh dear, I have forgotten, you earth-people tire and sleep. I have to confess, my friend, here in Magical World, there never is night. The time always stays the same."

"So where are these cowchees?" asked Joey, scrunching his nose and frowning.

"They are not easy to find. They could be anywhere. They travel all the time. I haven't seen them for a while. The druggons can never know where they are."

"But you said the unicorns and cowchees are more powerful than the druggons. Can't they fight them or destroy them," asked Joey, scratching his nose.

Alcon drew closer to Joey, carefully looking around him as though someone might see or hear them, then he whispered, "You must never think bad or ever suggest such a notion. Cowchees are like angels. They would never harm any creature. You must promise never to talk about destroying anything ever again, not on this world. Bad—"

"Yes, yes, I know," interrupted Joey. "Bad things could happen to me, but I'm getting tired of all this. I just want Olivia back." He sat on the soft ground to rest his legs. He was becoming agitated and frustrated with the situation he was in. "What if we never find these cowchees? I just want to take my little sister home where she can be safe."

"Calm down, my friend. You have to be patient. We will find the cowchees! I always find them. Besides, they shouldn't be too far away."

"I am patient. I just wish Olivia was here with me. I'm feeling very tired." Joey could not say anything anymore. He placed his head on the soft ground. The smell of the dirt reminded him of grape jelly crystals. His mum always made grape jelly. He wished he were at home. Joey fell asleep and dreamed of being home with his sister.

* * *

Slowly Joey opened his eyes. He had to try and remember where he was, and then he realized he was still in Magical World and that this was not a bad dream. After he rubbed his eyes for a few minutes, he noticed something move in front of him.

What he was seeing was the most beautiful creature he had ever laid eyes on. It was a white horse with wings and a horn between the ears on its head. Its wings glittered in many different colours. Joey sat up and stared into the creature's eyes. Then he remembered what Alcon told him about the unicorns. "Are you here to help me find my sister? You're a unicorn, aren't you? Alcon told me about you having great powers over the druggons. Could you please help me rescue my sister?"

The unicorn didn't move or make a sound. Joey was not sure whether it could speak. Normally, animals did not speak, but Alcon did, and this was Magical World. Something rustled in the yellow bushes behind the unicorn. Joey had to rub his eyes again just to be sure of what he was seeing was true. Next to the unicorn appeared the most beautiful girl he had ever seen. She wore a shiny red gown, and a red cloak hung on her back. Her skin was white, and her eyes were bright blue. She smiled at Joey and walked closer to him. He could see glittery wings on her back, just like the unicorn's wings. They were a glorious sight to see together.

"Joey, my name is Astina. I'm a cowchee. Alcon told me about your situation with your sister, Olivia."

"Astina," Joey smiled as he instantly fell in love with her. "Hey, you look like my age. I'm eleven, how old are you?" asked Joey.

"No, I'm eight years old, I think, so my father says." She turned around to look at the unicorn. "And this is Erac, my unicorn friend. Erac, come and meet Joey." She held her hand towards Erac.

Erac trotted close to Astina with the glorious various colours continued to flow behind him. Joey quickly stood up and walked towards Astina and Erac. He tried to touch Erac, but Erac pulled his front legs up high. "Neigh."

"Erac, it's okay, Joey won't hurt you. He is Alcon's friend, and I'm sure he wants to be our friend too." Astina held her arm up high to try and reach for his head to calm him down. Erac settled and slowly moved nearer to Joey. "Go on, you can touch him now," said Astina graciously.

Joey touched Erac's mane and his head; his white fur felt soft and silky. He was careful with his sharp horn that poked out from his head. Erac stood still while Joey wrapped his arms around his head. He hugged him like a soft toy and closed his eyes. Joey felt a wave of energy go through his body, with tingly feelings surrounding him. He felt good, a little overwhelmed, but totally relaxed. When he opened his eyes, he noticed his arms had changed colour—to bright blue. He pulled away from Erac and stared wide-eyed at his hands, legs, and feet. His whole body had changed to a bright blue. "Astina, why has my body turned blue?"

Astina looked surprised. She went silent for a few minutes, then smiled and held Joey's hand. "Erac likes you. He has energized you with his powers. Only a special creature can receive this from a unicorn. Apparently, you are the Chosen One, and we are very lucky to have found you." With that, she kneeled on the ground and bowed her head down in front of Joey.

Joey carefully lifted up Astina. "Please don't do that, please stand up. What do you mean I have powers? Will I stay this colour all the time?"

"In this world, yes, your skin colour will stay blue. But don't be ashamed of it. The druggons will never harm you. They will think you're powerful, and yes, you can be very powerful now. But if the druggons realize you haven't been here very long, they may very well still harm you. You have so much to learn about your new gift before you are able to use your great powers." Astina carefully peered around as though someone might see or hear them.

"What great powers? I'm just a boy. How can I have great powers?"

"There are always reasons why things happen. Your sister being taken by the druggons has brought you here. You were supposed to come here—this proves it. The unicorns were waiting for you. They have helped you receive your great powers."

"Is my face blue too?"

"Yes, I'm afraid so, your face is very blue, but you look very nice." Astina giggled.

"What if my sister doesn't recognize me? Will I ever be able to go back home with her? And will I be blue on Earth?" asked Joey anxiously, still staring at his blue hands and legs in disbelief.

"Trust me, your sister will recognize you. Remember, this is Magical World, you may never want to go back to Earth. You might like it here more." Astina put her arms around Joey and comforted him.

Joey pushed Astina away. "*No!* My parents will worry. I can't put them through that. Anyway, apart from the nice free food here, I love my home on Earth, and so does Olivia!" shouted Joey. "Now tell me, how I can get my sister back? Where are these druggons? Now that I'm blue, I'm sure there won't be a problem for me to frighten them away."

"You don't understand, Joey, these druggons are very intelligent. You cannot just walk up to them and demand Olivia back. We need to work a plan. You really need to learn more about your powers. Believe me, no other earth-being has, or could ever have, the power you have. There is so much you can do here apart from just saving your sister. You are the Chosen One, the one we have been waiting for. Even though this is Magical World, there is so much wrongdoing here. The druggons, especially Villazian, the master of all the druggons, plot horrible situations to a lot of creatures in our world." Again, Astina briskly moved her head around as though someone or something might have heard or sighted them.

Joey stood there and watched Erac and Astina. He slowly peered over his right and then his left shoulder. "Where is Alcon?"

"Oh, Alcon went back to his cave. He will be visiting the cowchees later. I gave him directions to our home. He said he would meet us there. Come, I will show you the way."

Joey followed Astina and Erac through the bushes. The air smelt like lollies. Astina and Erac were beautiful. Joey could not keep his eyes off them. He admired their glittery wings and the flow of colours they left behind as they walked. "Astina, what colour is my hair now? Is that blue too?"

Astina smiled. "No, your hair is still brown. Just your skin and your eyes are blue."

"You know, you and Erac are the most stunning creatures I have ever seen."

Astina's face blushed in different colours and then she giggled. "Thank you, Joey, that's nice of you to say."

"Why is your face changing different colours?" asked Joey.

"I'm just a little embarrassed by what you said. I suppose it's my way of blushing." Astina blushed more colours.

Erac also understood; he moved closer to Joey and bumped gently on his side. He then lowered his front legs to the ground in front of him. Joey stopped to pat Erac. He didn't know why Erac had lowered himself. He turned and glanced at Astina.

"He wants you to sit on his back so that you don't have to walk. He knows how much you humans tire so quickly. Go on, jump on."

Joey carefully climbed on Erac's back. He was so soft and cuddly, his wings so colourful and glittery. Joey snuggled close to him and enjoyed the ride. It was nothing like a horse ride. It was very smooth, like being in a car but gliding through the air. This was very magical indeed.

Bang! an explosion of fire flamed in front of Astina.

Erac and Astina quickly turned and flew in the opposite direction. "Hold on, Joey, we must try to escape. Erac, go quickly, a druggon has sighted us!" yelled Astina.

Erac and Astina flew very fast. Joey held tightly to Erac's mane. They were going so fast that he had not had the chance to look back. All he could hear behind him was the loud screaming roar from the druggon. Flames swished past them in midair, scarcely missing them and hitting a tree instead. Joey kept thinking about his powers and what he could quickly do to save their lives. He wished he knew how to use his powers. After what Astina had said, he tried to imagine being powerful.

Erac flew at lightning speed followed by Astina only a few centimetres behind as they raced and dodged the colourful trees, rocks, and mountains with the druggon only a few metres behind them. Joey quickly turned his head and saw a strong flame blaze from the druggon's mouth that almost touched Erac's tail. "Quickly, Erac, he's catching up!" yelled Joey.

CHAPTER 3

Crystals and a Castle

Erac glided between some trees and then suddenly swooped inside a small cave. He was much smaller than the druggon, and the cave entrance was much too tiny for the druggon to fit through. Because of their speed, Erac and Astina managed to slip into the cave, out of the druggon's sight.

The small cave progressively became larger once they were well inside the entrance. Joey guessed that the cave covered quite a large area of Magical World. It was like a huge city, and it looked like they had lost the druggon.

On a clear patch of ground, Astina landed gracefully, followed by Erac and Joey. "That was Megram. He's one of Villazian's allies. He's not as powerful, but he will do anything for Villazian. We still have to be careful, they can make themselves small and try to look for us here, but something stopped them. Tell me, Joey, what were you thinking while we were escaping from them?" asked Astina.

Joey jumped off Erac and gave him a good hug for saving him. "I was thinking about what you said earlier, the great powers I should have now that I am blue."

Astina sighed and looked relieved. "Good. Megram saw your colour, he probably read some of your mind. You did very well—I mean, while you thought about your powers, he must have read your thoughts, which would have made him think you knew how to use your powers. That must have scared him away."

Joey walked around the cave. It was covered with crystals. He could feel their energy. The walls were purple, but the crystals were radiant and had so many different colours. "Wow, just look at this place, this is heavenly," said Joey. He turned around and looked at Astina and Erac. "Are these crystals magic?"

Astina nodded. "Every one of these crystals is magic with healing powers. Each of these crystals are on Earth too, but scattered all over the countries. On Magical World, you can find all the crystals that are scattered on Earth in these caves, including gold. Also, their healing powers are far greater than the ones on Earth." She picked up a pink stone. "Look at this one." Astina handed Joey the crystal.

He held on to the crystal with his right hand. After a few moments, the crystal made him feel warm and relaxed. The small scratches he had on his skin instantly healed in front of his eyes. "Wow, this would be great on Earth. Can I take some home with me?" asked Joey.

Astina smiled and stared at him. She shook her head. "No, I don't think you'll be able to take any of these crystals back to Earth with you. Don't ask me why, but that's just how it is."

"Oh . . . I see." Joey waited until Astina and Erac had turned their backs. He then quickly slipped the pink crystal into his pocket. All Joey could think about was how many lives the crystal could save on Earth. "Does that mean if people die here, you can bring them back to life?"

"We do not worry about death here. We only worry about magical powers and viruses that are cursed upon others. Sometimes they are trapped forever. That is a worse fate than death." Astina held out her hand. "Come, Joey, let's continue our journey. We shouldn't be too far away from the cowchees. I can't wait to introduce you to my father. He has especially been waiting for the Chosen One."

Joey followed Erac and Astina through the crystal caves. "Can we eat these crystals like the plants outside the caves?"

Astina brushed back her long silky black hair and turned to Joey. "No, these crystals are special healers. They can cure viruses and magical powers. But you have to know which ones to use for the different viruses and powers."

"Do you know how to cure these viruses?"

"Some I know, but I still have a lot to learn. My father knows so much. He is the master teacher in our school. Every day he teaches us. But some powers are beyond our capabilities. You have to be born with special powers."

"Do you have school every day? Don't you have weekends or days off?"

"We can have time off from school if we want to, but none of the cowchees or children wish to have time off from school. All the students decide for themselves if they want to go to school or not, it's not forced on them. They enjoy the classes." Joey was confused; he could not understand why any kid would enjoy school.

Astina took Joey's hand and stood directly in front of him. She gazed into his eyes. "You are the one who was born with special powers, that is why you are blue. You truly have a great gift. This gift comes from the great white universe."

They continued to travel a further kilometre. The smells inside the caves were overwhelming. All the various crystals had their own smell. The pink crystals smelt like roses, purple smelt like violets, red smelt like cherries, green smelt like apples; yellow smelt like lemons, orange smelt like peaches, white smelt like lily of the valley, and blue smelt like blueberries. The cave gave Joey a feeling of happiness and peace. At that moment, nothing made him feel afraid or sad, and he sensed the crystals had a lot to do with his mood.

"Astina, if people or cowchees feel depressed, do these caves heal them?"

"Yes. It looks like you're learning very fast, Joey. These caves heal the mind, body, and soul of all creatures."

Erac stopped in front of a large white crystal, followed by Astina.

"Why have we stopped?" asked Joey.

Astina turned to face Joey and smiled. "We are here now, this is our home."

Joey was confused. "Where is your home? All I can see are crystals and this huge white one in front of us."

"Be patient, remember, this is Magical World. This large white crystal will take us to my home, but first, I have to say our magical words." Astina stood in front of the crystal and held out her arms. She slowly whispered, "White Polishion."

The crystal gradually turned into a white light. "Wow, what do we do now?" asked Joey.

"Come, we can now walk into the white light. This will take us home." Astina took Joey's hand, and Erac followed behind them into the white light.

The cave disappeared. A huge white castle stood before them. There were glorious plants and trees similar to what Joey had seen when he first entered Magical World. Joey was stunned, and he immediately loved the castle. It had a huge white bridge and a stream of red river.

They walked on the bridge, and when they reached the end, Joey noticed a statue of a red bird above the huge front door. "Wow, what a fantastic castle." Joey pointed his finger high into the red sky directly at the statue. "What type of bird is that?"

Astina and Erac continued to walk to the castle, still holding Joey's hand. "That bird is a phoenix, it's very sacred to us. It flies from the south and warns us if the druggons are coming. I don't think I've ever seen one yet. But Father has in his time. We've been very lucky though. Since I've been here, we haven't had any druggons find us. As you can see, they need to know which crystal and our secret password to come here. We're safe here."

Joey scrunched his nose and frowned. "But we've just had a druggon chase us. Wouldn't it have read your mind and found out about the crystal and the secret password?"

"Yes, the druggons can read our minds, but my father placed a spell on that thought for our home. There is no way they can read our minds when we think of our home or if we are home. Anyway, the druggons can only read our minds if they are a kilometre within our range. There is absolutely no need to worry."

Joey wiped his forehead with the back of his hand. "That's a relief. He looked like he would have ripped us into pieces."

Astina opened her arms up high and glanced at Joey. "Here is our home. We call this Riddells Withals. This castle goes everywhere with us. My father has magic that can move this castle to any part of Magical World. We never have to lose our home to the druggons or any other bad creatures in Magical World. There is also a secret code to enter Riddells Withals."

From inside her red cloak, Astina pulled out an orange crystal in the shape of a five-point star. She carefully held the star high above her head, closed her eyes, and said, "Umm, umm, open Riddells Withals, umm, umm." A huge white light shined from the crystal star and changed the door into thousands of tiny glittering stars. She carefully put the crystal back inside her cloak and walked through the glitter. Erac pushed Joey with his nose to follow her.

Slowly the glitter cleared, and in front of Joey stood the huge entrance of the castle. Unicorns, cowchees, and people were everywhere. It was busy.

Joey observed everyone helping one another. He could see people going inside the shops and taking whatever they wanted without paying for it. To Joey's surprise, he noticed the shelves automatically refill with more items. It looked like no one needed money. This truly was a fairyland.

There were people flying in winged cars. They were like ordinary cars on Earth, the difference being the feathered wings used to fly them.

"Joey, would you like a milk shake?" asked Astina. "There's this favourite restaurant I go to. They serve the best milk shake ever."

Joey nodded his head though he did not know what he wanted. Everything he saw had almost taken his breath away. The people and cowchees looked like they worked in the shops for pleasure, just like the children willingly went to school. All these chores were happily achieved by the people and cowchees in Riddells Withals as if they were an enjoyable hobby.

"Right, Joey, this is it, my favourite restaurant," interrupted Astina. She showed him inside a big banana-shaped food shop. "Lena, could we have your wonderful banana milk shake, please. Oh, by the way, this is Joey, he's new here. Joey, this is Lena, she is a human too."

"Hi, Joey, so what do you think of Magical World?" asked Lena, blending the milk and banana ice cream together.

"This is a great place. I'm still not sure how I ended up here, and this shop is very nice." Joey observed all the colours inside the shop. The chairs were in the shape of a large banana and looked very comfortable. The tables looked like strawberries. Joey sat on a banana chair in front of the strawberry table opposite Astina, who was smiling.

"You will love it here, Joey. You won't want to go back to Earth," said Lena, serving him and Astina a banana milk shake.

"No, I'm going back with my sister. You see, I have to save her from the druggons, then we'll be going back to Earth to be with our parents," said Joey firmly.

"There are no such creatures as druggons. I mean, I've heard stories about them, but that's all it is—stories. There are only good-luck dragons, unicorns, and cowchees here. I do not believe in druggons. This place is good. Everything here is what any person would dream of," said Lena, fixing her long plaited blond hair into a curled bun.

"Well, there are druggons here. We've just escaped from one while we were coming here, just outside the caves," replied Joey blankly.

Lena looked puzzled and frowned. "I don't believe you," she said offensively. Without another word, she swooped back into her kitchen.

Joey stared at Astina. "Why didn't you back me up? We both saw the druggon."

Astina moved closer to Joey. "Lena has never come across a druggon. There hasn't been a druggon in Riddells Withals for years. She has never been outside the castle. She's only been in the caves where the crystals grow," whispered Astina, taking a slurp of her shake.

"Surely she must believe there are druggons. She can't be that stupid. It was just outside the cave."

"She does not know, and besides, we don't talk about it unless it is absolutely necessary. Lena is happy in her own world. She loves it here. Father wants the people to believe they are safe here. We have been for years, and we will be for many more as far as Father is concerned. It is best if we keep the druggons to ourselves, we'll only tell Father."

"The people have a right to know. You're wrong in not telling them. Those druggons are very powerful. They should always be prepared for them."

Astina shifted her head from side to side. "My father would not agree with you. He makes the rules here. I would never disobey Father and neither should you. Come on, I'll show you our home."

Joey did not agree with Astina or her father, but he did not want to argue with her.

Outside the banana-milk shake shop, Erac waited for them. Astina led the way. Riddells Withals was crowded with joy and happiness. Joey noticed the red paths were only for walking and the purple roads were for flying. It was like a city on Earth, but everything here in Riddells Withals was so colourful, clean, and pure—nothing was dull. It seemed perfect.

Joey noticed everyone knew which direction all the people and cowchees were going. No one bumped into any one. Even Joey sensed someone was around the corner, and then a mother cowchee appeared with her baby. He could not figure out how he knew they were there. He was very careful not to run into them. They stared and smiled at him while they walked pass. It was as if they knew his thoughts. In fact, all the creatures in Riddells Withals smiled as they strolled past him. Some of them waved and said, "Welcome to Riddells." Everyone knew everyone. Joey felt very welcomed with all these people and cowchees being so kind to him.

* * *

At last, Astina stopped in front of the largest building in Riddells. It was huge and looked like a mansion. In fact, it was a mansion. It was painted red, purple, orange, yellow, and green, with a fine line of black along the trimmings of the round windows. The roof was a golden dome. The entrance door was white, and above it hung a statue of the same phoenix Joey saw before he entered Riddells Withals.

"This is my home. I think Father will be home, probably in his sacred room practising his spells and studying our old testimonies. Come, Joey, I can't wait to show you to Father." Astina grabbed Joey's hand, and they ran up the front steps. A huge latch hung on the front door. Astina pulled the latch, and it opened creakily until she pushed it wide open and they raced inside, with Erac still following behind.

Astina's home was certainly huge, and Joey thought he could get lost inside it. In the entrance hall was a water fountain flowing into a huge pond. Crystals and plants added to the beauty.

"Father, it's me, Astina. I have someone here to introduce to you. Father, where are you?" She ran into a room. Joey ran to keep up with her. Joey stopped and looked down. He noticed the floor was yellow; in fact, it resembled gold. He bent down to touch the smooth, cold, hard floor. He could not have imagined how expensive it would have been to have a gold-covered floor on Earth. It was obvious to Joey that no one had to pay for anything in Riddells Withals.

"Oh, Father, there you are." Joey heard Astina talk to her father. He quickly stood up and tried to distinguish where her voice was to try to catch up with her. Finally, he turned into a room and saw her hug her father. Astina turned and held out her arm, motioning to Joey to come closer. "Come, Joey, this is my father."

Joey was stunned. Her father did not look anything like Astina. He was a short, chubby bald-headed man with Chinese-like eyes and a long white beard. He wore a long white baggy robe with red trimmings, and a tiny red cap sat neatly on his head. The room they were in was enormous yet, at the same time, cosy. A table stood directly in the centre of the room.

The gold floor shined brilliantly, and the windows were decorated with rich red drapes. They were round to fit the windows and parted to the sides to show off the glorious garden view outside the room. The table was covered with purple cloth that dangled to the ground, and on top, books, crystals, and objects were neatly piled. Every wall in the room was covered with shelves filled with books from the ceiling to the floor.

"Welcome, Joey, my daughter is good to bring you here. I am very honoured to meet you. My name is Budda. Everyone calls me Lord Budda, but you don't have to call me that, just Budda is fine with me."

Joey was speechless, but he quickly answered, "Yes, Budda, it is an honour to meet you too. Astina has told me so much about you."

Budda gazed at Astina and smiled at her adoringly, and then he turned to face Joey. "I suppose she has told you I am a master teacher here. All creatures here respect me. I care for all of them. They are like my children. It is my responsibility and duty to care for all of them."

Joey was surprised to hear Budda say creatures. He wondered what he meant by that. To Joey, it sounded offensive to call humans creatures, but then he brushed it off and figured it was probably his way of saying people and cowchees were one.

Budda bowed his head to Joey. Joey was not sure what to do, so he quickly bowed back. When he stood up, he saw Budda smiling. Budda placed his hand on Joey's right shoulder. "Has Astina told you about you being the Chosen One because of your colour? I can see you are the one, and everyone else here would have been aware of that before you came to my home."

Joey looked at Astina, and then he turned to face Budda. "Yes, she has told me, but I only came here to find my sister, Olivia. The druggons captured her, and they look very dangerous. Could you please help me find her?" asked Joey.

Budda quickly turned to Astina. "You've seen a *druggon? Where?"* he roared.

Astina ran to her father's side. "Oh, Father, please don't be upset with me. We came across Alcon in the caves. He told us he was looking for us to help Joey. Joey needed our help. If we didn't go to him, the druggons would have taken him. We didn't have time to tell you first when we found Joey. On the way back, we came across Megram a few miles outside the caves, but we escaped." Astina lowered her head in shame.

"You shouldn't have gone out on your own. *Don't you ever do that again. You must tell me first!"* shouted Budda.

"But Joey needed our help. Like I said, we didn't have time. The druggons would have captured him. He is the Chosen One, the one we have been waiting for. Father, please don't be angry with me," cried Astina.

Budda grabbed her and held her close to him. With his chubby cheeks shaking, he shook his head. "I'm not angry with you, darling. Promise me you'll never try to do that again, you must come and see me first. You should never be outside the caves."

"But Alcon told me about Joey out there, and I wanted to do something good on my own. Father, I thought you would be proud of me."

"You could have caught a virus. Darling, don't get upset. I am proud of you, but no matter what the circumstances are, you must always come to me. It is too risky for you and Erac to be out there alone." Budda comforted her closely.

After a while, Astina stopped crying, and then Budda let go of her, and they both turned to Joey. Joey stared at both of them. He tried to see where the resemblance between Astina and her father was. How could she be his daughter? She looked so different.

Budda and Astina smiled. Budda moved closer to Joey and put his hand on his shoulder. "It's okay, Joey. Astina is my adopted daughter. Her parents were banished when she was just a baby. At that time, the druggons invaded our castle. Her parents were sent to Earth and never allowed to come back to Magical World. I am still trying to find a cure to reunite them with Astina, but that's going to take some time yet. I do not even know what they look like on Earth as humans. I think that will have to be the first cure I'll need to find."

"How did you know what I was thinking?" asked Joey.

"Well, Joey, here in Magical World, we have strong telepathy. Even you have it. Sometimes we know what the other is thinking."

"Oh, so that's why I knew people and cowchees were walking around the corner just outside. I guess I'll have to be careful with what I think from now on," said Joey, scratching his head.

"Yes, Joey, the longer you are here, the more you will learn all about your powers. Now how about we fix you something to eat?" Budda placed his hands on his large belly and shook it. "I'm getting hungry!"

"Okay, but it is very important for me to find my sister, Olivia. Astina says the unicorns can help me get her back. I don't think I have much time."

"Yes, yes, we'll talk about it over dinner. Come along, Joey." He escorted Joey and Astina out to the dining room.

The dining room was elegant and even bigger than Budda's workroom. The walls were bright red. The drapes were sky blue with small yellow stars. The room was just like being outside with its red sky and puffy yellow star-clouds painted on the ceiling. The windows were twice the size as Budda's workroom and were also round. The floor was still gold, and the dining table was made of oakwood, oval-shaped and very long. The chairs had high backs and were covered with white silk covers that overlapped onto the golden floor. There were so many chairs Joey could not count them. He guessed there were probably over a hundred.

The table was full of delicious food and drinks, all of Joey's favourites—potato cakes, dim sims, shepherd's pies, Pavlovas, Cokes, milk shakes, chips, chicken drumsticks, and so much more. The smell was mouth-watering.

They sat at one end of the table and started eating. Huge crystal chandeliers dangled from the ceiling, producing rainbow colours around the room. Budda waved his hand and instantly soft, gentle music played. Joey felt at home; it was as if he had known Astina, Erac, and Budda all his life. They were just like his family. Budda was so kind and thoughtful. Joey felt the creatures (as Budda described them) in Riddells Withals were lucky to have him as their master.

Budda glanced at Joey and smiled. He instantly knew that Budda had just read his mind. "Joey, you are most welcome to stay here as long as you like. After we eat, Astina will show you to your room, and if you like, we could give you a grand tour of our home. The wardrobe will also have fresh clothes for you to wear."

Joey nodded his head. "That would be very nice. I really need a bath," replied Joey. He remembered the crystal inside his pocket. He would have to make sure no one takes his clothes.

"Of course, freshen up after dinner, and then we will give you a grand tour. I can also help you on your first lesson to help you get Olivia back. I have plenty of books you can read up on just in case I miss out on anything. We have a huge library," Budda assured Joey.

"Oh, thanks, that would be great," replied Joey, taking a large bite from a chicken drumstick.

After they had finished eating, Budda picked up a stick with a red feather on the end. He waved it in the air and said, "Clanipp." In one instant, the table was empty and clean, just like the rest of Budda's mansion.

Everywhere Joey turned, it was immaculately tidy, not a speck of dust.

"Wow, can I have one of those sticks?" asked Joey.

"All in good time," answered Budda.

"Is that some kind of wand?"

"No, it is called a fettal. The red feather comes from our sacred bird, the phoenix. The feather is the important part of the fettal. Without it, I cannot use the power." Budda placed the fettal inside his cloak.

They all walked out of the dining room and followed Budda. With Astina by his side, he showed Joey his entire home. There were so many rooms, and every room had its own magical purpose. Budda explained how each room worked and how certain rooms were not meant for every creature. Joey understood what he meant because some rooms made him feel good and others did not. It still annoyed him to hear Budda say *creatures* instead of *people* or *cowchees,* but Joey was beginning to get used to his expression. The grand tour took almost an hour.

Finally, he stopped in a corridor and faced Joey. "Now, Joey, would you like to freshen up?"

Joey was immediately distracted and stared at a room behind Budda. It was a room with white floating balls. "Wow . . . Look at those balls, what are they for?"

Budda turned around and smiled gracefully. "Oh yes, I almost forgot to show you this room. This is for flying. These balls are called balons. Go on, jump on one and give it a whirl," answered Budda.

Joey carefully stood on a balon. He feared he would lose his balance, but as soon as he was on the balon, he felt as if a shield helped him keep his balance. His balon lifted him high up into the air. Joey's instincts were strong now, and somehow, he knew how to drive it. He flew around the room, and his speed depended on how many times he stamped his foot. If he tapped the right, he could turn right, and tapped left to turn left. Nobody needed to show him.

Magical World was full of surprises, and Joey especially enjoyed his flying balon. He was having so much fun. High up near the ceiling, Joey noticed a large round open window. Budda stared at Joey; he read his mind and understood Joey wanted to go outside. He only had to smile, and with that, Joey knew it was okay for him to go out. So off he went on his white balon into the red sky.

He had a good view of Riddells Withals. He glanced behind and noticed Astina was following him. But she didn't need a balon; she had her own wings. *Boy, is she fast.* Astina and Joey were very high. Below they could see the winged cars and all the cowchees and the people pacing everywhere. They were like ants. The higher they flew, the more colours Joey could see down below. It was all like a huge rainbow.

"You know, Joey, those winged cars don't fly as high as the balon. They are not as fast either," said Astina. She stopped and sat on a yellow star-cloud. Joey was amazed she did not sink through the cloud. He decided to join her and jumped onto the cloud. It was like a trampoline, only much softer and bouncier. They both jumped up and down; it was much better than a trampoline! Astina and Joey laughed, thoroughly enjoying themselves.

After a good bounce, they decided to rest on the cloud. To Joey, it felt like a soft bed. Astina glanced and smiled towards him. "What are your parents like, Joey?"

"My parents are great. I miss them a lot though. Hey, why don't you come with Olivia and me when I go back to Earth? I can introduce them to you."

"I would love to, but Father wouldn't allow it. If I go to Earth, I would be banished from Magical World, just like my real parents were, and I would never be allowed to come back here. Besides, I love it here. This is my home, just like yours is on Earth, and I couldn't leave Father."

"Oh, I'm sorry. You would have loved my parents, and they would have loved you. Mum and Dad are so modern. They let Olivia and me do anything we liked. One time, Dad took us on a great holiday. Mum and Olivia went shopping, and Dad and I went fishing. We caught a great big carp. Mum cooked it for dinner on the barbecue. We had a lot of fun and games together.

"My dad is very good to Mum. There was this one time the old lady next door grew a plant right outside Mum and Dad's bedroom window. It was a creepy-crawly plant—the strong vine-type, you know. Anyway, it grew and grew and broke through the roof and the plaster in Mum and Dad's bedroom. It did a lot of damage.

"Mum decided to try and cut the vines off our roof. The old lady ran out and yelled at Mum. She told her if she didn't leave her plant alone, she would get her son to call the police. Mum got really upset that time. So Dad decided to wait until two o'clock one morning when everyone was asleep. He got the saw and the plant killer. Mind you, he had to use a torch, so Mum held the torch for him. He cut the plant down and made sure it was poisoned. It was so funny—Mum and Dad looked like robbers. But really, they had no choice. It's not right to plant plants on other people's properties. To me, my parents are the greatest. They're always doing bizarre things. But at least they're having fun."

"You're so lucky. I sometimes wish I knew what my parents were like and what they looked like. I am so lucky Budda took me in. Nobody else on Riddells lost their parents. Father is still trying to figure out why they banished my mother and father. He has worked constantly on spells and magic ever since. But so far, he can't find anything to help bring my parents back." Astina looked very sad.

"I'm sure he will find your parents."

"Yes, I'm sure he will," nodded Astina, then she smiled.

Joey looked up and saw Alcon flying in the air. "Hey, look, here comes Alcon."

He jumped up and down and waved his hands. Alcon almost did not see them. But once he saw Joey and Astina, he quickly joined them on the cloud. The poor cloud felt like it was going to sink; Alcon was so heavy.

"Hey, Alcon, I can fly too. There's my balon," said Joey, pointing towards it. "Watch me fly." Joey stood on the balon and flew around the cloud.

Alcon sat still and carefully observed him. "I'm impressed."

Finally, they decided it was time to fly back to Budda's mansion. It was fortunate the window was very large; Alcon just squeezed through it.

"Budda, we're back. That was such fun," said Joey while he leaped off his balon.

Budda nodded and smiled. "Astina, will you show Joey how to freshen up, and when he is done, I'll be in our study quarters. Both of you can meet Alcon and me there, and we'll start on the lessons."

Astina nodded and jumped with delight. "Come on, Joey, it's easy," said Astina, leading him the way.

CHAPTER 4

The Wardrobe

Joey slowly followed Astina. "You're not going to watch me bathe are you?" he asked nervously. Astina laughed and turned to face him.

"No, of course not, we freshen up differently in our world."

Before Joey had a chance to say another word, Astina ran past him and pushed open the round wooden red door to his room. She ran inside while Joey stood near the entrance, wide-eyed. The room was huge, with the same gold floor. A large round window showed a view of beautiful colourful plants and a strawberry-soda feature. Astina ran to the window and carefully opened it. The glass window was like a door opening out.

"If you ever want a snack, there's this lovely apple pie tree outside this window. Oh, and over there is a small shrub with strawberry chewing gum," said Astina, pointing her finger towards it.

"Don't worry about how much you eat from the trees and plants, they grow back in a few minutes, and they never go off—if anything, they become so much tastier."

Astina went back inside the room and left the glass window open. "This is where you freshen up." She placed her hand on a wardrobe. It was an odd-looking wardrobe—long and skinny, with doors on each end. "All you do is walk inside this door and come out the other side."

She opened the door for Joey to enter. Joey was confused. "Don't you use a bath?" he asked, staring at the wardrobe.

Astina laughed. "No, Father says that's how earth-people clean up. We don't freshen up that way here. Anyway, this way is a lot easier and quicker. You don't have to do anything yourself, only walk through and come out the other end."

"What about my clothes, will I be wearing the same clothes?"

Astina moved her head from side to side and giggled. "No, of course not, the wardrobe chooses the clothes for you to wear. But don't worry, the wardrobe is magic. You never run out of clothes. It always finds the clothes that suit you best," said Astina, still holding the entrance door of the wardrobe and smiling.

"But what if I want to keep these clothes, especially Olivia's sweater? *I'm not going in there!*" said Joey very loudly. Astina instantly stopped smiling. Her eyes and head lowered.

"I'm sorry, Astina, I shouldn't have yelled at you."

"No, it's okay. You don't have to apologize to me. In our world, we don't worry about possessions. But if it's really that important to you, you can take your clothes off before you go inside the wardrobe and leave them here on the bed." She patted the bed with her hand. "And don't worry, I won't look at you while you undress. I'll turn my back, and when you're ready, you can walk through the door and close it behind you, then I'll open the other end, okay?"

"Okay," nodded Joey, making sure she turned around. He was relieved because he knew he still had the crystal in his pocket, and he treasured Olivia's sweater. Quickly he undressed and stacked his clothes on the bed. While he faced the wardrobe, he quickly turned his head back to the bed and noticed it had no legs. The bed was floating on air with only a thin layer of blanket floating over it.

"Joey, are you ready?" interrupted Astina, still looking away.

Joey quickly covered his private parts and looked at Astina to make sure she did not peek. "Yeah, yeah, in a minute." He stopped staring at the bed and entered the wardrobe, closing the door behind him. Before he could blink, the other side opened, and there was Astina smiling at him. Joey quickly covered his private parts, but he soon realized he was not naked anymore. He was dressed and cleaned. Phew, what a relief!

"You look great!" exclaimed Astina. Joey stepped out and looked down.

"Gosh . . ." he wore baggy gold-coloured silk pants that were gathered with gold bands on his ankles and a wide blue belt material around his waist. Joey noticed his chest was bare—no shirt, only a blue cape behind his back. He wore two wide gold bracelets on each of his arms and gold chains around his neck. His feet were bare with gold rings on his two large toes. He touched his head and felt some sort of crown with metal pieces dangling from its right side. "What's this on my head? And why am I dressed like this?"

Astina moved closer to examine the crown. "That looks like a gold crown. You see, the wardrobe knows you are the Chosen One, so it dressed you accordingly, and it looks like a perfect fit."

Joey looked around the room. "Is there a mirror in this room?"

"Yes, behind the wardrobe." Astina showed him the way.

They both stood in front of the mirror. Joey smiled and stared at his reflection. "Wow, this looks great. Look, Astina, I've got so many pockets in this cape."

"Yes, and the best part about our clothes is using the pockets. Anything you put inside will never come out unless you think about taking it out. Then it releases it."

"Cool, then I can never lose anything," Joey stared at all his pockets.

"Also, the pockets carry the weight of all the items and allow you to put as many things as you like in them. If you put anything heavy inside one of the pockets, you won't feel it. You probably already have quite a few things in there. Go on, take a look inside," explained Astina.

Joey carefully put his hand inside one of the pockets. "Wow, a flute! I play this in music lessons at school. Music is my favourite subject." The gold-coloured flute was made out of a special type of wood. Even though it was light in weight, it seemed very strong. It was the finest instrument he had ever seen.

Joey started to play the flute and played a wonderful tune. The music he played was far better than what he had played during his school lessons on Earth. His fingers somehow knew where to move, and his mouth blew fluently on the instrument. He had never played as well as he did at that moment.

He closed his eyes and continued to enjoy playing the tune until he heard a loud thump hit the window. He instantly stopped playing and opened his eyes. To his surprise, a flock of birds and small animals were trying to make their way inside the window. Joey also felt some weight on his shoulder. He found Astina resting her head on him, smiling with her eyes closed.

He gently shook her. "Astina, look at the window, those birds and animals are trying to get in. Do you think there might be something wrong?" asked Joey, placing his flute back inside his pocket.

Astina opened her eyes. She looked like she had just woken up from a deep sleep. After a few moments, she regained herself and then gazed at the window. "I don't see any birds or animals."

Joey looked back at the window only to find the birds and animals were gone. It was as if he had seen ghosts. "They were there a minute ago, and you had your head on my shoulder with your eyes closed. You looked like you were dreaming about something happy."

Astina moved her head from side to side. "I don't know, I can't remember. The sound of your flute, it must have hypnotized me. You play so well. Hey, we'll ask Father, he'll be waiting for us. Come on." Astina signalled with her head and pulled Joey by the arm towards the door.

* * *

They ran through Budda's mansion. There were so many rooms. Joey had no idea where Astina was taking him. He was relieved she was leading the way, and at last, they reached the study quarters. There were so many classrooms. But of course, Astina knew precisely which room Budda was in.

Joey stood in the doorway and peered around the room. All the walls had the same-sized books neatly shelved in alphabetical order. Budda was standing in the middle of the room with Alcon beside him. They were in front of a large long table that floated in midair at about arm's length in height. It was floating just like the bed Joey had seen in his room.

A few large books were stacked on one side of the table. One book was already open, and liquid formulas, herbs, rocks, and crystals were neatly piled in small groups on the table.

Budda glanced up and smiled. "My, Joey, you look wonderful. The wardrobe chose your outfit well. I am so glad you're here with us. Come in, I have some things to show you."

Astina was already standing beside her father, helping him sort the herbs. "Father, Joey found a flute in one of his pockets. He said when he played it, a huge flock of birds and animals tried to come through the window. I didn't see it because while Joey played his flute, I had my eyes closed and my head rested on his shoulder, and when he stopped playing, all the animals were gone."

"Let's have a look at your flute, Joey?" asked Budda.

Joey thought about taking his flute out from his pocket, which, of course, made the pocket slip open. He pulled it out and handed it to Budda.

"No, no. I only want to look at it, not touch it. This is your gift, and it's only for you." His hands were pushed out as if to protect himself.

So Joey placed the flute on the table. "It plays fluently. I mean, I play much better here than when I played on Earth at school," said Joey. He picked up the flute and flicked it through his fingers.

"Yes, of course you do. You have a fine instrument there. From what I can see, only the Chosen One is allowed to have that flute, and it is magical. You have the power to bring all good creatures close to you when you play it. You can put it back in your pocket now. It may just come in handy," said Budda, nodding his head.

"Would you like to hear me play it first?" asked Joey, holding it close to his mouth.

"No, only use it when you need to. From what I have read and heard from my books, if you play that for too long, you will have more than just birds surrounding my home."

"How can you hear the songs from a book?" asked Joey, dumbfounded.

"The books here are very different from those on Earth. When I read these books, it's like another voice speaks to me in my mind. Therefore, when music is read, it plays in my mind. My books make sure that anyone who reads them keeps the information in their minds forever. Every word. Come closer, Joey, and I'll give you an example." Budda opened one of his books and pointed to some of the words. "Here, read this."

Joey started to read where Budda pointed:

In order to find the cure for the virus that was cast from the druggons, only the Chosen One can cure the unfortunate ones. The blue-coloured human is the Chosen One. He has the power. In order for the Chosen One to accomplish his mission, he must find the charmal stone. This particular stone is emerald green with orange specks and can only be found in the magical well. The magical well is located directly under Rockwell Mountain.

While Joey was reading, he heard a voice speak in his mind. Then an image came to him—an image of the stone, the druggons, and the people and cowchees who were infected and suffered with the virus. The people and cowchees had sealed mouths. Their bodies were skinny and worn-out. They also had infected scabs all over their faces. Their clothes were filthy and ragged. They walked with bare, bruised, and scratched feet.

Even though they were sick and infected with the virus, it was clearly obvious the druggons were treating them like slaves.

The druggons had healthy mean-looking servants with ugly pointed teeth, long tongues, and skinny red bodies. They were almost naked, with only a small piece of black animal skin around their bottom half. They were called rebs. Joey could see the rebs had injected some food-type serum inside the people and cowchees. He quickly took his eyes off the book. He could not stand to watch them suffer.

Joey read more about himself as the Chosen One. With the charmal stone in his hand, he would use it to cure the people and cowchees. He went back a few paragraphs to find out exactly where the stone was. In his mind, he continued to see the charmal stone hidden in a well in the caves of Rockwell Mountain.

Joey pulled himself away from the book and stared at Budda. "Wow, I know exactly what to do now, and I know where to find the stone. This type of learning is incredible," said Joey. He touched the book again and stared at the words.

Budda nodded his head. "Yes, Joey, now you know how precious you are to all of us. Only you can save the people and cowchees who are infected with the virus," replied Budda.

Joey closed the book. "I understand. The people and the cowchees look like they are suffering, and they are obviously very unhappy, but I only came here to save Olivia. Getting that stone looks almost impossible," said Joey. He crossed his arms and turned his back on all of them.

"But, Joey, just look at all those people and cowchees suffering, only you have the power to save them. And besides, what if your sister has caught the virus, you would then need the stone to cure her."

Joey quickly turned to face them. *"No way."* He gazed at Budda's library. "Have you got a book where I can see Olivia?"

"These books do not show the future, they only teach us," replied Budda.

"But I'm just a boy. I don't want to be the Chosen One," cried Joey.

Budda approached Joey and put his hand on his shoulder. "We're all here to help you get Olivia back. I understand you do not want to believe your sister might have the virus, but there is that possibility. Magical World is very different from Earth. Don't be afraid to be the Chosen One. If I could take your place for you, I would, but I'm not the Chosen One—you are."

Joey turned to face Budda with tears streaming down his face and gave him a big hug. A rainbow came down from the ceiling window and shined on them. Joey looked up at the glorious colours. He wiped his tears and smiled. "Well, that means I've got work to do. Better go find that stone and save all those creatures."

They all smiled and looked relieved. Alcon and Astina came forward. "We'll be right beside you every step of the way," said Alcon, brushing his tail on the floor with excitement.

"Yes, we will," agreed Astina, and then she gave Joey a hug and a kiss on his cheek.

"I'm so proud of you, Joey. This proves you have a caring, wonderful heart. And yes, we will help you find Olivia," said Budda, nodding his head.

"I have to admit, your books are great learning tools. I know exactly where to go to find the charmal stone although it will be very difficult," said Joey, straightening his cape.

Budda placed his hand on Joey's shoulder. "Outside the caves is very dangerous, not only from the druggons but from other bad creatures. You need to go through your pockets and learn more about your gifts. Now that we have found you, we can't risk losing you. You've got so much more to learn," said Budda with a frown on his forehead.

Joey nodded and smiled. The only learning he wanted to do was find a way out of Riddells and go straight to Rockwell Mountain. "Budda, do you mind if I read more now? I'm not really tired yet," asked Joey.

"By all means, the more books you read, the quicker you can learn about your powers." Budda held and shook his stomach. "I'm feeling a bit famished, would you like something to eat first?"

"No, I'm not hungry. You go ahead and eat. I'll be fine here by myself. I know what to do now. Learning is fun and easy here." He was flipping through the pages in the book titled *T. T* was for the Chosen One. Maybe he could find more information about himself? He also noticed the book had an eye on the front cover. The eye was so real. And then it blinked. Shocked, Joey almost dropped the book, but instead, he gripped it tighter. The book felt very warm; it actually felt like human skin. This was no ordinary book—it was very much alive. He tried not to let the others see his surprise about the book. He just wanted them to go so he could be alone with the book.

"Okay, let's go, Astina, Alcon. We'll grab a bite to eat, and we'll be back later. I'll leave the food on the table if you feel hungry after your study, Joey."

"Thanks, that would be great."

CHAPTER 5

The Healer

Joey continued to study the book and was so completely focused, he did not notice them leave. The room was quiet, and he was alone at last.

The entire book was about the Chosen One with pictures of him on almost every page. The Joey in the book was so good at using his powers. Joey was not sure he could be as good as the Joey in the book, but he did know that he must try to learn it all.

He came across a subject about a wet blanket. This was also located in the inside pocket on the back of his cape. It was revealed that it was a very powerful weapon to be used against bad enemies. But it had to be wet in order for Joey to use its power.

Further inside the book, Joey pictured in his mind the blanket soaked in the soda water from the red river. He saw the druggon pounce towards him, blowing fire, but before the druggon had the chance to burn him, he swooped on it with the wet blanket. He flicked the blanket across the druggon's mouth. The druggon squealed in pain, his nose deeply burnt, and he was unable to blow fire, only a small puff of smoke came out from his mouth.

Joey continued to turn the pages until he came across a flute, but he decided to quickly skip that part because he already knew how to use that power. He read the next chapter about a healing woman. The woman gave the Chosen One a particular herb. Joey saw her in Riddells inside Budda's Mansion. Her room was an ordinary bathroom that was just like the bathrooms back on Earth. Joey noticed she was human; she had no wings like a cowchee, and she was not beautiful. In fact, she looked vulgar and quite ugly. Joey's mind suddenly went blank. He tried to read it again, but there was a blank spot on the page; the book would not allow him to see more about the healing woman. He wondered why he could not see her anymore. What was the book trying to hide from him?

Budda, Astina, and Alcon were making noises outside the room. Joey quickly shut the book. They must have finished eating. They entered the room and smiled at Joey. "Hey, Joey, learn anything interesting?" asked Budda.

"Yeah, heaps. I'm supposed to have a magic wet blanket. Then I got to the part about a human woman healer. She is supposed to be here somewhere, and she looked quite ugly. I tried to concentrate harder on her appearance, then the book blanked my mind."

Budda nodded his head and turned away. "That's an old description in the book. She is not here anymore."

"Why? What happened to her?"

Budda continued to nod his head even more and looked nervous about Joey's question. "She is an evil woman. We were disappointed with her spells. She banished herself from here. I'm not sure where—it was a long time ago."

"But I pictured myself visiting her. She had a particular herb for me. It was orange with pink specks. Boy, was she ugly, and she was in a bathroom, just like the bathrooms on Earth, unlike the wardrobe here." Joey scrambled through the pages in the book to try and find the human woman healer just to show Budda.

Budda quickly grabbed the book from him. "That's not necessary. I've read this book. I know what she looks like, but she is not here now. So you don't have to worry about it. That page is irrelevant," said Budda. He carried the book and placed it back on the shelf. He was not too happy about the topic and quickly brushed it off.

"Astina, could you take Joey to his room. Joey, you must be tired or even hungry by now. We can continue with our lessons tomorrow. Now if you don't mind, I have some work to do." Budda used his fettal to clear the table of the books, herbs, and crystals, and went into another room. Joey did not have a chance to say another word. Only Astina and Alcon were left in the room with him. They were all flabbergasted with Budda's sudden change of behaviour.

"Astina, have I upset your father?" asked Joey.

"Father has never been like that before, and he did seem upset."

"I was really getting to know more about myself. I'm not really hungry or tired. I wish I could read more from that book."

Alcon was peering at the book. It was back in its usual place under the letter *T*. "I'm sure Budda will let you read the book later. Maybe you should have something to eat and get some rest," said Alcon with a big wink at Joey.

"Yes, Alcon's right, Joey. Let's go, I'll take you to your room. Father sent your food there," Astina said, leading the way. Joey was right behind her. He also noticed Alcon had taken the book and hidden it under his scaly wing. This made Joey happy. He knew Alcon was on his side and would somehow allow him to have the book in his room to read, with no interruptions.

"Here we are. I'll leave you here to eat and get some rest. We cowchees don't sleep, instead, we meditate. It's a good form of relaxation. I'll teach you some time, Joey. So I'll see you later. Come on, Alcon, better let him rest," replied Astina. She pulled her head to the side to indicate to Alcon to leave the room with her.

"Oh yes, I would like to tell Joey something before I go, if you don't mind, Astina. It'll only take a few minutes," said Alcon, still clutching the book under his wing. Alcon knew how to stop anyone from reading his mind. So Astina had no idea why he wanted to stay behind.

"Okay, but don't be too long." Astina left to meditate in her room, which was across the passage from Joey's room.

Alcon waited until she was completely out of sight. Then he gave the book to Joey. "Now, normally humans have eight hours sleep, so I'll be back in eight hours to take the book back before anyone notices it's missing. I know how badly you want Olivia back. So here you go, Joey, read as much as you can. I'll leave you to it."

Joey smiled. "Thanks, Alcon, you're a great friend." He gave Alcon a big hug. Alcon licked him with his huge tongue and left Joey's room, closing the door behind him.

CHAPTER 6

The Coin Gift

Meanwhile, Joey sat on his bed and quickly opened the book to the part where he had stopped reading. Of course, there was no picture in his mind about the healing woman anymore. Maybe Budda was right about her not being relevant now. But Joey sensed Budda was keeping something from him about that woman. He decided to use the eight hours wisely and read every topic about his powers.

He remembered every magical word and spell as he went through the book; it was all absorbed inside his mind. Now it was only a matter of trying out all his powers. But the book warned him that he was only allowed to use his gifts when he needed to. If he used his powers for fun, they would all be lost. The book also mentioned that the words written in red were only visible for the Chosen One to read. Not even Budda could have read it.

There was a particular hidden gift Joey found very interesting. It was a coin attached to his crown. All he had to do was remove the coin from his crown simply by pressing his finger hard against the coin. The coin would then attract to his finger like a magnet. He would then place it inside his mouth. This would give him the power to visit other planets within the universe—that is, any one of the nine planets.

For Joey to visit any particular planet, he would just have to imagine the planet he chose. The coin would then disappear, and instantly, he would be travelling to the planet he imagined. But Joey's first priority was to read the topic about Earth. Once he had finished reading all about Earth, it clearly showed him that when he reached Earth, he would only be allowed to visit for ten minutes and that he would be like a ghost. Nobody or nothing would be able to see or hear him. He could walk past any person, and it would only be like a slight breeze and nothing more.

Joey stopped reading and felt the coin with is other fingers. He kept his pointer finger away from the coin because he was not sure whether he would use his new gift there and then. Then he decided to do it. It would only take ten minutes of his time. He felt he had to check on his parents. No one would know. Everyone here thought he was asleep.

Without another thought, he immediately pressed his pointer finger on the coin. The book was correct. There it was, sitting on the end of his finger—a shiny gold coin with an engraving of a turtle. He shoved it inside his mouth and imagined going home to Earth.

All of a sudden, Joey was inside a bubble. The bubble was a clear ball with Joey standing directly in the middle of it. Suddenly, the bubble travelled at fast speed through a white light. That was all Joey could see.

At last, he burst out from the white, and then it slowly disintegrated into black space. From a distance, Joey could see all the planets, comets, and asteroids. First he went past Pluto, then Neptune and Uranus. He saw the orange planet with the ring around it. Yes, it was Saturn. Wow, Jupiter was huge and green! And then he saw Earth.

Joey really wanted to visit the other planets, but he only had time to visit Earth. He even had a glimpse of Mars. He continued travelling at lightning speed until he saw Earth looming large in front of him. He approached the white clouds, then the blue sky and the sea, and finally, his home—Number 487, King Avenue, Seaford. When he landed, the bubble around him instantly disappeared.

Joey climbed the steps to the front door of his home. As usual, he could see Mum and Dad's shoes on the porch. *Great, they had to be home.* Joey could not wait to see them. He tried to open the door, but his hand simply went right through the door handle. He then touched the glass front door with his fingers; again, his fingers went through the door. He remembered he would be a ghost on Earth. So he pushed his whole body through the door until he was inside the lounge.

Everything was just the way it was the day he lost Olivia on the beach. His schoolbooks were on the coffee table, and his runners were under the green couch. He could hear his mum singing in the kitchen. He could not see his dad anywhere; he was probably out in the garage, working on his car. It had been a couple of days since Olivia and Joey had left Earth, and yet everything seemed the same.

Joey hurried into the kitchen, thinking about his time running out. He saw his mother making an apple pie. She looked very happy. Surely his parents would have known by now that their children were missing. Joey stood directly in front of his mother and stared at her. He waved his hand in front of her face. She did not acknowledge him. All she did was look up and stare into midair. Then she smiled and continued to roll out the dough for the apple pie. Maybe she sensed Joey's presence. He wished he could talk to his mother and tell her what was happening to her children.

Joey went through the back door into the garage to look for his father, and sure enough, he was there. His father sat on the old lounge chair with the radio close to his ear. He had a spanner in one hand, and his other hand was shaped into a punched fist. He punched into the air and yelled, *"Go, you beauty, go!"* His dad enjoyed listening to the football. It did not look like his dad was worried about anything either.

Joey was confused. His parents seemed happy and normal. It was as if his parents were not aware of their children missing. Maybe they were happier without their children. Joey suddenly felt depressed.

Joey's ten minutes on Earth was now over. The clear bubble appeared in front of him. He was still outside his father's garage. While he slowly started to travel away, he watched his dad, who was still yelling and punching his fist into the air. He continued to stare at him until he disappeared back into space. He was travelling faster now. Again, he passed the nine planets and, finally, through the white light.

Joey was lying on the bed with his eyes wide open. He could see Budda, Astina, and Alcon all standing in front of him. He touched his crown and found the coin was back in its place.

"Joey, are you with us? Joey!" yelled Budda, shaking him.

"How long have you all been standing there?" asked Joey, searching for the book he left on the end of his bed.

"Long enough, what happened to you? We were worried about you. You were lying on the bed in a trance," said Budda, frowning.

"Do you mean my body was here all this time?" asked Joey.

"Of course, but I noticed you somehow have the book. Have you been trying magic, Joey?" asked Budda.

"Oh, I'm sorry I took the book, we were going to put it right back," said Joey, staring at Alcon.

Budda turned to face Alcon and frowned at him. Alcon looked away and pretended he had no idea what was going on. "Joey, you have to be very careful with this magic. I know you're keen to learn, but you have to be cautious. Now tell me what happened to you?"

"I was back on Earth," smiled Joey.

"*What!* I mean, how did you do that?" asked Budda, looking very nervous and fiddling with his fettal. Now everyone was staring at Budda.

"There are a lot of pages about the Chosen One in the book that no one else can read. Not even you, Budda. It only allows me to read it. I'll show you." Joey grabbed the book and turned to the page. He pointed to the words in red that were only visible to him.

"What are you pointing at, Joey? There's nothing on that page," said Budda, still frowning.

"That's what I've been trying to tell you. I can see the words. Here, it tells me how I can visit other planets." Joey pointed to the coin on his crown. "See this coin here. All I have to do is press it with only my pointer finger. Then I have to put it into my mouth and imagine which planet to visit. The coin disappears, and I'm in this sort of glass bubble that travels through the universe at lightning speed. Oh boy, you should have seen all the planets. There was tiny Pluto, then Neptune, Uranus—"

"You must have been dreaming, Joey. We saw you here on the bed in a trance," interrupted Budda, shaking his head in disagreement.

"It must have been my ghost because on Earth, I could not feel anything, and nobody could see me. Even the book says I'm a ghost on Earth. You should have seen it. I was going through doors. And another thing, Mum and Dad didn't look upset or worried."

"Why should they be upset or worried?" asked Budda.

"You know, Olivia and I have been away for a few days. My parents would have sent a search party by now," said Joey, placing the book back on his bed.

"Oh, I'm sorry. I forgot your parents would worry. Did you see anything with a date and time? Maybe the time was different on Earth."

"Well, I had noticed my school books and runners were in the lounge room. I'm sure I left them there the same day I was at the beach with Olivia."

Budda placed his pointer finger over his mouth and waited, as if he had to think. "It must be the time. The time must be different on Earth than here. Let's have a look at the book."

Joey and Budda flicked through the pages in the book. Budda looked up at Joey. "Have you read the whole topic about the turtle coin gift?"

"The turtle coin gift?" repeated Joey, dumbfounded.

"I've heard about that gift somewhere from my great ancestors, but I've never read about it in that book. It's the coin with the turtle symbol." Budda glanced closely at Joey's crown where the coin was shining. "Yes, that's definitely the turtle coin gift."

"Oh, so you do know about the coin?" asked Joey.

"No, not all of it, just a little. That is a very good gift you have. I should have known you would have that. It allows you to help other planets other than Earth and Magical World. Now, have you read all about that gift? There must be more on it?" Budda questioned Joey.

Joey's face coloured a darker blue. He shuffled through the pages in the book. "Actually, no, I didn't. There was more, but I had to see my parents first."

Budda paused for a moment and frowned, "Joey, you must never start any magic unless you have read it all. That is very dangerous," Budda said firmly. He looked most annoyed.

"I'm sorry. I won't do that again." Joey pointed at the words in the book about the turtle gift. "Yes, this is the part I stopped at, after I read about being a ghost on Earth. Actually, further on, it says that I am a ghost on Earth. On the other planets, I am not, and here, it says, 'Warning, before visiting other planets, be prepared for dangerous creatures.' Also, it says I have more time with the other planets, and I am able to breathe on each planet using a mask from one of my pockets."

Joey opened the particular pocket inside his cape, which was once again shown to him in his mind from the book. He quickly pulled out the mask. It was black and large enough to cover half his face with holes for his eyes and a nosepiece that filtered fresh air. Joey tried it on. He imagined it to stay on his face, and it did—again, the book told him to do this. Once it was on his face, there was no way the mask could come off unless Joey imagined it off.

"How do I look?" asked Joey, smiling and touching his mask.

Budda did not look happy at all. "Joey, you were very lucky you did not go to the other planets. You must promise me not to try any magic unless you've read all about the gifts. If you went to any other planet, you could have died or even be killed. This is not a game and not a joke." Budda paced around the room, staring at the floor with his hand over his chin. "Well, I believe the reason why you're a ghost on Earth is because that is where you came from," said Budda, continuing to pace around the room in deep concentration.

Joey was about to say something, but Budda raised his hand to stop him from speaking. So Joey waited while Budda was deep in his thoughts. Joey was disappointed with himself. He never meant to upset Budda or put his own life at risk. He realized he was wrong and should have taken more care to fully understand his powers.

"Now, back to the time frame with the other planets and Magical World, Joey. I don't think your parents would have realized yet that you and Olivia are missing. I think time is faster here. On the other hand, maybe time stays the same on Earth until you return," said Budda staring at Joey.

Joey kept flicking through the book. "There must be something about that in this book for us to be certain," replied Joey.

Budda moved closer to Joey. "Check the index page at the back of the book, it's a lot quicker to find." Budda helped Joey find the contents page. Joey scrolled his right pointer finger under the letter *T* and found *Time frames on the other planets, page 684*.

"Ah, here it is," said Joey, his finger still pointing to the description.

Budda shook his head again from side to side. "I'm sorry, Joey, but you do remember that I can't see the words?"

"Oh, I'm sorry. I forgot, anyway it's on page 684." Joey quickly turned to the page and read it in his mind. Once again, he pictured Earth and himself on Magical World. The voice from the book told him exactly what Budda had suggested. "You're right, time stays the same on Earth until I return. Mum and Dad have no idea we're gone. That explains why they looked so happy."

"At least we're sure now your parents won't worry," assured Budda.

"Are you sure this book is right? I remember you told me the mistake it made about the healing woman," Joey said while he looked at Budda.

"How can I not forget? You keep reminding me," snapped Budda.

Joey, Astina, and Alcon stared wide-eyed at Budda in total disbelief.

"Father, is something wrong?" asked Astina with a worried look.

Budda turned to face her and then back at Joey. "I'm sorry, I didn't mean to snap. Don't be concerned, the book would not make a mistake about the turtle coin gift. It has nothing to do with humans, you can trust it," said Budda, who looked calmer.

Joey just nodded. He didn't want to upset Budda anymore than he already had, but he did not like his comment about the humans.

Budda picked up the book. "Now, I'm going to let you rest, Joey. I think you've done enough for now. We'll be back later, come on Astina, Alcon."

"Oh, Father, can I please stay here with Joey? I'll do my meditation here while he rests. The bed is big enough for both of us," pleaded Astina with an innocent look.

"Of course, darling, how can I say no to you? In fact, I think that's a great idea. You can make sure Joey does not use any more magic until our next lesson." Budda gave Astina a kiss on the cheek. With the book still clutched under his arm, he waved for Alcon to leave with him. Quietly they left Joey's room. Joey and Astina were alone at last.

"Astina, how did you all know I was reading the book?"

"Father and I read your mind. Remember, we can read minds. Even Alcon came rushing in the second you tried to go to Earth. We were all worried about you." Astina lay beside Joey on the bed.

"Can you teach me how to stop anyone from reading my mind?"

"Well, I think I'd better. If no one else is allowed to read parts about the Chosen One in father's book, then you need to know how to stop anyone from reading your mind. I must admit though, we were worried about you returning to Earth, especially Father. You should have seen him. Honestly, Joey, he does not want to lose you. He really does care about you."

"He has a funny way of showing it," said Joey as he slapped his hand on the bed.

"Don't be upset with Father. He does care about you and Olivia. Father is wonderful and caring to all of us."

"He seems to have something against humans. It's as though he doesn't trust us. Besides, he doesn't have wings like cowchees do, and he looks human to me. Is he?" asked Joey.

"Father is not human, he is a budda. A budda is like the Chosen One. He has great powers too. You shouldn't speak like that about Father. Maybe you should get the book under *B* for "budda" and learn about his great powers and understand how important he is to all of us."

"I'm not interested in learning about his great powers. I really don't care who your father is. All I want is my sister back so we can go home."

Joey turned his back and pretended to go to sleep. All he could think about was how he would get back to Earth once he found Olivia. He was totally reliant on Budda, the cowchees, and the unicorns. Joey sensed Budda was trying to hide something from him and that it had something to do with the healing woman. For hours, he thought long and hard about it all, but nothing came to him. Finally, he fell asleep.

CHAPTER 7

The Phoenix

After eight hours of much-needed sleep, Joey awoke. He could smell breakfast. Of course, in Magical World it was always daylight, but to Joey, it felt like morning and his stomach was making loud noises. He gave himself a huge stretch, feeling that it was the best sleep ever.

Then he remembered Astina. He turned to his side and noticed she was not beside him. Floating in the air, he could see a tray with bacon, eggs, toast, and Milo. Mmmm, this was his favourite breakfast. Maybe Astina left it for him, but how did she know this was his favourite breakfast? Then Joey remembered that she could read his mind. Anyway, he was so hungry he just wanted to eat, and so he ate every last bit.

The door creaked open. Joey was startled, but then realized it was only Alcon poking his head through. "Hey, Joey, did you have a good sleep?" He opened the door wider to let himself in. His tail swished from side to side.

"The best, thanks, Alcon. Where's Astina? I want to thank her for this great breakfast. I guess she must have read my mind, bacon and eggs are my favourite."

"No, I don't think it was Astina who made you your breakfast. She's still in her room, meditating. I've been with her the last eight hours," said Alcon, chewing on some of Joey's leftover bacon.

"Oh . . . I wonder who made this breakfast. Anyway, I thought Astina was staying with me."

"Didn't you notice her leave? She didn't look very happy. In fact, she was crying."

"Oh no, I must have upset her. Where is she? I've got to see her." Joey frantically jumped off his bed.

"She should be in her room across the hall from yours, you can't miss it, come on, I'll show you." Alcon led him the way. "What did you say to upset her?"

Joey did not answer Alcon; he simply knocked urgently on her purple door. But there was no answer. "Astina, it's me, Joey, can I come in? Please, Astina, I'm really sorry I said those things before."

Joey continued to knock; still there was no answer. Alcon came forward. "Right, out of the way," he insisted. Alcon pushed himself in front of Joey and slowly opened the door. He poked his head inside her room. "Astina, are you in here?" He turned back to Joey. "It doesn't look like she's in her room.

"Let me see." Joey pushed open the door and entered her room. He looked around. "You're right, she's not in her room." Joey stood still and gazed around her room for a few minutes. He found himself fascinated. It was so beautiful, and it instantly reminded him of Olivia. Astina had a huge dollhouse and mobiles with stars, moons, and planets near her window. It was very similar to what Olivia had. He sat on her glittery, colourful bed and enjoyed the moment. At that moment, he felt like he was at home in Olivia's bedroom.

Alcon waited patiently for Joey, then suggested, "Hey, let's go and find Budda. He'll probably know where she is. I'm sure she'll be fine. And about breakfast, sometimes when you dream of your favourite meal, when you wake up, it appears for you. It depends how badly you wanted it. My guess is that's how you got your breakfast. You magically made it yourself without even realizing it. It came from your dream." He licked his lips. "You should dream more of that bacon stuff, it's very delicious."

Joey smiled at Alcon. They both headed off to find Budda. Once again, they passed the room with the balons. Joey stopped and turned to Alcon. "Do you think I can put one of those balons in my pocket? You just never know when I might need it. Everyone does a lot of flying around here. Do you think Budda would mind?"

"I doubt very much that Budda would mind, yeah sure, take one. He's not the possessive type. He gives away a lot of his stuff to his students." Alcon handed Joey a balon. A pocket opened in his cape, and he quickly placed it inside. The balon shrunk neatly inside his cape.

Budda was standing near the doorway. He looked very pleased. "Alcon is right, Joey, you are most welcome to have a balon. I'm sure you will need it, so enjoy it. I was going to give you one anyway. Now, would you like to meet some of my students?"

Joey nodded. "By the way, have you seen Astina?" Joey glanced around the corridor to see if she was near Budda.

"Actually, Astina is helping me with my class. Come, I'll show you the way."

The classroom Budda showed Joey and Alcon was much bigger than the one they had been in previously. There were probably twenty or more students. Some were human, but most of them were cowchees. Astina was at the front, writing magic on a bright-purple board. It was nothing like a blackboard on Earth. She wrote very neatly, and while she did, Joey thought about Olivia.

Budda walked to the front of the classroom and stood beside Astina. "Can I have everyone's attention, please? Astina?" Budda smiled at Astina; she nodded back. The class turned in Budda's direction. "I would like to introduce you all to Joey, he is new here, and he will be joining our session."

Instantly there was complete silence. All the classroom students stared at Joey. Joey smiled and waved his hand. "Nice to meet you all," he said. Still no one said a word, and they continued to stare at him.

"Okay then, Astina, carry on," Budda instructed as he showed Joey a seat. Joey sat quietly on an orange padded chair. It was very comfortable. There were no tables in this classroom. It was clear to Joey they did not need tables because no one needed to write anything down. The lesson was magical, just like the books. Everything written on the purple board and explained by Astina would be absorbed into their minds.

Astina looked towards Joey's direction, and she did not look happy. Joey waved and smiled at her, but she quickly turned her back and continued to write on the purple board.

"I'm going to introduce you all to a very important spell. I will show you all how to control your minds so nobody can read what you are thinking," said Astina, and then she looked at Joey. He smiled because that was what she talked about teaching him the last time they spoke. She must have read his mind when he went looking for her earlier to apologize. He was glad she had forgiven him.

"First of all, I want you all to look inside your pockets and imagine looking for your mind-reading dust." Astina glanced at every student in the classroom. It was clear she wanted to make sure everyone of her students knew what to do. "Now a pocket should open, and don't worry, the wardrobe gives everyone this special pocket.

In the pocket, you will find the powder. Once you have found it, I want you all to take a handful and throw it above your heads like this." Astina threw her own dust above her head to demonstrate. "This dust will create a shield around you. No magic word is necessary. It's an invisible shield. No one can see it. If you taste the dust, it is very sweet. It won't affect you because, as you all know, almost everything here is edible."

Joey observed all the students following Astina's instructions. They all threw their dust in the air above themselves. The dust cleared as it landed on their heads. He found his own pocket with the magical dust. Only he could see the white powder. It looked like icing sugar. He tasted it. It did have a light, tangy, and sweet flavour as Astina had described it. He threw it above his head. The dust created a white shield around him, and then it disappeared. All the students discussed the magic between themselves.

Astina clapped her hands three times. "Can I have everyone's attention, please?" Everyone went quiet. This reminded Joey of school back on Earth.

"To take the shield off, you must throw the dust over your head again. I suppose you're all thinking not to take the shield off permanently. But may I suggest, it is only a good idea to have the shield on when you don't want someone to read your thoughts because this shield can also stop you from reading other minds. Reading minds is a good gift to have. You can learn so much from reading minds, and sometimes, you may need it to save someone. Okay, class, that's enough for this lesson. We'll see you all during the next lesson." Astina pulled out her fettal and quickly cleared her floating table.

All the students went to Budda and bowed in front of him. Joey sat next to Budda and watched him wish all the students well and praise them for their efforts. The classroom became empty very quickly, only Budda, Astina, and Joey stayed back.

"Why do all your students bow to you?" asked Joey.

"They were not bowing to me. They were bowing to you," replied Budda.

"Me?"

"Yes, you, Joey. They know you're the Chosen One. We all adore you. We are greatly appreciative that you are here with us."

Joey moved his head from side to side. "If they want to be my friend, could you please tell them not to bow to me? I don't want to be treated differently. I'm no more special than they are." Joey smiled at Astina, who smiled back. He was glad she was not upset with him anymore.

"Very well, I will make sure no one bows to you if that is your wish," replied Budda.

"Do you think I can go and look for the charmal stone now? I know what to do," asked Joey.

"No, not yet. You still have a lot of learning to do," Budda said firmly.

"I still have a lot of learning to do," Joey repeated sarcastically before he kicked the classroom door shut in frustration. "I cannot wait any longer. Anything could have happened to Olivia by now."

"You have to be patient. The time will come. We've been through this before, Joey. There is no use getting angry. Your angry energies will only make things worse."

"I'm sorry. I don't mean to be angry. I just feel as if I'm ready to go and you're trying to stop me."

"I would never do that. I am only being cautious. I don't want anything bad to happen to you. You need to give yourself time to learn more. You're still young, and you've just come here. My instincts sense that Olivia is safe at the moment, and you know Earth stays the same while you're here. So your parents are fine too."

"I don't trust those druggons. I've seen that virus in the book. And besides, there are other people and cowchees suffering too. They need to be cured and brought here so they can be safe in Riddells. You said you care for every creature in Magical World. You of all people would want them safe. Don't you?"

Budda stared wide-eyed. His face went pale, and he was not paying attention to Joey anymore.

"Well, don't you want them to be safe?" asked Joey again. But Budda was speechless. He pointed his finger towards the window. Joey turned around to face the window. There, standing near the window, was a red bird.

"That's a phoenix isn't it? Oh no, doesn't that mean the druggons are coming?" asked Joey.

"Father, what shall we do?" cried Astina.

"We must prepare for battle. They must have found a way to get into the castle, probably when you and Joey escaped from Megram."

Budda opened the window and let the phoenix in. "My little Ruddi, it's been a long time since I last saw you. How many are there?" asked Budda. Gently he stroked the bird's feathers.

The bird started to chirp until a high pitched voice came out. "There are five druggons coming. They should be here soon."

"Have they got Olivia with them?" interrupted Joey.

Ruddi continued to chirp but did not speak again. Budda gave Ruddi some breadcrumbs. "Good girl, you've done well, Ruddi," said Budda. He patted Ruddi again and placed her on the table to rest.

"Why didn't she answer me?" asked Joey.

"Her job is only to let us know if the druggons are coming. She won't talk anymore."

Joey patted Ruddi too. "How will we prepare for battle?" he asked.

"First we have to ring the bells. Astina, quickly, go and ring the bells."

"Of course, Father." Astina flew out of the window, and only minutes later, bells could be heard. Cowchees and people swarmed around Budda's front door. They knew that the bell meant it was an emergency, and they sounded frightened. But they were not aware of the druggons.

CHAPTER 8

The Magic Blanket

Budda opened his front door and stood in front of the crowd, with Ruddi perched on his shoulder. Budda took an object from his cape—a light-pink crystal in the shape of a five-point star. Except for its colour, it was almost the same as the crystal Astina had used to enter Riddells.

He held it close to his mouth. "*Can I have everyone's attention, please!*" he roared. The crystal star made his voice echo loudly. It was like a microphone. Everyone could hear him, and instantly, they all became silent.

With the star still in his hand, he announced, "I want you all to imagine the rainbow, all the colours in the rainbow. Please don't lose that thought, concentrate." The star Budda was holding glowed a brighter pink. After a few moments, all the cowchees and people disappeared. Then he glanced around. "Astina, Joey, why didn't you concentrate? You are not supposed to be here."

"Father, I can't leave you. What if something terrible happens to you?" she cried.

Budda moved his head from side to side. "I can take care of myself. You and Joey should be with the others. We don't have time to argue. Now concentrate, I will do it again."

"No, Father, I'm not going," snapped Astina.

"Me neither. You need us to help fight those druggons," said Joey. He pulled out his wet blanket. "Where's the nearest soda tap? I need to get this blanket wet," asked Joey, looking around him.

"Let me check," interrupted Astina. She flew around Riddells in search of something wet.

Crash! Bang! It was too late; the druggons had already found their way into Riddells. *"Aaaarrrggh . . . Father!"* screamed Astina. One of the druggons had swiftly grabbed her wings. She was kicking and screaming. *"Helppp!"* she yelled.

"Put her down, you filthy druggon!" roared Joey. *"I am the Chosen One, and I have great powers."*

The druggon that held Astina blew fire towards Joey. Joey quickly ran for his life and then jumped behind a brick wall. The fire just missed him, but he could feel the raging heat pass behind him. His heart pounded and sweat dripped down his face. He was shivering with fear.

The druggons trod heavily around Riddells, destroying anything that came in their way. Joey remembered his balon. He desperately needed to find something wet for his blanket. He knew the balon would be fast and easy to fly and dodge around the druggons.

Without hesitation, he pulled his balon from his cape and held it tightly. Suddenly, another blaze of fire hit the wall he hid behind. *"Aarrgh!"* he yelled. The wall instantly became red-hot like an oven. Joey had to move quickly before the fire went through the wall. But first, he had to use the nonmind-reading powder. This was not a time for the druggons to read his mind. He found the pocket with the powder and threw it over himself. He was pleased Astina had showed him this spell, and now he was confident the druggons were not able to read his thoughts.

Joey looked around again, wondering where he would be able to find soda water. Suddenly, a thought came to him—he remembered the pond in Budda's mansion. He would have to find a way to get to the mansion without the druggons noticing him. Glancing around, he found a small hole to his right near the partly crushed brick wall that stood in front of him. He squatted and carefully peeked through the hole. The entrance to the mansion was only across the other side. The door was wide open, and the druggons were nowhere near it.

Finally, the coast looked clear. Without another thought, Joey produced his balon and jumped onto it. Druggons or no druggons, he was determined to move. He quickly flew between the damage and ruin. A short distance away, Joey could see a huge druggon towering behind the mansion. The druggon was almost taller than the building.

Astina was screaming and crying, *"Let me down! Help! Arrrgh!"* Budda was frantically throwing blue stones, which sparked every time they hit the druggons. He fought very hard. Some of the blue stones eased the fire from their mouths and helped keep them from directly attacking Budda or burning Astina. But Budda looked as if he was struggling with the battle.

One of the druggons looked up and saw Joey. The druggon hastily pounced in front of him. Joey instantly flew behind him, missing the flames. He continued to fly around the druggon. It abruptly turned to try and catch him, but Joey used his quick reflexes with his balon and swooped past the druggon.

The druggon suddenly turned around again and blew more fire towards Joey. Once again, the fire missed him. He quickly drove the balon between the druggon's legs and grabbed its tail. He hung on to the tail with all his strength. Joey knew the druggon would not throw fire on its own tail. The tail swished in every direction, but Joey did not let go. The druggon tried so hard to get Joey off but could not do so.

Joey then briskly jumped onto the druggon's back. The druggon slammed his tail hard on the ground. *"Eeeeeeeee!"* squealed the druggon; he had obviously hurt himself and was in tremendous pain. Joey quickly climbed to the top of the druggon's head, holding on to the druggon's neck with both his hands. This made the druggon become extremely angry. The druggon rigorously shook its head in all directions. With every move, the druggon roared more loudly, and fire blew out with the movement of its head.

With great difficulty, Joey hung on as tight as he could. The druggon was very strong and fast. Joey thought about his cape, but he could not free his hands. His legs were dangling in the air with the balon still stuck to his feet. "*Helppp!*" he cried.

Budda turned and saw Joey in trouble. He could see that the problem was the fire coming out of the druggon's mouth, so he quickly threw a blue stone into its mouth. The blazing fire only stopped for a moment, but this gave Joey enough time to fly off the druggon. He flew around its head to avoid its huge rigorous tail. But the tail was too quick. Just as Joey was about to land near Budda's mansion entrance, the tail swooped across his legs. Joey stumbled onto the ground with the balon bouncing beside him. His leg was badly hurt. It could have been broken. Joey could not stand up and walk, so he crawled as fast as he could towards the entrance until, finally, he was inside the mansion. He stared at the pond that was only metres away. He could briefly see the goldfish swimming inside it.

On the slippery, shiny gold floor, Joey pulled his body towards the pond. He had to get to the pond as quickly as possible. It was lucky the gold floor was slippery; it helped him move more quickly. But he was not quick enough. The druggon poked his head inside the door. Joey instantly slid to the side of the entrance to avoid more fire from the druggon's mouth. But the druggon saw him and blazed fire directly at him. Joey screamed, "*Aaaarrrgggh!*" The fire burned half his face. He cringed with pain.

The druggon was so huge that it had to break the door and part of the wall to get inside the mansion. Joey breathed heavily; the burn on his face was stinging. He held his magic blanket tightly in his hand, but the pond was still too far from his reach. The druggon towered over Joey, who trembled with fear. He closed his eyes tightly and waited for the next blaze of fire to kill him.

"*Eeeee!* So you are suppose to be the Chosen One? *Eeeeeeee.* The most powerful one—Hey, you don't look powerful to me, *eeeeeeee,* Joey," screeched the druggon with a strong "eeeee" accent.

"Who are you?" demanded Joey, shivering in pain.

"I am Villazian, *eeeeeeee,* your cowchee friends must have told you all about me. I've been watching you and your sister from the beach, *eeeeeee*. Your little sister is quite nice, *eeeee*." He laughed.

"*What have you done to my sister?*" yelled Joey angrily.

"Well, *eeeeeee,* we've been experimenting with her. *Hahahaha,*" the druggon said with a spooky laugh.

This time, Joey could not hold back the tears that started to flow down his face. He quickly used the blanket to wipe them away.

"*Eeeeeeee,* now, I'm going to kill you. I certainly don't want the Chosen One hanging around, saving all those creatures, *eeeeeee.*"

Joey looked down to his blanket and, to his surprise, noticed that his tears had wet the blanket, and it was dripping with power. This was his chance to save himself and his sister.

"Wait, please wait, if you're going to kill me, could you do it with me standing up?"

"*Eeeeeeee,* one last wish, hey? *Eeeeeeee,* very well, it will give me a chance to see your whole body burn."

Joey leaned on the wall and pulled himself up with one hand to stand on his good leg; at the same time, he gripped the blanket in his other hand.

"*Eeeeeee,* ready to die?"

"No, wait . . . if you're going to kill me, I want you to do it quickly. Could you please come closer and blow your fire directly in front of me? The burning should hurt me more, I'm sure that would please you," nodded Joey.

Villazian gazed at the blanket but did not suspect it was a weapon. "*Eeeeeeee,* nothing would give me greater pleasure than to watch you die in pain, *eeeeeeee.*" Villazian shifted directly in front of Joey just as he had asked him. He bent his head down to be face-to-face with Joey.

Joey clenched his teeth with anger and determination, "I've got a present for you."

Villazian looked startled, but before he had a chance to blow fire, Joey thrashed the blanket across his mouth.

"*Eeeeeeeeeeee!*" squealed Villazian, with only smoke coming out from his mouth. He jumped up and down in horrendous pain. The blanket had burnt right through his mouth and nose. While he jumped, the floor and building shook like an earthquake had hit it. The pond cracked in half; all the nine gold fish scattered, flickering across the golden floor in search of soda water. Villazian, screeching in pain, finally flew away.

Joey quickly grabbed the pink healing crystal from one of his pockets. He held it tightly and imagined his burns and injured leg healed. Instantly, a glow of white light struck him. The pain was gone; his face felt smooth, and he stood easily on his feet. He was back to his normal self.

Joey thought of Budda and Astina; he wanted to make sure they were safe. He ran out the door with his wet blanket still in his hand. Joey saw Budda on the ground. He looked breathless and very weak. Joey quickly ran to his aid. "Budda, where's Astina? What happened out here?" He briskly looked around. "Why are all the druggons gone?"

Budda spoke breathlessly, "V-vill-lazian com-manded the-them to lea-leave. Ohhh, Joey, they've ta-taken Ast-tina w-with them, m-m-my b-baby."

Joey gazed around. Riddells was destroyed, and there was no sign of Astina. "Don't worry, we'll find the charmal stone, and then we're going to get them back—Astina and Olivia. I only hope they don't hurt them or kill them. Villazian ran off because I burnt him with the blanket. Here, take this crystal, it will heal you quickly." Joey handed Budda the pink healing crystal.

"Thank you, Joey, you've saved me."

"Don't thank me yet. Come on, let's go inside the mansion."

Budda used the stone Joey handed him, and he too was quickly healed. They both ran inside the mansion. Joey pointed towards the pond. "Look over there. That mean Villazian jumped up and down and shook the place. The pond cracked, and all the fish slid on to the floor. I think the fish are dead, they're not moving."

Budda ran towards the pond. He pulled out a new pond from inside his cape and waved his fettal over the pond. Instantly, it refilled with soda water. He placed the pink crystal inside the new pond and carefully, one by one, placed the fish back inside the pond. Budda glanced at Joey. "Let's hope they were only hurt. This crystal will only heal wounds." Budda touched each of the fish and encouraged them to swim. The fish then became very much alive.

"Budda, do you know where the druggons live? And where did all the people, cowchees, and unicorns go?" Joey preferred to call them who they were rather than creatures.

"They are all in here," Budda held the pink crystal star. He then pulled out a purple stone. "And this is where I shall put Riddells once we go back to the caves. But to find the druggons, you will have to take the book from the library. It will show you how to find them."

Before Budda could say another word, Joey raced to the study room to get the book about the Chosen One. "I'll meet you at the *cave*!" he yelled as he ran.

CHAPTER 9

Travelling with Toodles

Joey had no problems finding the book. He could see the book was sitting on Budda's floating table. It was as if the book wanted him to find it. Once Joey grabbed the book, he remembered to store it inside his cape, and sure enough, one of the pockets was open. The book shrunk neatly inside his cape.

Joey quickly ran to the cave. Outside the entrance to Riddells stood Budda with the purple stone in his hand. "I never thought it would come to this. We've been here for so long, and now we'll have to find a new place," said Budda. He moved his head from side to side with great sadness and disappointment.

"Where will you take Riddells now?"

"That, Joey, will take a while for me to find. It took me seven earth years to find this place. It would be a miracle if I found a new place soon."

Joey put his head down. He felt it was his fault. "I'm sorry."

"Why should you be sorry? It's not your fault. I should be thanking you. You did a great job with Villazian. He and his companions would have destroyed this place completely. And who knows how long I would have been able to fight them off. It was a hell of a battle. Oooooh, but I couldn't save my little Astina."

Budda pulled out his pink hanky from one of his pockets and cried loudly.

"Don't worry, I've got the book from the library, and we have magic on our side. We'll find those horrible druggons. Everything will be the way it was. I'll even help you find a new place for Riddells if you want me to."

Budda nodded his head. "You're right, I shouldn't be sad. I'm so glad you are here." He smiled and held the purple stone up high and closed his eyes. A strong white light shined from the stone and travelled towards Riddells Withals. Instantly, the castle zapped inside the stone. Joey and Budda were now in the cave, alone and surrounded by all the crystals.

The crystals immediately made Joey feel good and motivated. Even Budda appeared so much better. Budda rigorously searched through his cape until he pulled out a small boat that looked like a toy. He held the boat up high in the air and slowly let go of it; the boat then floated in midair. Slowly the boat increased in size until it turned into a huge boat. The boat was now big enough for anyone to live in.

"Wow!" yelled Joey. They both stood in front of the boat. It was gold and red and shaped like a turtle. Budda smiled, and reaching his hand up, he touched the bottom of the boat with his hand.

"Yes, Joey, many Earth years ago, this was my travelling companion. I call it Toodles. Come inside, I'll show you what Toodles can do."

The huge boat let out a rope ladder. It was as if it had read Budda's mind. The boat had a house built inside it, and it looked very cosy to travel on. While they climbed the ladder, Budda said, "I think it would be best if we travelled together to Rockwell Mountain."

"I agree," replied Joey.

Once they reached the top deck of the boat, Budda led Joey inside the house. It was enormous and identical to Budda's mansion. Budda carefully placed the rocks that contained the people, cowchees, unicorns, and Riddells Withals on his floating table.

"I can't believe all those people, cowchees, and unicorns are inside that crystal. Won't they be hungry?" asked Joey. He stared at the stone in disbelief.

"No, they are only in there for a brief moment. Inside this crystal, time stands still. It will probably take me a long time to find a new place, but to them, it will be like being inside the crystal for a minute. Not even that. It is just like Earth is to you. Your parents still don't know you and Olivia are gone."

"Oh, I see. Is Alcon inside that crystal too?"

"No, as soon as Alcon heard about the druggons, he went back east to his caves. Alcon is too soft. He can't fight the druggons. They could have quite easily had him for dinner." Budda put both stones in a gold chest in a compartment hidden under the floor. He sealed the floor with a power through his hands. No one would ever know there was a hidden compartment there.

"Now you know where the stones are, if anything should happen to me, you'll know what to do."

"Yes, I've read your mind. I know how to bring them back. But nothing will happen to you. I know you're powerful too. Astina told me a lot about you."

Budda smiled and walked back towards the entrance of the house. "Come, Joey, I'll show you how to fly this thing."

They both walked back outside. Joey was amazed; he assumed they would still be inside the cave. But magically, they were outside the cave, floating high in the red sky with all the yellow star-clouds around them.

"How did we get out here? We were in the cave a minute ago," asked Joey.

"Well, once we enter Toodles, he immediately prepares us for our journey. Toodles can read my mind. I just have to imagine being out of the cave, and he vanishes to where I want to be. But I have to think of a likeness of the place I want to be. For example, see that huge red river down there?" Budda pointed his fettal over the edge of the boat.

Joey looked down towards the direction Budda pointed. "Yes, I see it."

"I was just thinking of that red river. That was how Toodles knew where to go. So you see, Joey, you can't just think of any place without you being there before. There has to be some likeness of the place in your mind. This is partly how we travel in this world. If there is a place we have never been, then we follow our instincts, or I just let Toodles take us. Toodles always travels north." Budda patted Toodles as though it was his pet. "Okay, Toodles, take us to Rockwell Mountain, and follow Joey's mind."

Joey gazed at Budda and smiled. He felt proud that Budda understood him so well. Joey knew exactly where to go, and he felt even more confident now that Budda trusted him.

"Now, you have to concentrate on the destination you saw from the book so Toodles can understand you," said Budda firmly.

"Don't worry, I've made it perfectly clear for Toodles to understand my thoughts, you can relax."

Toodles started moving through the air. Joey could see his turtle feet wave rapidly until, eventually, the boat moved faster like a jet plane. While they glided through the red sky, Joey could see and hear the yellow star-clouds bump the boat.

"You treat Toodles like a person or an animal. He looks like he is only made out of wood," said Joey. He paced around the boat and stared into the sky.

"Of course, everything has its own energy. Wood, metal, dirt, water, trees, glass—anything. Even on Earth everything has an energy source in it. These everyday items don't talk back, but in Magical World, everything is magnetized and, therefore, much more real."

"So you're saying every object has energy, even a pencil?" asked Joey, dumbfounded.

"Yes, even a pencil. Everything has to have energy, otherwise, it would not exist. You should treat everything with care because there are good and bad energies floating around us. You can't see them, but they are there, and you don't want to attract the bad ones."

"Yes, I remember Alcon told me about that. So I should stay calm in every situation. Being angry or hurting anyone or anything only makes it worse."

"I am very glad Alcon explained that to you, Joey. You are a fast learner. I am very proud of you," Budda patted Joey's shoulder.

At that very moment, Budda reminded him of his father. Joey's thoughts drifted to his home on Earth. He missed his family. To him, it felt like months had gone by, but in reality, time would stand still on Earth until he returned. Yet he still had no idea how he was going to return home.

Joey and Budda walked back inside the mini mansion on the boat. Budda waved his fettal in the air and instantly, with magic, created a banquet of food neatly served on a floating table. "Hungry, Joey?"

Joey quickly nodded and licked his lips. "Mmmmm, I'm starving, this looks delicious."

"Then sit down and eat with me. We're going to need all our strength and energy for our journey. There are a lot of places I, myself, have never seen in Magical World. We have to be very careful not to bump into danger."

Joey looked around the mini mansion. "Do you have the books that were in Riddells Withals in here? Because if there are other problems other than the druggons, we should read up on it and be prepared."

Budda poured himself a cup of tea and nodded his head. "Yes, I do have books here. Everything in here is the same as my mansion in Riddells, and there is so much about Magical World in all my books that it would take you a lifetime to fill your mind with it all. Usually, when I encounter a problem, I normally look up that particular topic and deal with it there and then."

All of a sudden, Joey did not feel like eating. His stomach churned. For him, this meant something was not right, and he had a feeling something was going to happen. "I understand there would be so much to read about Magical World, but is there a topic on Rockwell Mountain and the charmal stone?" asked Joey. He watched Budda eat while he eagerly waited for his reply.

"Well, yes, I suppose there would be." Budda carefully sipped his tea.

Joey immediately stood up. "Where is the book? I want to be prepared before we get there, and according to Toodles, it won't be long."

"Sit down, Joey, let's finish eating first, and then I will show you the library."

Joey slammed his fist loudly on the table. "*No, no,* I need you to show me now. We don't have time." Joey was feeling irritated and very impatient.

Before Budda had a chance to say anything, Toodles shook. There was a loud bang; the food and the table flew across the room, and Joey fell onto the floor. He searched for safety and tried to grab on to something stable while Budda flew to a corner. A falling bookshelf just missed Joey by a few centimetres. The earthquake-type movement suddenly stopped. It felt like the boat had cracked in half.

"Joey, are you okay?"

"Yes, I'm fine, let's get out of here."

They both ran out of the mini mansion. "Oh no, Toodles is hurt!" cried Budda.

The boat was no longer in the air. Toodles was stuck in a cave. It was as if something had pushed the boat towards the ground, and Budda was correct. Toodles was very badly damaged.

CHAPTER 10

Riding with Sess

Even though Toodles was damaged, Budda quickly shrunk the boat and placed him back inside his cape.

"Toodles will be okay now. It may take some time, but while Toodles is inside my cape, he will be repaired, and the stones will still be safely inside Toodles," said Budda as he gazed around. Joey stood beside him, also looking around.

"This place does not look like Rockwell Mountain. But it shouldn't be too far from here," said Joey.

"Well, then, where to now?" asked Budda.

Joey searched around the area; the trees, the plants, and the ground appeared dull and dark. "This place gives me the creeps. It doesn't feel right here," said Joey. His body shivered; he did not know whether it was suddenly cold or it was the fear of the unknown that lay ahead of them.

"Do you think we should go through that cave? Is that the way to Rockwell Mountain?" asked Budda.

"That is one way to Rockwell Mountain, but I don't think it's a safe way. I must admit, I came here from a cave, and I don't trust caves anymore," Joey declared.

"We've got to take the risk. It's our only chance to save the suffering and Astina and your sister, Olivia. Come on, let's go," demanded Budda, leading the way. Joey hesitated, but then realized it was not the time to debate Budda, especially about the part of finding his sister. It was what Joey wanted most. So he caught up and kept close to Budda. At the same time, he pulled out his blanket and, with it, held on to a small bottle of soda water. This time, he was making sure he was prepared for the unexpected.

The cave became darker and darker. Even the smell changed. No more sweet smells, only a foul, stale vomit-like smell.

"Yuk, it stinks in here," said Joey.

"I think you're right, Joey. This place doesn't feel safe. The smell tells us everything." Budda stopped and turned to face him. Suddenly, there was a loud swishing noise.

"What was that?" asked Joey. He felt his whole body sweat, and his hands and legs started to shake with fear.

They stopped as directly in front of them were three different cave entrances. Two large and one small. Joey was confused; the directions all looked the same. At this point, he could not identify which was the true direction from the book he had read.

"My instincts are not good on this. Which direction should we take now, Joey? We'd better do this quickly." Budda looked very pale, and his eyes grew wide.

Before Joey had a chance to say anything, out came a huge snakehead that covered the entire cave.

"*Aaaaarrgh!*" they both screamed together.

"Quickly, to the smaller cave," howled Joey. But the beast was too fast. It quickly cornered Budda and Joey, and then it opened its huge mouth, showing its two large, long, sharp yellow fangs.

"Oh my god, it's a huge snake. What will we do?" shrieked Joey. His whole body shook with terror. Without a moment's hesitation, Joey prepared his wet blanket. Instantly, he whacked the snake across its wide-open mouth. To his surprise, the snake did not flinch; it was not harmed in any way.

Budda tried the power he used on the druggons, but the snake still did not move. Its long tongue slithered out, almost touching Joey and Budda. They both curled in the corner of the cave, desperately searching inside their capes for other alternatives. Joey pulled out his flute. He had to try something, or the huge snake was going to swallow them. He quickly started to play his flute. The snake closed its mouth and stood still for a few moments.

"Keep playing, Joey, its working, it looks like you've calmed this monster down," said Budda.

Joey carefully studied the snake while he played the instrument. The snake danced to the music, moving its head from side to side, enjoying the tune. Then it stood still again, staring at Joey while he played. Joey stopped. It looked like the snake was getting ready to strike him; it briskly swirled towards Joey.

Joey stood directly in front of the snake with Budda behind him. He stared into its huge, wide green eyes. The snake was so big that it could have easily swallowed him and Budda together in one whole gulp.

"*Sssssssss,*" hissed the snake, as its long red tongue spat out from its mouth. It could have wrapped completely around them. Instead, it delicately touched Joey's face.

"*Sssssssss,* you play well, Chosen One, *sssssssssss*. I've had this annoying toothache, and now it's gone. Your music must have healed the pain, *sssssssss*. I am now in debt to you, *sssssssss*." The snake stood high on his long shiny bright-green body.

"N-n-n-n-no, no, that's fine, Mr. Snake. I'm glad to have helped you," said Joey. His hands felt shaky and wet with sweat.

"I insist, *sssssssss*. By the way, my name is Sess, *sssssssss*. That's what all the humans call me, *ssssssssss*."

Joey was instantly relieved and realized the snake was harmless to begin with.

"Nice to meet you, Sess. My name is Joey." Joey turned behind him and put his hand on Budda's shoulder. "And this is my friend, Budda."

Budda bowed his head. "Yes, yes, lovely to meet you, Sess." He then quickly pulled back. Budda did not appear comfortable near the snake.

"You've mentioned other humans?" asked Joey.

"*Sssssssss*, yes, they are my friends too, *sssssssssss*."

"Where are they?"

"*Sssssssss*, near Rockwell Mountain, *sssssss*."

Joey glanced at Budda and then turned back to Sess. "Could you please show us how to get to Rockwell Mountain?"

"*Sssssss*, I can do better than that. We are still very far from Rockwell Mountain. To save you time, you are both most welcome to travel inside me, *sssssss*. The humans do this all the time, *ssssss*."

"Do you mean go inside your mouth?" asked Joey flabbergasted.

"*Sssssss*, how else? All the humans back at Rockwell Mountain use me to take them to many places, *ssssssss*. They say it's like travelling on a train. Just make sure you don't go near my digestive system, *ssssss*."

Joey turned close towards Budda's ear and whispered, "Can we trust this snake?"

"I can trust your flute. Your flute only brings good to you. I'm sure Sess is very trustworthy," said Budda quietly. He stepped forward and stood directly in front of Sess. "We would be honoured to travel inside you, Sess. Thank you for your kind hospitality."

"*Sssss*, it's my great pleasure, *sssssss*."

Sess opened his mouth wide. Joey and Budda looked at each other and slowly walked inside Sess's mouth. His insides were pink and soft. Joey felt warm; it was like being inside a sauna. His feet wobbled as he climbed farther inside Sess, and he felt like he was walking on jelly. They found Sess's digestive system and kept their distance from it. They rested near his scaly skin. Joey could see his new skin almost shed through.

"Look Budda, we can see through Sess's skin. It's just like a window. Wow, this is a bit like being on a train."

Sess quickly slid through the caves. Joey noticed he left his mouth slightly open, so they could have air to breathe.

"Wow, Sess is very fast. Man, can he move," said Joey, smiling at Budda.

"We are very lucky we found Sess. He may be able to help us with the druggons. Have you noticed how strong and fast he is?" Budda peered through Sess's scales and blinked at the cave that flashed past. But it was difficult to see anything clearly because of the speed they were travelling at.

"I noticed all right. My wet blanket didn't do anything to him, and neither did your stones. I wonder what the other people are like. I hope they're as good to us as Sess is." Budda nodded in agreement.

They sat comfortably inside Sess. They were wet and slimy, but the ride was very enjoyable. Budda pulled out a staff from his cape and used it for light. He had placed it beside them so that they would not be completely in the dark. Joey looked at Budda and noticed he had closed his eyes and was meditating. Joey also closed his eyes; the warmth of Sess's insides made him slowly drift off to sleep.

* * *

Budda shook Joey awake. "How long have I been asleep?" he asked.

Budda stared at Sess's mouth. "A few hours." He pointed his finger towards Sess's mouth.

"Look, Sess's mouth is open. We must be . . . come on, let's go." Budda helped Joey up. They both carefully headed towards Sess's open mouth.

Once they climbed out of Sess's mouth, Joey noticed they were still inside the cave. But the cave looked different; there were many assorted closed doors scattered along its walls.

"Are we in Rockwell Mountain?" asked Budda.

"*Sssss,* not yet. You have to wait for the doors to light up, when the doors light up, you can then find the way. I'm not sure how it works, but I think it could lead you to whatever destination you desire, *sssssss.*" Sess placed his head on the ground. "*Sssss,* I need my rest now. The humans shouldn't be too far away, *sssss*."

Joey patted Sess on a small part of his head. "Thank you, Sess, the ride was great, and both of us are happy to have you as our friend. We'll take it from here, you get your rest."

"*Sssss,* it was my pleasure, Joey. If you need my help again, wake me up, *sssssss*." Sess closed his eyes and drifted off to sleep.

"I wonder how long it will take for any one of these doors to light up?" asked Budda. He carried his staff closer to the doors. Every door was different in colour and shape, and some doors were made up of square frosty decorative glass.

"Look, over there is a glass door. Bring your staff closer, Budda, maybe we can see something through the glass," Joey demanded.

They both raced to the door and peered through. "Look, Budda, there are people in there." Joey knocked hard on the door.

"Hey, open this door," he yelled. The people walked past. It seemed like no one paid any attention to Joey's calls. It was as if the door did not exist to them, and only Joey and Budda could see them.

"They can't see us. The door must be invisible to them," said Budda. They both continued to stare through the frosty glass.

"I guess you're right. They're all looking this way, but they can't hear or see us. We are like ghosts to them. I doubt very much there'd be a door on their side. They're obviously not in a cave, and it looks like a hospital."

"What makes you think it's a hospital?" asked Budda.

"Just look at them, they're all dressed in doctor's and nurse's uniforms, and there is hospital equipment around them. This door is hopeless."

Just as Joey was about to turn away from the door, he noticed a boy stare in his direction. Joey quickly put both hands on the glass and yelled, "Hey, can you see me?" He waved to the boy.

The short, small red-headed boy waved back. "Did you see that? He waved at us. Hey, how do we get in, little boy?" Joey waved for the boy to come to him. The small boy walked towards Joey. Suddenly, a nurse appeared behind the little boy. She grabbed his hand and spoke to him. Joey could not hear what she was saying. Then she started to walk away with the little boy, but he stopped her and pointed towards Joey and Budda. She turned and glanced in Joey and Budda's direction and turned her head from side to side. She looked as if she disagreed with the boy, and then she took him into another room.

"Oh no, only the boy could see us. That lady could not see us. Why didn't she see us?" asked Joey.

"I have no idea. The boy looked very young. He would have been about five or six years old. I doubt it if the lady would have believed him. I think the place behind this door is somewhere on Earth. There are a lot of ways to enter Magical World. But once a person is in Magical World, they cannot go back to Earth that easily. Not as real beings anyway. That child was innocent, that was why he could see us." Budda put his hand on Joey's shoulder. "Come on, we'll have to wait until one of the lights light up on one of these doors like Sess said. Then we can figure out how to get to those humans in Rockwell Mountain. Let's not get side-tracked, I'll fix us something to eat."

Budda pulled out his fettal and waved it in the air. There in front of them appeared a round floating table with loads of delicious food and two floating chairs to sit on. The glorious food on the table radiated with bright colours and yummy smells. It made the cave appear dull.

"Wow, how did you do that? This looks yummy, I'm starving."

Joey quickly sat on the bright-yellow floating chair. It was very similar to the chair at the banana restaurant Astina had taken Joey to. He paused for a moment and felt sad. It felt as though his heart had dropped and the life in him was taken away. He missed both Astina and Olivia. He then thought about what Budda had just told him, it being difficult to go back to Earth. He wondered if that meant for him too.

Meanwhile, Budda sat in the other banana chair, grabbed a sario fruit, and glanced at Joey. "What's wrong? Have I done something to upset you?" Budda took a huge bite from his fruit.

"No, you've done nothing wrong. These chairs just reminded me of Astina when she had first brought me to Riddells Withals. You know that banana milkshake shop, it had the same chairs. There was this blond human lady, I think her name was Lena." Joey was quick to cover his true thoughts about going back to Earth.

"Ah yes, that banana shop." Budda sighed and placed his food down. "Joey, you must never be sad. I know it's a sad situation, but in Magical World and even on Earth, you must realize that if you are sad, the situation only gets worse. For good things to happen, you must always be happy."

"Really? Is that how it works?" Joey replied sarcastically.

"Yes, of course. Didn't you notice when bad things happened on Earth, people always got depressed? And then more bad luck appears," explained Budda. He smiled at Joey, completely ignoring his sarcasm.

Joey then smiled back. "Come to think of it, I can remember the time my Uncle Ben's daughter was killed in a car accident. A few months later, his wife, Auntie Faye, had a stroke. Uncle Ben had to close his business to take care of her full time. Then they had to move out of their brand-new six-bedroom brick house, into an old run-down weatherboard house. I remember Mum and Dad helped them move. There are still a lot of problems in that family, and I've never seen my uncle or aunt laugh or even smile."

"You're learning fast, so let's be happy. We will get Olivia and Astina back. They are safe. My instincts are good. And when I meditate, I always imagine the white light around them. This will always protect them, I assure you," said Budda as he sipped his herbal tea.

Joey smiled and enjoyed eating his hot dog and potato cakes. He kept quiet about his doubts of getting back to Earth, and he was glad Budda had not asked him about it. "Let's do something funny then. I need a good laugh. Do you have any suggestions?" asked Joey.

Budda made a funny face. He pressed his nose with his fingers, and at the same time, he made his eyes squinty and pulled his tongue out to his chest. Joey chuckled. He could not imagine ever being able to do that. Budda certainly had many talents. Budda then stood on the floating chair on his tiptoes; he almost looked like a ballerina.

"Hahahahaha," Joey laughed so much he almost could not breath.

Budda then bounced on the chair and went flying into the air. Just as he was about to land back on his chair, it moved, and Budda's buttocks landed smack bang on the hard ground.

"*Ooouchh!*" he cried.

Joey continued to laugh; he wanted to help Budda, but he was laughing so much he could hardly move. Budda was so chubby. A couple of times, he lost his balance and fell back down again. This made both Joey and Budda laugh even more.

Suddenly, to Joey's surprise, he saw a blue light flash on and off.

CHAPTER 11

Jack and Ben

Joey instantly stopped laughing. He pointed towards the lit door. "Look, over there, the light, it's flashing on that blue door," said Joey. He jumped off his chair and raced to the door. He tried the handle, but it would not open. Joey touched every part of the door to see if there was a button or a secret switch that could help him open the door.

"How do we get in?" asked Joey impatiently.

"I don't know. I've never come across this door situation before," said Budda, touching all parts of the door.

"*Help!*" cried another voice.

"Did you hear that?" asked Joey.

"Yes, I heard it. It sounds like someone is trapped somewhere."

Budda and Joey searched the cave but could not see anyone. Suddenly, the light on the door stopped flashing. The door opened and a grown man appeared. Not noticing Joey or Budda, he lifted up a huge rock, and from its deep hole, he raised a small boy. The dark-coloured boy was about five years old.

"There you go, son," said the middle-aged man, who towered over the tiny boy.

"Thank you, sir," answered the boy. Joey recognized his voice as the same as the one who cried for help.

"Er . . . excuse me, sir. My name is Joey Willis, and this is my friend Budda. Could you please help us find Rockwell Mountain? We were told one of these doors would take us there."

The little boy and the man stared at Joey and Budda. They looked bewildered and were speechless for a few minutes.

"Well, nice to meet you, Joey and Bud. My name is Jack Batson, and this is little Ben." He grabbed each of Joey and Budda's hand and gave them both a good shake.

"My name is Budda, thanks."

"Oh, sorry, *Budda*, I'm not really good with names. So where did you two come from?"

"I'm from Earth," said Joey. He pointed his hand towards Budda. "And my friend, Budda, is from Riddells Withals. Your friendly snake Sess brought us here. He says the humans from Rockwell Mountain can help us find our way there." Joey and Budda nodded their heads in agreement while the little boy, Ben, helped himself to some of the leftover food on the floating table. He seemed very hungry.

"Mmmm, yummy, yummy, this food tastes great," said Ben.

"What's this, some kind of picnic? Hey, where did you get all this food cooked out here in the cave?" asked Jack.

"It's magic. Budda used his fettal. Well, can you take us to Rockwell Mountain?" asked Joey.

Jack stared at Joey and Budda. He was wearing baggy worn-out, ragged clothes, and his beard was half-shaven. He also smelt bad and breathed heavily.

"Now why would you want to go to Rockwell Mountain so badly? Is there gold or something around there?" asked Jack mischievously.

"No, we really need to find a particular stone," explained Joey.

"Oh, even better, diamonds, hey!"

"Wrong again. The stone we are looking for is called the charmal crystal stone. The stone's colour is emerald green, and we can use it to heal particular viruses."

"I haven't heard of any charmal crystal stone. But I can take you to Rockwell Mountain if you want. Just let me have a bite to eat, if you don't mind?"

"Go ahead, there's plenty of food for you and Ben. Thank you so much, we really appreciate your help," said Joey.

"I don't think you'll be thanking me when we get there. I've never heard of a healing stone before. You mentioned before the humans can help you. Well, I don't think they can."

"Why?" asked Joey.

"It's not that they don't want to help you. It's just that they are very weak, and a lot of them are very sick," Jack said while stuffing his mouth.

"Why don't they use the crystal caves? It would heal them within minutes," asked Joey. He glanced at Budda, who was moving his head from side to side, trying to stop Joey from saying more. Joey then realized he should not have mentioned the healing caves or any magic.

Jack stopped eating and turned to face Joey and Budda. "I don't know anything about crystal caves. Don't tell me you're one of those freaks who thinks a stone can automatically make someone better."

Joey felt embarrassed and intimidated. "Oh, well, maybe I'm wrong about the healing crystals. I've just read it in a book somewhere." He realized this man was no different than a lot of people on Earth, who had no belief in crystal healing. Joey did not like this man. He had an attitude about magic and healing, and Ben was not taken care of very well, being stuck under the ground for who knows how long. In Joey's mind, this man, Jack, did not seem to be a nice person although Joey convinced himself to be nice to him. No matter what he said or did, they needed him to take them to Rockwell Mountain.

While Jack and Ben were eating, Budda grabbed Joey's arm and whispered close to his ear, "Joey, do you really think we can trust this man? I'm having problems trying to read his mind, and he does not come across a patient man to me."

"We have no choice. We've got to be nice to him. At this moment, he is our only guide to get to Rockwell Mountain. Maybe his nonbelief in magic prevents us from reading his mind, I doubt very much he would have a nonmind reading shield," whispered Joey.

"Yes, I think you're right, but there is something about this man I don't trust, especially keeping a hungry little boy underground. Now that's cruel!"

"I know. That's another reason why we should stay with him. When we get to Rockwell Mountain, we should take Ben with us. No one should be treated like that," said Joey seriously.

Budda nodded his head, "Yes, I agree with you on that. Poor Ben, he deserves a better life."

Jack seized Ben by the arm and turned him away from the floating table. "That's enough, no more food for you. The rest is for me, you little guts," he yelled angrily. He pushed Ben to the ground near the corner of the cave. Ben was lucky his head missed a group of rocks, and Budda quickly ran to his aid. He slid his hand inside his cape to give Ben a sario fruit.

"I can supply you with more food, Jack. There is always plenty to share," said Budda.

Jack turned to face Budda. "Oh yeah? And where do you think you can get more food, in midair or something? I can't see any bags of food with you. And there is certainly no food stores close by," he said sarcastically.

Budda did not answer; he only placed his arms around Ben and kept close to Joey.

"When can you take us to Rockwell Mountain?" asked Joey, quickly trying to change the subject so there'd be no arguments.

Jack finished eating the last piece of apple pie. While chewing, he mumbled, "We can leave when I'm finished with what I came here for . . . mmmmmm, very delicious."

Joey and Budda pretended to smile. It was now very obvious that they were right and Jack was not a pleasant person. He also appeared to be very selfish.

"Ah yes, before we head off, I have to get something. Ah yes, that's right, the burning stones. You'll just have to wait a minute." Jack was searching the ground. He bent down and grabbed some black stones and then bundled them inside a mesh sack that he flipped over his shoulder. "We use these stones to keep our fires going. They are much better than wood, they last a very long time." Jack threw a sack to Joey, Budda, and Ben. "Come on, you farts, help me fill these sacks, and then we'll be on our way."

"We'll be happy to help," said Joey, pretending he did not hear Jack's nasty tone. He pointed his head in the direction of a pile of black rocks and eyed Budda to start filling the sack. He also wondered if the rocks were the only reason Jack came here.

"Ah yes, of course, we'd be happy to help," repeated Budda. Joey, Budda, and Ben stayed close together while they filled the bags.

"I have a much better way to carry these rocks," whispered Joey. He gazed inside his cape.

Budda grabbed Joey's arm. "That's not a very good idea, Joey. I don't think we can trust this man with our magic. We'll play along with him and do everything his way," whispered Budda.

Joey released his cape and nodded his agreement. They spent a good half hour filling the bags. Jack carried them as if they were as light as a feather; he looked extremely strong.

"Right, follow me this way." Jack led them towards another door, a red one this time. "Okay, all done!" yelled Jack. "This door will take us to Rockwell Mountain. Watch this!" He waved his hand very slowly across the door.

"Now this is magic." He had a smirk on his face that gave the impression that Joey and Budda knew nothing about magic. Budda frowned and looked upset. The lights on the door started flashing. Jack counted every flash, "One, two, three, four, five, six, seven, eight." On the eighth flash, he grabbed the door handle and turned the knob. Before he fully opened the door, he turned to face Joey and Budda. "Every door has its own number of flashes. If you don't turn the handle on the required flash, you won't be able to enter. Rockwell Mountain is always eight. It's really important to know what number each door is or you'll be guessing forever, and you may never be able to get out of these caves. It's just like having a secret code."

"Wow, that's amazing,' answered Joey.

Jack nodded and smiled. He threw the sacks of rocks over his shoulder. "Okay, everyone follow me," he said as he made his way through the door.

Ben, Joey, and Budda followed. In front of them were grey rocks and green trees and, in the distance, a huge purple mountain. Everything around them apart from the mountain seemed to be like Joey's real world on Earth, and nothing appeared edible.

Jack pointed towards the purple mountain. "There's your Rockwell Mountain."

"Yes, I know, I saw a picture of it, thanks, Jack," answered Joey.

"Why are you thanking me? We are here, but there is no way you'll be able to get on that mountain."

"And why not?" asked Joey.

"That place is infested with huge snakes. And those snakes are not ordinary snakes. They spit poisonous fire.

Nobody has ever been able to get on that mountain." He laughed.

Joey and Budda were so disappointed. "There must be some way of getting there. We'll have to find a way," said Joey desperately.

Jack vigorously shook his head from side to side. "Sorry, mate, many people have tried and been killed. Even if one of the snakes only slightly burnt you, their poison will kill you instantly. Those huge snakes are ten times stronger and faster than any ordinary snake. Even if you tried to fly over them, they'd be able to grab you. Not only are they lethal, they are also smart."

Joey and Budda looked at each other, but they kept quiet because they knew Jack would disagree with whatever they suggested. Jack continued to walk along a dirt track with the others behind.

"Where are you taking us?" asked Joey.

"To my people. We have to get these rocks to them. It gets so cold at night, we need fires to keep warm, otherwise more of our people will get sick and die."

CHAPTER 12

Curash Virus

Joey glanced at Budda and noticed he was using a floating table to carry his bag of rocks. He pointed his finger to Joey's cape and then his floating table. Joey knew what he meant. He looked inside his cape and thought about the floating table. A pocket opened, and he placed his hand inside and pulled out his own floating table. At the same time, Joey peeked at Jack to make sure that he kept the floating table hidden behind him. After loading his sack of rocks on the table, he grabbed Ben's sack. Ben was so small he was struggling to carry his sack.

"Don't you use wood to burn?" asked Joey.

Jack continued to walk ahead of them without looking back. "Yes, we do use wood, but these rocks have twelve months of burning in them. I don't know what these rocks are made of, but they save a lot of work, especially when there are so many of us sick."

Joey realized the black rocks were magic. "What type of sickness do your people have?" he asked.

"I wish I knew. I have some friends who come to help me with the sick. Sometimes their cures help, but it doesn't help them all—many still die. My friends take them away when they die as whatever the sickness is, it is very contagious. They promised to give the dead a good burial."

"What are the symptoms of this type of illness?" asked Budda.

"My friends call it a curash virus. And as for the symptoms, you'll soon see for yourselves when we get to the village. Now that's enough with the questions," grunted Jack angrily.

"Okay, but just two more questions, what are your friends' names, and how long has this curash virus been around?" Joey asked.

"My friends' names are Victor and Max, they visit every month. We've only had this virus for around three months, just before I met Victor and Max in the caves. Now, if you ask me any more questions, I'll leave you both here," said Jack impatiently.

Joey wanted to ask more questions, but he had no desire to upset Jack anymore. Budda and Joey wanted to help the sick people. They decided to ignore Jack's unpleasant behaviour. Budda moved closer to Joey. "We'll try and use our healing stones to help cure the people," whispered Budda.

"I was thinking the same thing," said Joey quietly.

"Yes, but we'll have to do it without Jack knowing. He doesn't believe in healing stones. We really can't afford to get him upset."

"I agree," Joey agreed, nodding.

They walked through the bushes for a few hours. Ben looked exhausted, so Joey put him on his floating table, and a few minutes later, he fell asleep. Luckily, Jack kept on looking ahead although Joey made sure he was always in front of the tables just in case Jack turned around.

The ground was very hard under Joey's feet, unlike the comfortable ground in the real Magical World. Budda was also struggling to walk through the bushes and rocks. Joey suggested he sit on a floating chair, but Budda refused, fearing that Jack might turn around and notice. Although the way Jack was moving, he did not look as if he cared about how they were coping.

Finally, they approached a huge cave entrance. Joey was feeling slightly cold when they stopped. He searched inside his cape pocket and found a yellow powder-like substance. He threw it over his head. Instantly the powder made him feel warm. He gazed downwards and saw that his feet were not bare anymore. The powder had given him black boots that made his feet feel very comfortable.

Joey quickly woke Ben and gently lifted him off the table. Budda also unloaded his table, and swiftly they put their tables back inside their capes.

As Ben was about to say something, Joey gently placed his pointer finger over his mouth and quietly said, "*Sssshhh,* don't tell Jack about the table. Let's make this our little secret, okay?"

Ben smiled, and nodding, he happily agreed.

"Anyway, you won't need a ride now, it looks like we're here," whispered Joey.

Jack stopped, slamming his bag to the ground. He had not rested once during the entire trip, and he made it look easy to carry the heavy sack of rocks. He pulled out a canister from his pants pocket and drank from it.

"Is that soda drink?" asked Joey.

Jack turned the canteen over and out poured ordinary water. "Does this look like soda drink to you? Sorry to disappoint you, mate," he said sarcastically. He didn't offer any of them a drink, so Budda gave Joey and Ben a drink from his cape.

Budda whispered to Joey, "This place . . . apart from Rockwell Mountain is just like Earth. The people here don't believe in magic even though magic is here, which means they are living just like people on Earth."

"I see. That's why everything here is like Earth, because they don't believe in magic. Oh no, if only they would listen to us, then there would be plenty of food for everyone, and little Ben wouldn't be hungry." Joey patted Ben gently on his head. Ben stared up at him and smiled.

"This is why we are here. To show the people there is magic and beauty beyond their suffering. And I think little Ben is starting to believe it. That's why only he can see it. He is the innocent one, and we are here to save him and anyone else who wants to believe and are good to themselves and others."

"You're right, Budda. We've got to help these people and take them with us to Riddells Withals." Joey held Ben's hand, and Budda nodded.

All three of them stood in front of Jack, who pointed his finger to an entrance of a huge dark cave. "Here is where my people live. We've made this cave our small village. There's a special door here that allows us in. We never stay out here during the night as it is very dangerous. Monsters fly in and take people back to their nests for food. That is why we had to travel quickly before nightfall."

"What are these monsters?" asked Joey.

"We call them lexus creatures. They are like prehistoric creatures. Huge hairy, winged beasts with the head of a white tiger. And it's no ordinary tiger's head, it's about five times the size. They have vicious mouths that could rip you in half with one bite."

"How long have you all been living like this?" asked Budda.

"For many years. Every day, the people in the village are getting fewer and fewer, now there are only a few of us left. We've been using this cave as our hideout.

Luckily, nobody has been eaten yet. I'm sure by now the lexus creatures are getting very anxious because they haven't had human flesh for so long."

"So what do they eat instead?" asked Joey.

"Anything, I guess, maybe other monsters or even their own. I don't know. I've certainly never hung around to find out. At least now we're safe. Come in and have a look, we've even disguised the doors with bushes and rocks."

They all walked inside the cave. Jack moved some branches away from a black-coloured door, which was a very good colour disguise. He waved his hand slowly over the door and closed his eyes. He looked as if he was in some deep concentration or meditation. He then opened his eyes and a light started to flash. He counted each flash until it reached twenty-five. When a flat door handle appeared, Jack quickly turned the handle, and with Ben close beside him, he turned to face Joey and Budda. "Welcome to our home. Come in."

"Will the door be disguised again once we're inside?" asked Joey.

"Don't worry about that, the branches always settle back on the door once it's closed. I don't know how that happens, but it does. Come on, let's go, it's getting late."

This place did not look anything like the cave. It looked more like an old-fashioned village. There was light as if it were day, and people and animals, houses and gardens and trees. You would not guess they were in a cave, but it was nothing like Riddells Withals and the real Magical World, where everything was beautiful. The only magic in the village was the fact that it was inside a cave and resembled an ordinary life on Earth.

The people stared at Joey and Budda. Joey realized it must have been the way he and Budda looked and dressed, which was very different, especially Joey's blue skin. These people looked so poor in their ragged clothes.

They continued to walk through the village, and the people continued to stop and stare at them. Joey could not take his eyes off a small black-haired girl. She would have been about six years old, and she had a very pretty face. She wore a faded blue dress and was sitting in a wooden wheelchair. Then Joey noticed she had no legs. She smiled at Joey as if she were very happy to see him. He stopped and took her hand and smiled. "Hello, my name is Joey, what's yours?"

"Suellen. I haven't seen you here before. Where are you from? And why is your skin blue?"

"That's a long story. Have you ever heard of Earth?"

Suellen shook her head. "No, where is Earth?"

"Earth is in another world. Don't ask me how I got here because even I don't know. The fact is, I'm here and I have to make the most of it. And my skin wasn't always blue, it's normally your colour—I don't know how that happened either. Anyway, enough about me, tell me what happened to your legs?"

Suellen gazed down and suddenly looked sad. "I caught this horrible illness. It's called the curash virus. I almost died, and they had to amputate my legs. It was really lucky Victor and Max gave my father a vaccination, or I would have died."

"How did this curash virus start?"

"I started feeling tired, and my legs were pinching. It was like pins and needles. I got a really high temperature, and then I fell asleep. Papa said I was asleep for two months. When I woke up, I saw my legs were gone and my whole body hurt. A lot of the people here have this virus. The horrible thing about this virus is that it makes you feel cold all the time. Papa had to keep me warm."

"How are you feeling now?" asked Joey still holding her hand.

"Much better, but my body is still healing. You'd better be careful, they think this virus is contagious."

"Don't you worry about me, you just get better."

Joey wanted to give Suellen his pink healing stone, but he noticed Jack had been looking at him the whole time he was talking to her. Then he signalled for Joey to move along.

"I'd better go. I hope I see you again, Suellen."

"I'd like that. I live just over there, come and visit anytime." Suellen pointed to a small hut. Bits of wood were not nailed in properly, and it looked like it only had one room for her whole family. Joey felt so sorry for her and wanted to help her. In fact, he wanted to help all the people.

"I'll be back to see you, I promise," Joey said, giving her a kiss on top of her head. The more they walked, the more people crowded around. Everywhere Joey looked, everything seemed old, worn-out, and dirty. Joey felt like he would not fit in here, and he presumed it was because of his colour.

At last they stopped in an empty courtyard. In the middle was a huge well with empty baskets around it. Jack started to pile the black rocks into the empty baskets. "You can fill these baskets with the rocks. People always come here when they need rocks or water," he explained. He seemed a lot quieter and a little sad.

While they unloaded the rocks, Jack said to Joey and Budda, "Now you know what the virus is like and how much these people are suffering. We have a small hospital around the corner full of sick people. I noticed the way you cared for that girl. When you're both finished settling in, you can help out at the hospital. We could do with extra hands, everyone helps around here."

"Of course we'll help. We would be happy to do that," said Budda.

Joey nodded. "Definitely, we'll do all we can to help."

Jack blinked slowly and, with a slight smile, said, "Well, I'm glad I met up with you two in the cave. I'll show you to your room where you can rest. With so many people dead, there are plenty of empty rooms to choose from."

Jack escorted them to a block of huts near the hospital. He was right when he said there were a lot of empty rooms. As the doors were not completely shut, Joey could see the rooms were empty with the exception of a single bed in each of them. The dust and dirt inside and outside the huts made Joey feel very uncomfortable.

"Here you go. These will be your rooms—numbers 67 and 68. You're welcome to have a room each or can share, the choice is yours. As you can see, they both have two beds. These rooms are the biggest out of the lot. I'll leave you both to it. If you need anything, I'll be at the hospital, just go down this road and turn right."

Jack seemed to have the impression that Joey and Budda were going to stay for an indefinite period. He seemed to have forgotten the real reason they were there although, perhaps, this could be excused with all the suffering and the poor state of the village. It was a situation of who can help whom in desperate times.

Budda scrunched his nose and frowned in disgust. "Yuck, this is disgusting. Maybe I can let Toodles out, and we can stay in there instead of here," suggested Budda.

"I don't think that's a good idea. We don't want Jack to know about our magic yet. Remember, you were the one telling me to keep a low profile," said Joey.

"Yes, I guess you're right. Surely I'm allowed to clean and decorate our room."

"You can clean it, but forget about taking anything out from your cape to decorate the room. He'll wonder where you got the stuff from."

"Very well then," said Budda with a mild disappointed look on his face. He closed the door after Joey and quickly shut the curtains. He pulled out a doll from his cape. She wore a pink silk gown and robe, and she was very pretty, even for a doll. In fact, she looked like a genie. Budda waved his hand and threw pink dust over her and commanded, "Clean up!"

The doll moved like a robot, and with a blink of an eye, the whole room was sparkling clean. The dirt floor was now covered in bright-green grass. The grass was so soft you would have thought it was green carpet. The walls looked like they had had a fresh coat of white paint. The beds were made up with crisp, clean white linen and fluffy yellow blankets. There was not a speck of dust to be seen.

Joey gasped, "Wow, how did you do that?"

Budda quickly put the genie doll back inside his cape. "How else? I used magic. You can do that too, every wardrobe outfit has a genie doll of its own. There is so much for you to learn about your magic, Joey, even the basic stuff, such as cleaning up."

"Did you have to put that doll away? We might need her again, she's fantastic."

"Oh, Joey, you just told me to hide our magic from Jack." Budda looked disappointed again. Joey noticed that he seemed to be a little downhearted. Then he realized that Budda was simply not used to the poor conditions and surroundings they found themselves in.

"I know, I'm sorry, it just felt so good using magic. I wish the people here would believe in it. They would never have to worry about food, clothing, or shelter," said Joey.

"That's why we are here. We have to help these people and bring out the real Magical World they should be living in," declared Budda.

Budda smiled and sat on one of the squeaky clean beds.

"You call this Magical World? No, this is more like Earth. That door we went through must have taken us to another world like Earth. Maybe we're on another planet."

"Sorry to disappoint you, Joey, but this is part of Magical World. Just look at Rockwell Mountain, it has the colours of Magical World. The reason why this part does not look like Magical World is because these people don't believe in magic. They haven't experienced the real Magical World, and yet they are in it. Once they start to believe, then this will all change to the real Magical World."

"Maybe it's because of these beasts that come out at night. It looks like the people here live in constant fear. Earth can be like that in some places, especially in countries where there is war," said Joey. He flopped onto the other bed, his head down. Joey felt sad for these people.

"We are going to have to try and change that for them. That's why we are here. We have to find a way to help these people and to retrieve that stone from Rockwell Mountain."

"But those snakes are deadly. How are we going to get past them?"

Budda sat on his bed in quiet concentration. Joey kept silent, knowing he had to let him think. Meanwhile, he too tried to think of a way to pass those snakes. Then Budda looked at Joey. "I'll have to meditate on this one. Anyway, we can't do anything until tomorrow. We don't need the added problem of those beasts at night and the snakes. You should get some sleep while I meditate. In the morning, we'll first go to the hospital to help the people, and then we can sneak out."

Joey nodded. "That sounds good to me." He began to relax, and slowly he drifted off into a deep sleep. It was as though he had not slept in days. He could get very confused with time in Magical World, and Budda seemed to forget he still needed his sleep.

CHAPTER 13

Rockwell Mountain

Ten hours later, Joey woke up. He wondered where he was—was he at home in his own bed or at Riddells Withals? Then he remembered he was somewhere near Rockwell Mountain in a dirty village full of sickness. For a moment, Joey wished this was all a bad dream and that Magical World would just simply disappear.

Joey suddenly felt a wave of guilt. *What if I had slept too long*? He quickly sat up and pulled the blankets off. Budda would be at the hospital by now. Joey splashed his face with some water from a dish to help him wake up. There were no showers or special wardrobes to freshen up here. He was not sure how Budda had freshened up; maybe he used something from his cape. Joey decided he was not going to waste any more time figuring it out and set off for the hospital.

The hospital was made out of mud brick with a roof of tree bark. It did not look anything like a real hospital back on Earth, and Magical World did not need a hospital with all its healing crystals and magic.

Immediately, he was inside the entrance, and all Joey could see were beds and beds of sick people. Some were even lying on dirty old mattresses on the floor.

Helpless moans and cries filled the air—this was no modern hospital. No painkillers or anaesthetics and hardly any decent bed linen or bandages. This place looked more like a slaughterhouse, with the young and old slowly dying.

At one end of the large room, Joey saw Budda sitting next to a little blond girl. He was holding her hand and quietly speaking to her. Budda glanced up and signalled to Joey to come to him. Joey slowly made his way through the crowded beds and mattresses, carefully ensuring he did not step on or bump anyone.

The little girl Budda was with had only one arm and one leg.

"Lucy, I want you to meet someone," said Budda. He put Joey's hand on hers.

"Who is this someone?" she asked.

"Joey Willis is my very dear friend. And Joey, this is Lucy. She was telling me about her eighth birthday celebration yesterday. Everyone here sang her a happy birthday song and had made her this special quilt. Look at this," Budda said pointing to the quilt, which was covered with embroidered animals. "Lucy can feel the embroidered pictures." Joey was shocked to realise that this pretty blue-eyed girl was not only without an arm and a leg, but she was also blind. He quickly pretended everything was normal and used his other hand to feel the design.

Lucy smiled. "Yes, this is the best birthday I've ever had. Can you see the rooster? That one feels the best. Go on, touch it."

Joey touched the rooster and then looked back at Lucy. "Well, happy birthday, Lucy. If I'd known, I would have got you a gift." Joey carefully looked at the girl and thought of Olivia; she was the same age.

Suddenly, Joey remembered the healing crystal. He quickly pulled it out from his cape and glanced at Budda, who appeared surprised that Joey had the crystal. He nodded his head as if he knew what Joey was going to do. Joey turned to face Lucy again. "Actually, Lucy, I was wrong. I do have a special gift for you."

"You do? What could it be? Oh, you are so kind, Joey." Even though she was blind, Joey could see the excitement in her eyes.

"I have a beautiful pink crystal in my hand. Here, I'll give it to you to hold. This crystal has special energies. I want you to imagine it going through your body."

He placed the small crystal in the palm of her hand and gently closed her fingers over it.

"Oh, thank you, Joey, it must be beautiful—it feels warm and smooth."

"No need to thank me, just hold on to it tightly and imagine energy going through your body—pure, wonderful energy." Joey tenderly covered her hand with both of his hands.

"Okay, I'll try." Lucy closed her eyes. She looked radiant. Joey could see the energies of the stone go through her. After a minute, she slowly opened her eyes. Joey and Budda looked into her eyes. She was staring straight ahead as if she was still blind. Budda waved his hand in front of her face, but she did not respond. Her eyes did not move.

"Wow, I feel really good. I feel so happy and relaxed, and I don't feel any pain. Joey, you said something about energy going through me while I hold this crystal, was it that that made me feel so good?" she asked.

"Yes, Lucy, it was the crystal. But you have to promise to keep it a secret and take care of it. I don't have another crystal to give to anyone else. It wouldn't be fair to the others here. This is your special gift from me," said Joey quietly. He did not want to lie to Lucy, but for now, he had no choice. He had to keep the healing crystal a secret from Jack as Jack still needed proof and convincing of its healing and magic.

"I promise, I won't tell anyone. This will be our little secret. Thank you, Joey, this is the best gift anyone has ever given me." Lucy yawned and suddenly looked very tired.

"You'd better get some sleep now, Lucy. We'll come back and visit you later. You just get better, okay?" said Joey. He helped Lucy get comfortable in her bed and moved her hair from her face. This also reminded him of the times he tucked his sister into bed when his parents were busy.

"Okay," said Lucy, and soon after, she drifted off to sleep.

Joey and Budda looked at each other. They were both very disappointed.

"The crystal didn't work," stated Joey with sadness. He had been so sure the crystal would heal Lucy. Budda paced around Lucy's bed and did his thinking habit with his pointer finger over his mouth.

"That's it!" said Budda, his eyes lighting up.

"What is it?" asked Joey anxiously.

"It's a curse. And it looks like a curse only the druggons would use. Unless there are other creatures we are unaware of around here. No, it has to be the druggons."

"Are you sure?"

"Yes, I am very certain. My instincts are sure of it."

"But these people don't know the druggons, and I can't see any here."

"They must be in disguise. These druggons could even turn themselves into an insect if they wanted to. I also have a feeling they know we're after the charmal stone," said Budda, looking worried. Joey could tell by the frown on his forehead; it was the same frown he had when Astina told him about the druggons outside the crystal caves.

"We can't waste any time then. We're going to have to go to Rockwell Mountain now," said Joey. He was more determined than ever to get the stone.

Budda and Joey hurried outside. They were not going to waste a single moment. They had to do this without being noticed. Jack might try to stop them, and they were not yet ready to show any of their magic to the people in the village. Not until they had proof. If they had the charmal stone, it would cure the people, and that would be all proof they needed.

Their path instantly became crowded with the village people. They struggled through the crowd, and almost lost sight of each other until Joey decided to hang on to Budda's belt.

After a lot of pushing and shoving, Joey and Budda finally made it to the outskirts of the village, away from the crowd. And just as they turned in the direction of the door, directly in front of them was Jack.

"Joey, Bud, I'd like to introduce you to my friends Victor and Max," said Jack. He pushed himself between them and placed his hands on their shoulders. "Victor, Max, this is Joey and Bud. We met up in the caves. They are going to stay with us and help out at the hospital. We were very lucky we came across them, we really need the extra hands to help."

Budda moved his head from side to side. "Actually, no, Jack, my name is Budda. Joey and I are not staying here." He moved away from Jack and glanced at Joey.

"We are on our way out. Remember, we told you at the caves that our main purpose was to find the charmal stone at Rockwell Mountain," explained Budda.

Jack stopped smiling and had a stern look on his face. "Surely you're not still on about that magic stone are you?" he said, shaking his head and looking annoyed.

"Yes, we are," interrupted Joey.

Jack crossed his arms and stood tall, but just before he had a chance to say anything further, Joey intervened. He shook his pointer finger and said, "Now, I know you don't believe in magic and healing stones, but there is a good chance that the stone could cure these people."

Victor pushed himself in front of Jack. "*Eeeee,* maybe we could help you and Budda, *eeeeee,*" he suggested. Jack looked as if he was going to explode with anger, but Victor held his arm and nodded his head as though he were taking care of the situation. Jack seemed to calm down.

Unlike the people in the village, Jack's friends were well dressed. They were both wearing black suits with black shirts and ties. Max was dark-skinned while Victor was pale with blond hair and blue eyes. On the left side of his face was a bandage. He looked as if he had suffered some sort of burn. They both appeared interested in what Joey and Budda had to say.

"And how can you help us, Victor?" asked Joey. He didn't like the look of these men; he had a feeling they were not to be trusted. His instincts were working overtime, and he felt as if he had met these men somewhere before. Victor's accent reminded him of someone.

Victor pulled out a small black box and opened it in front of Joey and Budda. Neatly stacked inside the box were filled syringes.

"Theeese are the only way weeeee are going to cure theeeeese peeeeople. There is no other cure, you seeee," said Victor, using his other hand to secure his bandage.

"What happened to your face?" asked Joey.

"Had a little problem with a beast outside theeeese caves. You seeeeee, there are a lot of undesirables out there, and that stone you are looking for won't help you at all. You seeeeeeee, you're much safer here than out there."

The more Joey listened to Victor, the more he tried to picture the person or the situation he reminded him of. He desperately wished he could remember.

Budda nudged Joey and signalled him with his head to leave. "Sorry, Jack, Victor, Max, but we have other reasons to go to Rockwell Mountain. And don't worry, Jack, we'll find a way to handle those big snakes. If all goes well, we'll be back to help your people. Come on, Joey, let's go."

By this time, a crowd had gathered, and as Budda and Joey headed towards the door, they were shaking their heads in disbelief. Someone called out, "Those snakes will kill you!" And Joey could hear the people saying amongst themselves, "They won't be back."

"Have you thought of a plan to get past the snakes?" Joey quietly asked Budda.

Budda kept walking straight ahead, moving his head from side to side. "Nope, not yet," he replied.

Joey was feeling frightened, but he made sure no one saw his fear. Instead, he smiled and waved. Budda was racing to the door, and Joey had to run to keep up with him.

"No, wait, Joey, Budda, wait! Please wait!" yelled a voice from the crowd.

Budda and Joey stopped and saw it was little Ben running towards them.

"Ben!" shouted Joey. Ben raced to their side and grabbed Joey by his cape.

"Please don't go," cried Ben. "Please don't go, please," he cried again, over and over.

"Ben, don't worry. Don't cry. We'll be back, I promise," said Joey. He gave him a hug and looked at Budda.

Budda grabbed Ben and also gave him a hug. He held his shoulders and looked at his face. He wiped his tears with a pink hanky from his cape. "Ben, it will be okay. We'll be back to get you, I promise," said Budda.

"No, No, you won't. Those big snakes will kill you. Please don't go."

Budda gave him another hug and whispered in his ear, "Ben, remember the floating tables."

Ben nodded his head. "Yes, I do." He sniffed loudly.

"That was magic. Joey and I have special magic. We will use our magic to get past those snakes, and we are going to get the charmal stone to save all your people. So don't worry, we'll be safe, and we'll be back before you know it. I promise. Now stop crying and go back to your home."

"Magic, oh yes, I remember the secret."

"That's right, we have magic. We'll be okay, I promise," Budda assured Ben again.

With tears still running down his cheek, Ben managed a smile. He stepped back and allowed Joey and Budda to continue their journey to Rockwell Mountain.

Before they disappeared through the black door, Joey turned and had a last look at all the anxious faces. Ben waved from the distance. Joey waved back and quickly followed Budda back inside the cave.

Joey noticed the branches quickly cover the door again. Jack was right about that; nobody could ever suspect it was there. But Budda was not taking any chances; he placed a brown stone near the door.

"Why are you doing that?" asked Joey.

"These caves are very confusing. Once we walk out of here, it will be very difficult for us to find the door again. Only you and I will know what this stone means here. This way, we'll be able to find the door quickly and easily."

"Good idea. I suppose once we get back, we won't want to worry about the time the lexus beasts come out."

"It's not the lexus beasts I'm worried about, Joey, it's the people. We need to save as many of them as we can. I'm sure the charmal stone will help them. And as for the lexus beasts, I don't think they will be too difficult to handle. I doubt they are worse than the druggons. We'll use our magic to fight them."

"Yes, you're right. I'll be getting my wet blanket ready."

"You can also get your balon ready because that is how we are going to get to Rockwell Mountain."

"But didn't Jack say those snakes can stretch high."

"I'm aware of that, Joey. So we'll use this for protection." Budda pulled out a glass bubble. It was exactly his height. He stood on his balon, and magically, the bubble went over his whole body and his balon.

"You have one that fits you too, Joey, look inside your cape," echoed Budda's voice from the bubble. It was just like a microphone.

Joey thought about his bubble and quickly searched his cape. A pocket opened up, and he pulled out his very own bubble. It was exactly his size; it was a clear blue colour, and it was shaped exactly like his body. Once Joey stood on his balon, his bubble magically covered him too. He had the overwhelming feeling that he was completely safe. When he spoke to Budda, it was like Budda was inside with him.

"Joey, nobody else can hear us talk, we can hear each other, but nobody else can hear us. Also, these bubbles make us invisible to others. The snakes won't hear or see us, and if they try to blow fire, we will be protected from getting burnt or poisoned."

"Are you sure they can't see us?"

"No, I'm not sure. This is Magical World, and I'm not sure what powers they have. I tried to look for it in my books back at the hut while you were sleeping, but I couldn't find anything on them. So we'll have to play it by ear and hope they can't hear or see us. And remember, Joey, if we break up by accident, while we are both wearing these bubbles, we can communicate."

"Wow, this is great."

Budda nodded his head in agreement and smiled.

"Once we get to our destination and all is clear, we'll have to take these bubbles off to locate the stone. When we do, be very careful, Joey."

"I will. Let's go. You'll have to follow me, I know exactly where the stone is from what I've read in the book."

"Then lead the way, my friend."

Joey quickly took off like a flash, followed by Budda. It felt so wonderful to be able to fly. He kept thinking about Rockwell Mountain, and in the far distance, he saw a glimpse of the purple mountain with the red sky above it, just as he had seen it in his book. It was quite a distance to travel on foot. He was glad to have the opportunity to use his balon and bubble.

Flying reminded him of the time his father had taken him on a small plane ride. Except on Earth, he had to have a paper bag ready just in case he was sick. His balon did not make him feel sick at all, probably because he felt safe because of its magic. Joey knew the magic would not allow him to crash, whereas with an airplane, there was always the possibility of a crash. Accidents seemed to happen on Earth. But here, he felt perfectly at ease gliding through the air on his magical balon.

"Can you see the mountain?" Joey asked Budda.

"Yes, I can see it. We should stay high, just in case the snakes sense us. Once we get closer, we will slow down."

"I can't see any snakes. Jack said it was infested, surely we'd be able to see at least a few." Joey did not take his eyes off the mountain.

"They could be camouflaged. Have a look inside your cape for a pair of goggles." Budda already had his goggles on. Joey wanted to laugh because Budda looked very funny wearing them; they almost covered his whole face.

"Why are you wearing goggles? There's no water. I don't think we'll need to swim." Joey joked, trying not to laugh out loud.

"These goggles are not for swimming, Joey. The goggles are magic and allow me to see the mountain at close range," snapped Budda. Budda was not impressed with Joey's sense of humour.

"Oh, I'm sorry. You mean they are like binoculars?"

"Just find yours and put them on. We don't have time to play around—this is not a joking matter."

"Okay, okay, hold your pants up. Here we go." Joey pulled out a blue pair of goggles. They were not as large as Budda's; they were a nice, neat fit. He quickly put them on, and to his surprise, the mountain was magnified. He had to let the balon drive by itself. Looking through the goggles made him confused as to where he was. The goggles also allowed him to hear movements around the mountain. He could see and hear as if he were standing right on the mountain.

"Wow, this is great. I can hear the trees moving," said Joey.

"Yes, so can I, but there's no wind. What is making the trees move?"

"The only way we're going to find out is when we get there," said Joey. He took off his goggles and looked at Budda. They stopped in the air for a moment. Budda briskly pulled off his goggles. Simultaneously, they nodded their heads.

"Let's go full speed ahead," said Budda firmly. They turned and faced the mountain on their balons and sped as fast as they could go. The mountain was getting closer and closer. While Joey was inside his bubble, he had no fear, and he knew the charmal stone was in the centre of the mountain. Nothing was going to upset him or make him feel afraid.

Somehow, Joey understood that the more he believed in his powers, the stronger he felt. All he had to do was believe in himself. He realized he was not only doing this for Olivia but also for Astina, Ben and Lucy, all the people suffering near Rockwell Mountain, and all the people and cowchees that were captured by the druggons. He also knew that that rock was not the only way he was going to save everyone. There was a huge battle ahead of him. Joey was ready to fight. He was not afraid; in fact, he had never felt braver in his whole life than he did at that very moment.

At last they were only a few metres from the top of the mountain, and still there was no sign of snakes. Their bubble shields were a very good camouflage, but Joey was beginning to believe this was too easy.

Joey and Budda were now directly above a cave in the middle of the mountain, and it was an enchanting sight. They stopped and floated in midair.

"Down there, somewhere inside that cave is the charmal stone," said Joey. They both peered down. If Joey had not seen the cave in his mind from the book, he would never have known there was a cave hidden there.

"Are you sure there's a cave down there?" asked Budda.

"That's what it showed in the book," said Joey, pointing to some trees that were shaking. "See, you can just see it there, those trees are moving."

"Oh yes. I can see now. But I can't help wondering why the trees are shaking so much. There's still no wind. Something is not quite right. Let's take a look with our goggles before we go down."

Joey could now see the cave clearly. "Those trees don't look like the ones in Magical World. There is no fruit or food on them." Joey pointed to a large tree. "And look at that—the branches are moving by themselves."

Budda was also examining the trees. "I see that too. Those are no ordinary trees. I'm beginning to think that's where the snakes are hidden," muttered Budda.

"What, I can't see the snakes. Where are they?" Joey quickly removed his goggles to face Budda.

CHAPTER 14

Battle with the Snakes

"The trees, you see, Joey, the trees. Take a good look at the trees—the snakes are the trees in disguise. I've just spotted an eye open on the end of a branch. Oh boy, we are lucky we didn't run into them. We would have been burnt to a cinder if we'd taken off our shields down there."

Joey took another look at the trees with his goggles back on. Peering towards the very end of a branch, he saw the eye of a snake move. "You're right, the trees are snakes. What a clever disguise! You're brilliant! I would never have guessed those trees were snakes."

Budda nodded. "You always have to be cautious in these situations. Now we're still going to have to find a way to get inside that cave without the trees—I mean, without being noticed by the snakes. And by the looks of that, there are a lot of trees—oh, I mean, snakes. It will be hard enough to fight one of those beasts let alone a whole mountain full of them."

"They look a lot meaner than the druggons," observed Joey.

"I wouldn't be surprised if the druggons had something to do with putting those snakes there. The druggons probably know about the charmal stone hidden in Rockwell Mountain. I dare say, those huge snakes won't be stronger than the druggons, but there's so many of them. I think this is going to be very difficult and probably impossible for the two of us to handle."

"I don't think it will be impossible for the two of us to handle them if we have to," said Joey, talking up the situation.

"And how is that? Tell me how you plan to fight all those snakes?" asked Budda with a sarcastic tone.

"There's a lot about my magic I haven't learnt yet. There must be a way we can defeat those snakes. I wasn't the Chosen One for nothing, you know." Joey had decided to trust his instincts and was becoming more and more confident with his magic.

Budda rolled his eyes but nodded his head slowly. "You could be right, Joey. But you haven't come up with anything yet. We will have to be so careful, and we can't take our shields off. The only time we can is to seize the stone."

"Well, let's hope those snakes are not inside the cave. But if the druggons did put those snakes there, then they may have prepared a trap. And I don't think the charmal stone will be that easy to grab. We will need time, and from my memory of the book, the cave is very big. I'm going to get my wet blanket ready anyway, just in case we come across something bad." Joey pulled out his blanket and a bottle of water and held it securely. Glancing down at the mountain, he thought he noticed something on the ground near the trees, and a little farther, on he saw a horse running away.

"Wait, can you see something moving on the ground down there?" Joey said, pointing.

Budda turned in the direction Joey was pointing. "Yes, I can see it. It's something in the shape of a shell."

"It's some sort of cover. Look, it's moving!" The shell–like cover tilted, and with shock, Joey shouted, "Oh no, it's Ben!"

"My god, why is he here? Is that boy suicidal?" asked Budda.

"We have to save him. We can't waste time. He must have travelled here on that horse. I'm going down!" yelled Joey. And before Budda could answer, he was down in a flash.

Joey's balon stood directly in front of the shell Ben was hiding under. The snakes had not noticed them yet. Budda had followed Joey and now stood behind Ben. Together their shields would be able to protect Ben, with Joey in front and Budda behind. Ben did not yet know they were there because of their invisible, soundproof shields.

"How will we be able to warn Ben?" asked Joey.

"Well, at the moment, the snakes haven't noticed Ben, but when they do, we're going to have to take our shields off and fight, but at the moment, we are like ghosts to them."

"Why did he come here? I told him we'd be fine." Joey was deeply worried for Ben.

"Yes, I know, but there must be a reason why Ben's here, none of the humans would dare come here," said Budda.

The cave was directly in front of Joey, and branches swished at the entrance. "I think the best way to save Ben is to enter the cave. I can't see anything inside, only those branches near the entrance. I'm sure my wet blanket can take care of those," said Joey.

"Good idea, but we're going to have to make a move now. We're running out of time, and it'll get dark soon. We don't want to have to deal with the lexus creatures as well."

Joey briskly wet his blanket and then placed the bottle back inside his cape. Budda pulled out a bucket full of stones. The same type of stones he used to fight the druggons.

"I'll keep cover behind you, Joey. You grab Ben, and we'll make a run for it to that cave. We'll go on the count of three. One . . . two . . . three!"

Joey and Budda simultaneously removed their shields but with their weapons at hand. The snakes immediately saw them and hissed loudly. Their disguise was gone, and although they were not as large as Sess—much smaller, in fact—they looked very fierce and powerful.

"Ben, it's me, Joey, I want you to get out and jump on my back behind my cape, I'll carry you to the cave," yelled Joey as he waited for the snakes to attack. Ben obeyed.

Joey took a good look around him. One of the snake's mouth was wide open and was steered in his direction. Joey waited for the snake to come closer, and with only a short distance between them, he quickly lifted his blanket and whipped it across the snake's head. The snake collapsed to the ground with severe burns to its head, but it still had some life in it. Just as it tried to move up to attack again, Joey gave it another whack. His blanket was so fierce it was like a burning whip. The headless snake was now lying dead on the ground.

Budda was still throwing his stones in every direction as the other snakes started to surround them.

"Come on, let's get into the cave quickly!" yelled Joey.

The three of them quickly made their way nearer to the cave to escape the poisonous blaze blowing at them from almost every direction.

Slam! Slam! Slam! Slam! went Joey's blanket. Underneath his cape, Ben was holding on to his waist tightly and shaking.

Budda stayed very close to Joey and Ben. In one hand, he now held a long shield, which was succeeding in throwing back the poisonous fire to the snakes. They had to be so careful not to have the slightest burn as the poison would instantly kill them. Joey and Budda continued to fight the snakes with all their strength. The snakes were fast and wild and doing all they could to try and stop them from approaching the cave. The situation was becoming unbearable; the cave was only metres away.

"We're almost there! Come on, let's make a run for it!" shouted Joey.

The three of them took the risk and ran for their lives to the cave. Finally, they were inside. But they were not safe yet, there was nothing to stop the snakes from entering the cave. They had to think of something fast.

Budda pulled out a red stone from his cape, and he threw it near the entrance and uttered the word *igger* very loudly. The small red stone, which was only the size of a hand, turned into a very large, heavy bright-red crystal ball. Just as a snake was about to enter the cave, the red crystal squashed its neck and slowly killed it. The stone had just made it in time to prevent the snake from throwing its poison fire. The crystal now covered the entire cave entrance, shining its bright-red light.

Joey and Ben gazed in amazement. "How did you do that?" asked Joey, dumbfounded.

"It's magic, and it was the best I could do. Those snakes would have swarmed in here and killed us all. Just look at that vicious beast," replied Budda.

They all stared at the dead snake's head, which hung over the large rock. Green slime oozed from its mouth.

"Oooooh, yuck, what's that green stuff coming from that snake's mouth?" asked Ben. He approached the snake for a closer look.

Joey pulled him back. "Don't touch it, it could still be poisonous." The green ooze was turning into a huge puddle.

"Joey's right, Ben, don't go anywhere near that snake," Budda said, carefully holding Ben's shoulder to keep him away.

Ben looked at Joey and Budda. "What do we do now?" he asked.

"The question is, Ben, why are you here? We told you to wait at the village. What could have ever possessed you to come here? You could have gotten us all killed," muttered Budda.

"I had to tell you something very important. I overheard Victor and Max talking to Jack. They are very upset with you two being here, and they are coming here to kill you. Victor especially told Jack that that stone you are after is evil and would cause more people to get sick. I had to come and warn you both!" cried Ben.

Joey comforted Ben. "It's okay, Ben, we're safe now. Don't cry. But you must promise us never to do that again. You must never risk your life for us," said Joey quietly.

He turned to Budda. "You know, I thought there was something suspicious about Victor and Max." Joey paused for a moment and looked towards the ground. A thought ran through his mind. He stared at Budda. "Yes, I remember now, I've heard Victor's accent somewhere. Didn't you say those druggons could disguise themselves into anyone or anything? I know who Victor and Max really are!"

Budda nodded his head slowly. "I know what you're thinking—Victor and Max are Villazian and Megram in disguise."

"Exactly, and I bet they are the ones who made those people sick. Remember, Jack told us the people started getting sick after he met Victor and Max."

"You're right, Joey. And it's obvious Jack isn't aware of it. We've got a lot of work to do. Let's go and find that stone," said Budda. He pulled out his staff, which lit the cave even more brightly than the red crystal. They all peered around the cave. It was huge and glorious, with all sorts of coloured crystals.

CHAPTER 15

Home Sweet Home

The smell that came from the crystals was heavenly. This was a much larger cave and even more beautiful than the cave near Riddells Withals. The colours were overwhelming. With Budda's staff lit up, the different-coloured crystals sparkled like diamonds; the whole cave glittered.

In Joey's mind, Rockwell Mountain was worth much more than any possession on Earth. As he wandered through the cave, he once again felt energized and happy. He looked at Ben and then Budda and noticed their faces were glowing and even Ben appeared much healthier than he did at the village. Ben smiled as he touched a few of the crystals.

"Mmmmmmmm, it smells yummy here," said Ben. He turned and looked at Joey and smiled even more. Joey admired his glorious white teeth.

Joey was wide-eyed too. "Yes, this is a beautiful cave. This is the most amazing place I have ever seen in my whole life. And you know what? This place is even bigger and more beautiful than the cave back at Riddells Withals," said Joey, who then gazed at Budda.

Budda nodded his head. "Yes, this is so much more beautiful. In fact, if it weren't for those snakes, this would be a great new place for Riddells Withals," said Budda. He too touched some of the crystals, enjoying the energy that came from them. Joey could tell from the look on his face, the way he closed his eyes and smiled, that his cheeks had turned pink and rosy.

They slowly walked farther into the cave. There did not appear to be an end to it; the crystals and stones went on and on.

"Do you think this cave will ever end?" asked Joey.

"This cave is very magical indeed. Every crystal has a purpose, and no, I don't think there is an ending. In fact, this must be the never – ending cave. There are entrances in and out, but certainly no end. I've read about this cave in my books."

They walked for hours through the cave. Keeping a close guard, Joey had his wet blanket ready at all times.

"I can't see the charmal stone, and it looks like we're not going to make it back to the village people before dark. Do you think the lexus creatures could come inside these caves?" asked Joey.

"Even if they can make it through those snakes, I've blocked the entrance. Nothing can move that crystal. Even if they blew up the cave, the crystal won't move," said Budda.

"But they could come into the cave from another cave entrance," said Ben, looking concerned.

Budda stopped and looked at Joey and Ben; he gently ruffled Ben's hair. "We can't have little Ben worried, now, can we? We'll have to find a safe place for us to eat and rest. You two are probably due for a sleep."

On a side wall of the cave behind all the crystals was a large, tall white diamond. It would have been almost the height of Ben. Back on Earth, it would have been worth millions—Joey was sure of it.

"Wow, look at the size of that diamond," said Joey, wide-eyed.

"Hmm, yes, I think this will do." Budda held Ben's hand and motioned to Joey to follow him. Budda then stood directly in front of the diamond and pulled out his pink crystal star.

"I'm going to bring back Riddells Withals, with all the people, cowchees, and unicorns. We're all going to live inside this diamond for a while. With the snakes outside the caves, everyone will be safe from our enemies. This place is an ideal home for Riddells Withals."

"Wait, are you serious?" asked Joey. He was surprised that Budda had selected Rockwell Mountain as the new home for Riddells Withals.

"Yes, I am serious. I want Ben to be safe. It would be ideal for him to stay here until we settle this business with Jack and the druggons. I'm sure Jack would be very upset with Ben if he found out he was here telling us about his plans. He probably already suspects that Ben is missing. The druggons may curse him with the virus. It's not easy to find a cure for these viruses. I have tried every option to help those cowchees and the people the druggons have captured. We don't even know if the charmal stone will help the curash virus. We may end up making a fool out of ourselves."

"You're right. This is a fantastic place for Riddells Withals. It's close to the people in the village and to the charmal stone. I think this would really upset the druggons though because we'd be close to a power greater than theirs," said Joey.

Joey held Ben's shoulder to comfort him. Then he looked at Budda. "I still think you should wait. We haven't found the stone yet, and it's still not nightfall. We don't know what the lexus creatures are capable of doing. They might find a way to get into Riddells Withals. There must be something in this cape of mine that could keep us safe for one night, and we'd be able to see what happens here during the night," pleaded Joey. He was still looking at Budda. Ben stood beside Joey and fiddled with his cape.

"Ben, please stop doing that," muttered Joey.

Budda quickly grabbed Ben and lifted Joey's cape. "What are you doing?" asked Joey, feeling a little annoyed.

"Take a look at one of your pockets, it's open," said Budda.

"What?" Joey quickly looked inside his cape.

"This must be answering my question about being safe tonight. This cape is amazing." Joey put his hand inside the pocket and felt something very small. He carefully pulled it out and placed it in front of him. It turned out to be a miniature model of a small house. Within a few seconds, the tiny house grew bigger and bigger until it was slightly taller than Joey.

"Look at that, it's a small house, but how can this keep us safe for the night? Any one of our enemies could easily attack this."

Budda and Ben stared at Joey with worried looks on their faces. "What are you talking about? We can't see the house," said Budda.

"You mean you can't see it?" asked Joey.

"No, we can't see it," answered Budda and Ben in unison.

"Then this house must be invisible to everyone except me. What a perfect disguise," Joey said proudly.

He opened the front door to have a look inside. As he did, Ben yelled, "Look!"

"We can see it now. You're right, Joey, this is a perfect disguise, and no one except you can see the house unless the door is open. This is just another one of your special gifts," said Budda.

"This is no ordinary house—this is my parents' house. Everything is exactly as it was the day Olivia and

I went to the beach. Come inside." Joey waved his hand for Budda and Ben to follow him inside.

"Cool, what a nice place," said Ben. Joey's house was like a palace to Ben. Ben quickly found Joey's room and sat straight down on his bed.

Budda was peeking into every room, and as he did, he picked up a few of Joey's mother's ornaments. "So this is your home? Is this what houses look like on Earth?" he asked.

"Yes, you've read my mind. This house is identical to my home back on Earth, but look, we can see through the walls to the cave. At least this will be a safe place for us to rest for the night, and at the same time, we can see what happens at night in this cave." Joey pulled out a can of Coke from the kitchen fridge, yanked the top off, and swallowed a large mouthful.

"I suppose this all make sense now. The cape decided the safest place for you is your home. That's why this house is identical to your home back on Earth. It doesn't necessarily mean it is your home, just a replica. This is a perfect hideout for us. Oh, you're right about waiting. I do want the people, cowchees, and unicorns to be safe in Riddells Withals. I suppose I got too excited with the beauty of this cave and the glorious healing stones. I was caught off guard." Budda smiled and nodded his head.

Joey shrugged his shoulders. "It's okay, that's why I'm here, to help out. But you should really wait until we sort out the druggons. We don't want them to attack

Riddells again. Anyway, at least we'll be safe now—at least, for tonight," said Joey

Budda nodded in agreement again as he continued to gaze around the house. "I'm pretty sure your cape chose this for you because you've always felt safe in your own home."

"Hey, maybe you're right. I've never thought of it that way, but I guess I have always felt safest at home." Joey picked up the remote control for the television and put it on. "Look at that, there's a program on TV. Hey, Ben, come and see this," Joey said loudly.

Ben raced into the living room and stared at the television set. "How did those people get inside that box?" he asked.

Joey laughed. "No, Ben, there are no people inside the television. We don't call it a box. Every television set will have this show on now. Actors make the film only once, and they play it on the television. Come and sit down on the couch next to me. You'll love this show." Joey patted the seat with his hand.

Ben looked at the show, wide-eyed. Even Budda appeared intrigued. Joey felt so good to be here. Even though the house was not really his home, he was reminded of being back at home.

"Joey," interrupted Budda.

Budda's voice startled Joey, and he turned quickly to face him. "What's wrong?" he asked.

Budda pointed to the front door. "I don't think we'll be safe if you leave the door open."

Joey promptly hurried to the door and slammed it shut. "Oh, I'm sorry, I must have forgotten. You're right, any creature could have wondered in, thanks, pal."

Budda smiled. "Remember, we must be very careful. Anyway, I've prepared us a banquet in the kitchen, let's have something to eat."

Ben was still staring at the television. He had not noticed what Budda was saying.

"Ben!" called Budda loudly. "Come and have something to eat. I was just telling Joey I've made us a banquet."

Ben frowned and made a funny face. "What's a banquet?" he asked.

"Food, come on, let's eat." Budda waved his hand for everyone to follow him to the kitchen. Ben hesitated; he did not want to leave the TV.

"Don't worry, Ben, the television plays programmes all night. We've got cable, there will be even better programmes later. Come on, you're going to enjoy the food Budda has prepared. Anyway, you must be starved," said Joey, putting his arm around Ben's shoulder as they walked to the kitchen.

Budda had prepared a great banquet. Ben's eyes lit up. He quickly sat down and started to eat; he tried almost everything on the table. Joey enjoyed watching Ben eat so well. It was lucky the food was magic and would not make him sick. That was the best part about Magical World—you could eat as much as you wanted and never get fat or sick. From the look of Ben, his mouth was not large enough; his cheeks were so round and full of food, it made Joey laugh.

"Be careful, Ben, you won't get sick, but you could choke," Joey warned.

"Oh no," Budda said, moving his head from side to side. "He'll be fine. The food is magic, he won't choke."

"I wish Earth was like this. Do you think my magic cape could work on Earth? I'd be able to give food to the kids at school, they'd love this stuff," Joey queried as he took a huge bite from his hamburger.

"I'm not sure, I've never been to Earth, Joey, but you're more than welcome to stay at Riddells with us. I mean, you and Olivia of course," said Budda. He licked his fingers after he put a cream cake inside his mouth.

"Didn't you say time stays the same on Earth while we're here in Magical World?"

"Yes, that's right. What's that got to do with you and Olivia staying at Riddells?" asked Budda.

"Well, doesn't that mean I'll never get older? I mean, I'll be eleven years old, and Olivia will be eight forever."

"I don't know what you mean." Budda frowned, and he looked very confused.

"I mean, don't you get older?"

"Older?"

"You know. Your body ages?" asked Joey.

"My body has always been like this."

"You mean you've always looked like you do now the whole time you've been in Magical World? What about Astina, wasn't she a baby when she came to you?"

"Oh, I see what you mean. Here in Magical World, babies grow up to eight years old. And any person who comes to Magical World older than eight stays that same age forever unless, of course, they contract a virus. Then their bodies change," explained Budda.

"So if Olivia and I stay in Riddells Withals, we'll never get older?"

Budda patted Joey's shoulder and smiled. "That's right, my friend. You stay young forever."

"So you're saying I'll never grow into a man."

Budda nodded his head to agree. "Why would you want to change? You look fine the way you are. I've had grown men come to Riddells Withals, and they have to shave all the time. They also take life too seriously. Children are fun to be around. It's no fun being a grown-up anyway. But you know what, Joey?"

"What?" Joey stared at Budda, anxiously waiting for his answer.

"It's your choice. If you want to grow up, you can go back to Earth. Or if you want to be eleven for a while, you can stay here as long as you like. The choice is yours and only yours. You are the Chosen One, and I'm pretty sure you're the only person who can do that."

"So I can come back here again even if I go back to Earth?" asked Joey.

Budda chewed on his chocolate mint dessert and then shook his head from side to side. "I don't know. I've never been to Earth myself. And if I ever was on Earth, I don't remember."

"Then where did you grow up? And who raised you?" asked Joey. He didn't take his eyes off Budda as he anxiously waited for his answer.

"I was raised by the cowchees and the unicorns. They gave me my great powers just as they gave you yours. But I was allowed to grow into a man. I am probably only about twenty-eight years old. I think if I did age, like humans on Earth, I'd be at least two hundred years old."

"Wow, no way. You don't look anything like an old man, and nobody lives to two hundred on Earth. So you mean to tell me you never die here?" asked Joey. He was baffled to think that Budda could be over two hundred years old in Earth years

"We never worry about death here. We only worry about viruses and curses. The truth is, Joey, nobody really dies here."

"Are there other places apart from Earth and Magical World?"

"Of course. You've seen the other planets. Why do you think the humans on Earth have never been able to visit other planets? Each of those planets have their own living creatures and life forms, but they are all completely different. The white universe protects all the souls," said Budda.

"How do you know all this?" asked Joey.

Budda sighed and looked more serious. He stared into Joey's eyes. "Because the white universe communicates with me every time I meditate. This has a lot to do with my gift and powers."

"Do I have this gift?" asked Joey.

"Everyone has this gift. It's only a matter of believing. The more you believe, the more it is willing to communicate with you. The truth is, it's there whether you believe in it or not. But if you truly—and I mean truly—believe in it, the white light will tell you many things that happen within the universe. But in Magical World, it's more apparent because we are closest to the white universe, closer than Earth or any other planet. All the planets, including Earth, have it too, it's just not as clear as it is here," explained Budda.

"So it's similar to the stones and crystals having more power here than on the other planets?" asked Joey.

"Exactly, the power of everything is stronger here than on any other planet because Magical World is closer to the white universe."

Joey's eyes wandered back to Ben, whose head was on the kitchen table. He was sound asleep. Budda also turned to look at Ben. He pulled out his fettal and waved it in the air a few times. Ben suddenly disappeared.

"Where did you send him?" asked Joey.

Budda smiled, "Don't worry, he's on a floating bed in your room."

Joey was having difficulty believing Budda. Budda noticed Joey's reaction; he would have also read his mind. "Go and check your room. He is in your bedroom asleep. If we carried him, we would have woken him up. It was better I used my fettal," assured Budda.

Joey hurried to his room. There beside his bed was Ben sleeping like an angel on one of Budda's floating beds. Joey felt happy again; he was glad to see Ben so well taken care of.

"Didn't I tell you he was fine?" said Budda from behind him.

"I never doubted you. I just wanted to see him for myself. You'll have to teach me how to do that," said Joey, smiling.

"That's easy. You've got a fettal somewhere in your cape too. All you have to do is imagine Ben moving from one area to another and wave your fettal slightly. Then you can have Ben safely asleep on a floating bed at whatever destination you want him to be."

"That did look easy. I suppose you're right about magic being stronger here in Magical World. So do you think if I did visit other planets, the strongest power I would have would be on Pluto because it's closer to Magical World?" asked Joey quietly; he didn't want to wake Ben.

"Maybe so, I'm not sure. Your powers could be strong wherever you go because the unicorn gave you your powers. I've never been on any other planet. My place is here. All I know is that the white light is greater here than anywhere else," said Budda softly. He gently placed his hand on Joey's shoulder. "I was . . . I'm still hoping you'd change your mind about going back to Earth. But that decision is entirely yours."

Behind Budda, Joey noticed movement in the cave.

"Are you okay?" asked Budda.

"There's something in the cave, I saw some movement behind you. Are you sure we're safe here? Look, there it is again," Joey said, pointing his finger.

CHAPTER 16

Confronted by a Lexus

Budda turned swiftly. There, standing in front of them was the ugliest creature Joey had ever seen. He shrieked with disgust.

"Oh my god, that must be the lexus. Are you sure he can't see us? He's looking this way."

"Quickly, we must check that the doors are locked. You go to the back door, and I'll go to the front," ordered Budda.

Joey didn't listen. He stood still and stared at the lexus wide-eyed. "No. We should keep still, he could see and hear us," whispered Joey.

They both kept still. The lexus roared loudly and looked directly towards Joey. Joey quickly pulled out his wet blanket. He held the blanket behind his back and slowly poured soda water over it, and instantly, it became his weapon. He held it very tightly. Joey was not sure whether the lexus was aiming at him or Budda. Jack was right about its head being five times bigger than an ordinary tiger's head. These creatures in Magical World would tower over the creatures on Earth.

The lexus roared again, and the sound was almost deafening as it showed its huge white teeth. The teeth were almost the size of Joey's bedroom doorway. No man would be strong enough to fight this beast. Even Joey doubted he could fight the beast with his wet blanket.

Budda quickly ran to Ben, who was slowly waking up following the beast's loud roar. Budda put his hand over his mouth. Ben's eyes opened wide, and his face was as white as a ghost. Budda whispered something in his ear and kept him down on his bed.

Again and again, the lexus roared, continuing to stare directly at Joey. With his last roar echoing, it simultaneously jumped up and flew straight to where Joey was standing. Ben screamed and Budda shouted, "Joey, get down, quickly, under the bed!"

Joey accidentally dropped his wet blanket. He had no time to pick it up as the lexus was so fast, and right at that moment, Joey didn't feel prepared to fight it.

"Arrrrrrrrrrrrrrrrrrrgh!" screeched Joey. The lexus lunged towards him. He closed his eyes tightly and tucked his head under his arm. This was the end for him; the moment he knew he was going to die. He waited for a while, and waited and waited. Time seemed to tick by and nothing happened.

Joey peeked through a gap under his arm, but the lexus creature was no longer in front of him. He heard another loud roar, but this time, it was behind him. Quickly, he scrambled under the bed to where Budda and Ben hid and peeped out. In front of the lexus was one of the poisonous tree snakes from outside the cave. The lexus and the snake rolled on the ground in a huge bundle and fought ferociously. At the same time, some of the crystals broke and scattered into small pieces. Finally, after a struggle, the lexus grabbed the snake's tongue with its claw and ripped it out from its mouth and, with one large bite, swallowed the snake's head.

"You wouldn't believe what happened to you, Joey," said Budda, looking deathly pale.

"Shhhh, we'd better keep quiet, the lexus might hear us. From the looks of that snake, he's a hungry pussy cat," whispered Joey.

"We can make noise, it's okay. The lexus can't hear or see us. He went right through you like a ghost. So it wasn't you he was angry at, it was that snake," said Budda. His normal colour returned and little Ben stopped crying. They were all relieved.

"Phew, that was lucky, I really thought I was gone. Seeing that, there's no way my blanket or your stones could have protected us. And just look at me, my pants are wet. How do I freshen up now? I can't stay in this outfit with wet pants."

"Just take out your fettal and point it to your pants," suggested Budda.

Joey did as he was told, and using his fettal—which, of course, was blue in colour—his pants immediately transformed to being clean and dry.

They now looked around the cave to try and find the lexus creature. But it was nowhere to be seen, and neither was the snake. The lexus had obviously eaten the remainder.

"Now we know what the lexus creatures eat if they can't find humans," said Joey.

"Yes, and it's very obvious the snake's poison doesn't affect them. They certainly are a rare species," said Budda.

"Well, aren't you lucky you didn't bring Riddells Withals into this cave? Any one of the cowchees or humans could have wandered through these caves for a healing crystal and would have become a meal for the lexus—or the snakes, for that matter. They are still finding their way into the cave." Joey paced around his house, still searching for any sign of movement in the cave.

"Joey, you need to stop walking up and down and get to bed. You must get your rest," said Budda as he carefully tucked Ben back onto the floating bed.

"How can I sleep after that happened and there is still danger out there?"

"I'll be awake, I promise. If anything should happen, I'll wake you. Now get some sleep," demanded Budda.

"You promise?"

"Yes, of course I promise. We'll get through this together."

CHAPTER 17

Joey's Dream

Joey lay under the familiar purple quilt his mother had made. She loved to sew; his mother was a very versatile lady who could sew or make almost anything for their home. When he closed his eyes, he felt as if he were at home again. Even the smell on his sheets reminded him of home.

His eyes became heavy, and within a few minutes, he drifted into a deep sleep. He dreamed of his family. They were all getting ready to go to the beach. Olivia ran out the door towards the beach. Joey raced out to catch up with her, leaving his mum and dad behind. His mother always took her time getting ready.

Olivia was already near the water. Joey wanted to catch her and throw her in. It was a very still and hot day; the sea was very calm. Today only small, light waves washed over Olivia's feet. She turned to face Joey and smiled and waved for him to come into the water with her.

"Joey, it's fantastic here, come and have a look at what I've found! Turtles!" called Olivia.

Joey smiled as he ran towards her; he really wanted to see the turtles. Sea creatures had always fascinated him, and he loved to catch them.

High in the sky, Joey noticed a dark patch. It was moving rapidly towards Olivia. He felt suspicious and decided to run faster. The dark patch in the sky moved closer and closer towards Olivia. He did not trust the dark patch.

"Olivia, come here!" he yelled.

Olivia only waved to Joey and smiled. As usual, she would not listen to her big brother. Joey ran faster. Just as he caught up with her, the dark patch in the sky turned into a swarm of bees.

Olivia looked up and shrieked, "Look at all those bees, Joey, we're going to get stung!"

"Quickly, get into the water," urged Joey.

They dived into the sea and, holding their breath, stayed under. The bees hovered above them. They both desperately needed air, but the bees were only centimetres above the water. Joey and Olivia were trapped under the water and were in danger of drowning. The bees were aiming for them no matter what; they were not going away.

Joey closed his eyes tightly and then opened them again. Suddenly, he woke up from his nightmare in a cold sweat, gasping for air. He waved his arms about and knocked the lamp down. Budda briskly opened his bedroom door and ran to his aid.

"Joey, what's wrong?" he asked.

He was still gasping for air. "It's Olivia, she's in danger. I had a dream. We were back home, and there was this huge dark patch in the sky coming down towards Olivia and me. It turned out to be a swarm of bees. We were under the sea, and we couldn't get air. They would have stung us to death if we tried to get air. We were drowning. It felt so real, I mean I didn't feel like I was dreaming—I felt like I was really drowning with Olivia!"

Budda held on to Joey's arm and nodded. "You were very lucky you woke up. Those bees have something to do with Villazian. He's trying to get inside your mind in your sleep. He is doing magic on you, Joey."

"*Magic?* What kind of magic?" asked Joey anxiously.

"It's like a curse. Villazian is trying to kill you in your sleep. If you hadn't woken up, you really would have drowned. Your dream would have become a reality."

"So are you saying that if I go to sleep now, I will die." Joey looked desperately at Budda for an answer. With a very serious look on his face, Budda nodded in agreement. "Isn't there anything I can use to stop this? What about the nonmind reading dust?"

Budda moved his head from side to side. "No, I'm afraid that won't help. It's a curse they've put on you. We are going to have to find a way to stop you from sleeping."

Joey looked inside his cape and pulled out his book. "Then we'll have to find Villazian and fight him. Otherwise, he'll keep putting curses and viruses on everyone in Magical World. And because he's been on Earth, he may even start putting them on people there. The charmal stone has got to be here somewhere. I'll drink lots of Coke to keep me awake. I'm sure we'll be able to settle this in a day."

Joey flipped through his large blue book. On the front cover, a blue eye looked at him and then it blinked. It was like a real eye staring at him. The book felt alive. All of Budda's library books were lifelike. Some, like this one, had an eye; on some, the binding felt like human skin and others were warm just like a living creature.

On every page, Joey could see and hear images and voices. It was as if he were dreaming the lessons from the book. Joey found the topic about the Chosen One searching for the druggons. Like all the books, it always kept up-to-date with recent events. He read the part about where Riddells Withals was located and confirmed it was inside Toodles's cabin floor where Budda had put it last.

Joey continued to read the information about the druggons, but for some reason, he could not picture a place in his mind. And he could not hear any voices either. Joey had to read the information manually, word by word, and what he read was

Well, may you find a rock, its mount is higher than any hill and tainted with the colour purple.

"What is this? This doesn't make sense," he stated flatly.

"What are you saying?" asked Budda.

"I've found the topic where the druggons live. But it won't let me see it in my mind, and the book only reads this message and I have no idea what it means." Joey handed the book to Budda. "Here, have a look for yourself."

Budda stared at the words. "This is a riddle. The druggons have cast a spell to avoid being traced. Of course their books would make the location clear, but any other book would only have a riddle. Now if they had their own way with magic, there'd be no riddle at all. You see, I've done this too. It's a spell. Not everyone can do this spell—it is very difficult. I've used this for Riddells Withals. I knew the druggons would do the same. We have to figure out that riddle, and normally riddles are impossible to work out." Budda didn't sound surprised.

CHAPTER 18

The Mirrored Pillow

Joey looked inside his cape. "There must be something in here that could protect me from dying in my sleep." He concentrated very hard and waited for one of his pockets to open. For a while nothing opened, and then on the very bottom of his cape, a pocket opened.

"I have something." Joey looked at Budda and then back at the cape. "One of the pockets is open," said Joey. He slid his hand inside the pocket and carefully pulled out a silver mirrored pillow.

Budda looked stunned. "You have amazing powers. There is always a solution to any problem you bump into," said Budda.

"This is a weird-looking pillow. I've never seen anything like it. I don't even think anyone on Earth has ever invented a mirrored pillow. I wonder what I am supposed to do with this pillow?" asked Joey.

"Sleep on it. The pillow is supposed to protect you from bad dreams. It's obvious, isn't it? Now you don't have to worry about having bad dreams." Budda grabbed the pillow from Joey and squished it between his hands. "Mmmmm, feels comfy and soft. You should have no problems sleeping on this tonight."

Joey smiled broadly and seized the pillow back. "I guess I'll have to trust my cape. At least now, I'll have a good night's sleep. The nightmare I just had was horrible. I just hope Olivia is okay."

Joey squeezed the pillow. It was soft and silky smooth and looked like a mirror. He could actually see his reflection. "This is an amazing pillow. I'm going to try it out."

"Maybe you should put it back in your cape. You haven't got time for any more sleep, Joey. We've got to find the stone and the druggons," snapped Budda. He paced around Joey's room, then shook his head and headed towards the kitchen. Joey assumed he was getting breakfast ready. Ben was still fast asleep and snoring. Ben's snoring amazed Joey; it was truly loud for a small boy.

Joey tossed the pillow on the bed and decided to try it out. He lay down on the bed and put his head on the pillow. His head slowly sunk into the pillow until the sides of the pillow creased past his ears. The image Joey saw on the pillow startled him; he could see his face as if he were staring into his bedroom mirror. While he continued to stare at his image, Joey realized he couldn't close his eyes, not even blink. It was as if the image was forcing him to stare into it. He was not able to move. His whole body was paralysed, frozen, and he could not call out for Budda to help him.

Joey wanted to get up; he was now wishing he had listened to Budda and put the pillow back inside his cape. How long was this pillow going to hold him down? Was this another curse from the druggons to try and stop him from finding them? Joey decided not to panic and remained calm. He knew it would not be too long before Budda returned. *Oh, come on, Budda, get back in here.*

After a few minutes, Joey noticed the image of his face on the mirrored pillow start to change; his whole face started to move. It was full of silver spots and became a swirl of colours. Joey was not looking at his face anymore; this image was now completely different. It was as if his image was floating on Rockwell Mountain.

The image moved inside the cave, past the crystals until it came to a huge black rock. This rock was not pretty like the crystals; in fact, it was quite ugly and looked like a burnt-out tree stump. The image continued to take him through the black rock. Joey could see a huge black hole.

Joey hoped he was not dreaming and that this was not another cursed dream concocted by the druggons. He remembered the only way he woke up from the other nightmare was when he blinked hard and opened his eyes again. Only this time, his eyes could not blink. Surely his cape would be protected against this curse?

The blackness lasted only a few minutes until he entered another deep cave. Balls of fire floated in midair with nothing to hold them. This certainly was magic. Joey could actually feel the warmth of the flames as his image guided him farther inside the cave. The image travelled fast towards another entrance way, which led in two directions. One direction continued farther inside the cave; the other led to a dead end.

Joey wanted to scream with what he saw in the dead-end cave. He was paralysed with fear but could feel his heart pounding. Inside cages children were sleeping. The rags they wore only just covered their skinny bodies; their feet were bare and scratched with sores. Joey was mortified.

The image then moved out of the dead-end cave to the other one. Joey could hear children crying. The image moved closer and closer to the crying sound. At last he could see them. They were all working; some were pulling cartloads of rocks while others were digging with spades. And then Joey saw some scrawny creatures whip the children with sticks, forcing them to work harder.

These were the reb creatures; he remembered them from his book. They worked for the druggons. It suddenly occurred to him that this was probably where the druggons lived. He searched hard amongst the children for Olivia. But the image only took him back to the main path where he had first entered.

The image quickly whisked past the fireballs until it finally reached the other end. Here was a large open area, probably about the size of ten football fields.

Huge rocks littered the floor, and between them, flares blazed. On the far end, Joey could see a clear area containing two small cages, one on top of the other.

The image took him all the way through the stones and fire until it reached the top cage. There inside the cell was what Joey and Budda had been searching for—the charmal stone. It was huge and beautiful, with glorious colours that sparkled. The stone was certainly out of anyone's reach; it would be virtually impossible to get near.

Slowly the image lowered to the bottom cage. It looked like a small girl's bedroom. A girl with wings sat on a lovely white bed. She looked very sad, her head down and her hands on her face. Joey peered closer. Then he recognized her—it was Astina. His heart felt like it was going to jump out of his body. He was shocked and in total dismay. He wanted to reach out and comfort her and tell her everything was going to be all right and that he would come to her and save her soon. This was what Joey wanted to do so badly; he wanted to save her, Olivia, and all the other children.

Suddenly, Joey started to lose this image of Astina. Her image and the whole cave swirled into smaller and smaller circles until Joey could only see his own reflection on the pillow. Then his eyes moved; he could see his room, and he could blink and move his body again.

He quickly jumped up and stared at the pillow and then put it back inside his pocket cape. He realized the pillow was not supposed to help him sleep without nightmares; it was given to him to help him locate the druggons, Astina, the people, the cowchees, and the charmal stone. Joey remembered his first thought about his desire to locate the druggons and then he thought about getting help to sleep without the nightmares. That was why the cape showed him the mirrored pillow.

Joey recalled the druggon's riddle: A well and a rock—well, rock. It must have meant Rockwell. Oh, and a mount higher than a hill is a mountain. Rockwell Mountain—the riddle was solved! The riddle meant Rockwell Mountain.

Joey felt numb, but he had to tell Budda. He raced into the kitchen.

"Budda, Budda, I know where the druggons are hidden, I know what the riddle means."

To Joey's surprise, Budda was not in the kitchen. Some of the food was half-eaten. He quickly searched the other rooms, but Budda was not in any of them. The television was turned off. It was very quiet. Joey then thought of Ben; he had forgotten to check on him. He quickly ran back to his room.

"Ben!" he yelled. The floating bed was still floating in midair. Joey pulled the blanket off, but it was empty; Ben was not there.

He ran to the front door. It was wide open. They must have gone into the cave. Though Joey could not understand why the food was left on the kitchen table hardly touched. Normally Budda would eat everything; he would never let anything go to waste. Joey ran out into the cave.

"Budda, Ben, where are you?" he shouted.

They were nowhere to be seen, and everything was completely quiet. Suddenly, Joey remembered his father's security camera; his father was always worried their home might get robbed. He quickly ran back, appreciating that he was the only one who could see his home; otherwise, he would have forgotten where it was. As he let himself in, he slammed the front door shut. He thought of his father and was very proud he was smart with cameras. His father had neatly installed a camera in each room inside the air vents that were connected to the cooling system. The cameras could clearly view and secretly film each room.

Joey dashed into his father's room. He opened the wardrobe and rummaged behind the clothes to where a small chest was hidden underneath the floor. Joey carefully lifted a square of carpet and pulled the chest from its hiding place. He yanked open the lid and grabbed the camera. From inside, Joey retrieved a small chip from a slot inside the camera. It had always baffled Joey how a small chip contained days of recording.

He raced into his father's study where, as a rule, Joey was not allowed by himself. But he had seen his father use the equipment many times, and he was confident he knew how to use the equipment. Anyway, this was not his real home; it was only a duplicate of it. His father would never know he had been in his computer room alone.

Joey turned on every computer and placed the chip inside the hard drive of the main computer. All his father's computers were networked. Within a few minutes, Joey could see all the rooms viewed on each monitor.

There were several monitors, one for every room—the kitchen, all the bedrooms, the living room, the bathroom, and even the toilet. He went back over the last hour of film and then played the views. Joey studied each screen. In his bedroom screen, he could not see himself on the pillow. He looked back at the kitchen view and saw Budda was preparing breakfast with his fettal. He checked his bedroom again, and there was Ben on his floating bed sound asleep. Joey knew at that time that he was on his pillow, but his body was not shown on his bed.

He played the film for ten more minutes and still he could not see himself. He decided to go back twenty minutes. He saw himself discover the pillow and Budda telling him to put the pillow away. He saw himself lay on the pillow, and then he and the pillow disappeared from the screen. He rewound the film again and repeated the part where he had disappeared just to be sure he had not missed anything. But when he played the film again, he had not been mistaken. He had disappeared along with the pillow.

He had to keep watching the bedroom and kitchen monitors to find out what had happened to Budda and Ben. He saw Ben wake up and gaze around the bedroom. "Joey!" he called. He jumped off his bed and stood beside Joey's bed. He touched the blanket and moved Joey's pillow as if Joey might be hiding under his pillow and blanket, but Joey was not there. Ben went into the kitchen. He stretched his arms high and yawned.

"Good morning," he said.

Budda looked at Ben and smiled. "Well, did you have a good night's sleep?" he asked.

"Mmmmm . . . yes, where's Joey?" asked Ben. He peered around the kitchen and selected some toast with vegemite.

"Isn't he in his bedroom?" asked Budda, frowning.

"No, his bed was messy, but he wasn't there."

Budda put down his cup of tea and stood up. "Joey, come and have some breakfast with us!" he called and waited for his reply, but there was no answer. He then walked into each room, calling Joey. Ben stopped eating and followed Budda. They both gazed at each other with worried faces.

"Where could he be? I've just searched every room," said Budda.

Ben shrugged his shoulders. "Maybe he's outside, I mean in the cave, looking for the stone," said Ben.

"Yes, yes, he must be, he's not anywhere in the house. Let's go out the front door and see. It should be safe now." Budda moved his head from side to side with disappointment. "He should have told us, he didn't even have any breakfast. Oh goodness, that boy is never patient." They both walked to the front door. Budda gently unlocked the door and slowly opened it. He stood still for a moment and carefully peeped into the cave.

"What are you waiting for? Let's go out," said Ben restlessly. He tried to push himself underneath Budda's arm, but Budda shoved him back inside.

"No, quickly, go back inside!" he roared. He tried to slam the door shut, but a huge red claw pushed the door open. Budda tumbled to the floor. Ben ran behind, screaming with fear.

It was a druggon; Joey could tell from the huge claws. The druggon was Villazian, but he quickly transformed into a human, a very strong human at that. Before Budda had a chance to stand up, a whole group of druggons had transformed into humans.

They all crowded into the house and grabbed Budda and Ben, who both kicked and yelled. They were never going to be able to fight off the druggons by themselves.

The druggons shoved Budda and Ben inside a huge black mesh bag and threw them into a cage, which was parked outside the front door. Joey could only see a glimpse of it from the film clip. Once again, Joey's heart sank as he watched his friends go through such an ordeal.

The druggons searched his whole house without moving a thing. It was obvious they were looking for him, but he wondered why they were so careful with his home; they touched nothing.

Joey adjusted his cape and noticed one of the pockets had opened. Once again, the cape must have read his mind. He stopped the film and carefully put his hand inside the open pocket and felt a piece of paper. As he pulled it out, he realized it was a message:

> *No creature in Magical World is allowed to destroy any gift from the Chosen One's special cape. Any such creature would be cursed and then banished inside one of the Chosen One's coins for all eternity.*

Joey knew he had quite a few coins, enough to banish every druggon. Now he knew why the druggons did not touch or break anything inside his house; they would have been trapped. If only they had broken one of his mother's ornaments; it would have been so easy to capture them. That was also why they transformed into humans, just to be small in size and easier to get around. This was the opposite to what they did to Riddells Withals though, by now, it would have all been repaired.

Joey placed the note back inside his cape pocket. He was relieved Budda and Ben had not accidentally broken anything in his home, and he wondered how the druggons knew so much about him. He ran out into the cave and carefully shrunk his house and placed it back inside his cape pocket.

Joey kept thinking about the images from his pillow and remembered where the druggons lived. He ran through the cave, but then he slowed down, and after a few minutes, he stopped. He remembered the druggons could mind read and could probably sense he had found them. He quickly searched for his nonmind reading dust and threw it above his head. Joey poked his tongue out, relishing the taste of the nonmind reading dust. Mmmmmm, it had its usual sweet-tangy flavour. He was now confident the druggons could not read his mind.

CHAPTER 19

Clipper the Frog

Joey pulled out his wet blanket. He knew he had to be prepared for battle, and his instincts were working overtime. What if there were too many druggons? He feared he would not be able to fight them all. He could not go to them now, not until he had a plan. From the images on his pillow, he remembered the caves were very wide and open, and there was nowhere for him to hide. And how was he going to get through the cave with the fallen rocks and fire flames?

Even if I had found a way to get to them, how am I going to get them out?

This was all another plot by the druggons. They wanted Joey; they wanted the Chosen One. That was why they kidnapped Olivia and Astina and now Budda and Ben. They kept them alive because they knew Joey would try and rescue them. Joey knew the druggons were smart, but he had to be smarter.

He sat down on a smooth cold surface on the floor of the cave and pulled his knees up towards him; he wrapped his arms around them and rested his chin on top of his knees. He stared at the crystals and rocks opposite him and tried to think of a way to save his sister and all his friends in Magical World. For the first time in his life, he felt helpless.

He began to remember what Budda had told him about the white universe and how he could communicate with it. But Budda had not told him how to do this. If only he could communicate with the universe, maybe the white universe could help him.

A strong feeling came to Joey. Perhaps he should close his eyes and concentrate on the white universe; maybe that was the way to communicate. So Joey closed his eyes and concentrated on the white flow coming down from the red sky. He concentrated hard for ages, but nothing came to him.

Joey opened his eyes and continued to stare at a purple crystal in front of him. Parts of the crystal started to move. Just as he was about to take a closer look, out jumped a small brown frog. It scared the living daylights out of him.

The frog quickly jumped all around the cave area where Joey was now standing. It was lively and very fast. There was no way Joey could catch it.

The frog finally landed on a very high red crystal. The crystal had a small crack in it, and the frog crawled inside. Even if Joey took out his balon and flew up near the crystal, his hand would have been too big to grab the frog through the crack opening.

Joey thought it was very unusual for a single frog to be inside Rockwell Mountain cave. Perhaps the white universe was giving him a sign; maybe this was how the universe communicated. Joey shook his head. What could a frog do to save his sister and friends? But he could not get that frog out of his mind.

If only he could change himself into that frog, he would be small and fast. To be a frog would be a great way to get through the druggon's caves, especially the cave with the flares and rocks. Was there a way Joey could change himself and his friends into frogs? If there was a way, surely his cape would be able to show him. He concentrated and thought hard about changing into a frog.

He opened his cape and carefully checked if any of the pockets had opened. In a bottom corner was a small red pocket. He almost missed it. Joey carefully slid his hand inside the pocket. He moved his hand around and felt something very soft, slimy, wet, and alive. He quickly pulled out his hand; whatever it was scared him a little. Out jumped a fluorescent tiny bright-blue frog.

"Wow, you're gorgeous!" Joey had never seen such a tiny bright frog. It was smaller than the brown frog he had just seen. He slowly approached the frog, and surprisingly, it did not try to jump away. He carefully picked the frog up and stared at it. Joey noticed something tiny inside its mouth; it looked like a folded paper note.

"Have you got a message for me?" asked Joey with a smile. He had always liked animals, and this little frog did not try to run away from him; in fact, it seemed friendly. Joey carefully held out his hand underneath the frog's mouth, and the frog instantly released the note and stayed still. It was as if it wanted Joey to read the note. Joey carefully placed the frog on a blue crystal next to him.

"Now don't you run away, little froggy. You stay right there while I read your little note."

The blue frog let out its long rainbow-coloured tongue; it was as if the frog understood what Joey said to him. This was definitely no ordinary frog.

The note in Joey's hand was so tiny he had to be very careful to unfold it. He was bewildered at how many times he kept unfolding it—and there were more folds. By the time he eventually completely unfolded it, it had turned into a poster. There was a lot of information on it, so Joey began to read.

Joey read that the frog's name was Clipper. He gazed at Clipper and said. "So your name is Clipper. Nice to meet you, Clipper." Out poked Clipper's tongue in response. Joey smiled and continued to read the rest of the poster.

He learned that he would need to pat Clipper's head four times and imagine he would turn into Clipper.

Of course, the real Clipper would disappear until Joey wanted to turn back into himself again. For him to turn into a human again, he would have to croak like a frog eight times. Otherwise, he would instantly turn back to his human self after four hours. The same would apply to any others who wanted to be a frog.

Joey had an idea. He could use Clipper to change himself into a frog until he reached the cage where Astina was imprisoned, then he would change back to his normal self. Once Astina realized who he was, he would convince her to change into a frog with him so they could find the others and escape. But first, he would have to change back into a frog and jump inside the cage above Astina's prison where the stone was hidden. He thought once he was in the cage, he could quickly change back into himself, seize the stone, place it inside his cape, change back into a frog, and leave with Astina.

Joey had it all planned out, but he wondered if it was all too easy. Of course, it still worried him that the druggons had a plan of their own, like capturing him and threatening to hurt the others. Ideally, Joey wanted to sneak into the cave, find his friends and all the prisoners, change them all into frogs, and escape from the druggons without them even noticing.

Joey stood still for a while and stared at Clipper. Again, his rainbow tongue flickered in and out. It was as if Clipper was trying to tell him something, but time was running out, and Joey had no time to work out what Clipper was trying to tell him; he had to save his sister and his friends.

"Well, here we go, Clipper!" Joey patted Clipper's head gently with his pointer finger four times and imagined himself as a frog. In the blink of an eye, he turned into Clipper.

Now the cave looked gigantic. His rainbow-coloured tongue flickered out, and his legs felt springy and light. Joey jumped around the cave, and after a while, he actually enjoyed being a frog. He continued to jump towards the direction of the black stone image he had seen on his pillow image, and it was not long until he had finally reached it.

With the black stone now in front of him, he wondered how he was going to get through it. The stone looked hard. If he jumped on it, he feared he might knock himself out. Instead, he decided to lean his head slowly on the rock and not jump through it. Surprisingly, his head slid through the rock. It turned out his head was half inside the rock, and this was just how he saw it in his pillow image.

The rock was very large, and being such a small frog, there was much darkness around him as he continued to jump farther and farther inside the rock until he reached the other side. There in front of him was the cave with the fireballs on each side.

Even though Joey was disguised as Clipper, it still bothered him that the druggons might see him. He decided to play it safe and jump towards the side of the cave where there were tiny rocks for Joey to hide amongst, and the fire balls did not radiate as much light there; it was just enough for Joey to see where he was going.

On his travels, he came across some druggon droppings. Though the smell did not bother him, it attracted a lot of mosquitoes and flies. *Mmmmm, this looks good thought Joey.* He quickly leapt on top of the sloppy droppings, his tongue flickered out, and he instantly caught a fly. To Joey, it was delicious, and he could feel it still alive and buzzing inside his stomach. He could not believe he was standing on druggon droppings, lavishly eating flies and mosquitoes. Before he got carried away with eating, he forced himself to jump away from the droppings.

Joey felt his stomach weigh him down, making it difficult for him to jump. He had obviously eaten too many flies and mosquitoes. He compelled himself to continue to jump farther and farther until his stomach started to feel lighter.

Joey continued his journey deeper inside the cave. He could hear children's voices nearby, and the sound was not pleasant voices. Joey remembered the images from his pillow where he had seen the children suffer. He jumped past the cave where the children were forced to work surrounded by the dreadful reb creatures. Joey sensed that once he had the stone, he could somehow change all the suffering that surrounded him.

A short distance ahead, he heard loud voices. Being a small frog gave him extra hearing senses, so he quickly hid inside a group of scattered rocks. Joey doubted any creature would notice him because of his size, even with his bright-coloured complexion, and he was also lucky he had his nonmind reading powder over himself. The position he was hiding in was a dark corner of the cave though Joey had a clear view of the entire cave. The voices became closer and closer until directly in front of him stood Villazian and Megram.

Joey desperately wanted to change back to himself there and then, just to be able to throw his wet blanket across their mouths. All the fear he had for them had instantly vanished; he loathed them. Instead, Joey stayed still and studied them.

"*Eeeeee*, it won't be long until we find the Chosen One, *eeeeeeee*, now we've captured his friends, *eeeeeeeee*," said Villazian. He flicked his tail in the air like a hungry lion.

"Yeah, yeah, that fat one squealed like a pig inside the sack. Hahaha," laughed Megram.

They both laughed harder and louder, the sound vibrating like a tremor throughout the cave. Not only did they laugh, they jumped and swished their tails vigorously in every direction until finally Villazian sat on his tail and gradually stopped laughing. He then jumped hard on his hind legs and, with his tail, slapped Megram across his head. "Shut up!" he roared.

Megram stumbled to the ground and ceased laughing. He quickly shook his head as if nothing had happened and stood up tall and still. "Yes, master, sssssorry, master," he replied, half-dazed.

"*Eeeeee,* we've still got to capture the Chosen One, *eeeeeeee,* Joey is his name, isn't it?"

"Yes, master, Joey Willis. A damn shame he wasn't in his house with the others." Megram punched his clawed fist into the air. "We nearly had him. He must have gone out to the cave before the others. Lucky we caught them though," said Megram, briskly nodding his head four or five times.

"*Eeeeee,* yes, lucky indeed, but does he know where we are? *Eeeeeeeee,* there's no point having them alive if he doesn't know where we are. We have to think of a plan, *eeeeeee.*"

Megram jumped up and down in front of Villazian. "What's the plan, master? What's the plan? Hey? Hey?"

Villazian whacked Megram across his head. "Be still, you idiot. I haven't thought of a plan yet."

Megram rubbed his clawed paw across his head where Villazian had whacked him. He moaned as if he was in pain. "Okay, master, sorry, master." Megram pointed his claw in the air. "Master, I don't think you really need a plan."

Villazian turned to face Megram and gave him a mean, stern look. "And why don't you think I need a plan?"

Megram slowly shrunk himself and hid his head behind his paw. "Well, he has that magic cape. I'm sure he'll figure out a way to find us. I mean his friends are gone, and he knew his house had cameras. He knows we have them. It shouldn't be too long before he comes to find them. Then we can catch him and kill him." Again he punched his fist into the air with excitement.

"*Eeeeeee,* maybe you're right. We'll just have to wait. *Rebs, come here at once!*" screeched Villazian.

His voice was so loud it could be heard far away, but then, this was Magical World. A group of rebs immediately rushed to Villazian's aid. They all bowed to the ground, then stood up with their heads down.

"Yes, master, I, Slogan and all of us are here at your service," replied one of the rebs bowing his head low.

"*Eeeeeee,* Slogan, make sure you organize reb guards to stand near the entrance of the cave. I want some of you outside the black stone and some inside the cave entrance, *eeeeeeeeee.*"

Slogan kept his head down, but his huge round eyes slowly peered upwards and gazed at Villazian. "Master, can I ask what are we guarding against?" he asked with a tremor of fear in his voice.

"*Eeeeeee,* the Chosen One, make sure you capture him and bring him to me. But don't kill him. I want to have the pleasure of doing that, *eeeee.*"

Slogan and the other rebs continuously bowed their heads. "Yes, master, we'll do that right now, and we'll bring our precious snakes to hold him once we capture him, master."

"*Eeeeeee,* yes, you do that, *eeeeee*. Now off with you all," demanded Villazian, pointing his paw toward the entrance of the cave.

The group of ten rebs instantly trooped towards the cave entrance. Each of them pulled off the red belts they had tied around their thin waists. The belts turned into live snakes. They held them high above their heads as if they were precious pets. From what Joey could see, the reb snakes were well-trained pets.

Villazian and Megram watched the rebs, and then they turned to face each other again. "*Eeeeeee,* once they capture Joey Willis, you make sure you kill the others, especially that Budda, *eeeeeeee*. We have no use for them, *eeeeeeee,* they're nothing but troublemakers."

"Hahaha, with great pleasure, master, with great pleasure," laughed Megram.

They both wandered off farther inside the cave, well out of Joey's view.

The cave became quiet. There was only the distinct sound of children crying. Joey squeezed himself out of the small rocks and leapt along the side of the cave in the direction where he last saw Astina and the charmal stone. He did not want to think about the rebs or the snakes; all he wanted to do for now was save his friends, but he had to make sure no one could see him. If they caught him, his friends and his sister would be murdered.

This was becoming such a mission for Joey. If Budda could not protect himself, then how was Joey going to save them? And now those snakes had become another worry for Joey because snakes love to eat frogs. His plan was ruined. He would not be able to change everyone into frogs; it was too much of a risk.

After some time, Joey started to feel an overwhelming thirst. He could not remember the last time he had a drink; he must be dehydrated. Being such a small frog meant he should have frequent drinks. Joey now understood why frogs hung around the swamps, lakes, and ponds. His legs were getting weaker, and there was still some distance before he reached Astina and the charmal stone. He was shuffling along now, searching for some water.

In the middle of the cave, Joey caught sight of something shiny. The closer he went, the more it appeared to be a puddle of water. But he was not sure whether it was a mirage or some sort of hallucination because of the way he felt and the fire balls were no help either. Their heat made him feel even more dehydrated and weak. Hopefully, Joey was not hallucinating; hopefully it really was water.

He got close enough to the puddle to see that it was definitely real. Luckily, Joey was still out of view hidden between the rocks. He desperately wanted to approach the puddle for a drink, but he still feared someone would see him.

He decided to take the risk. He would have a quick drink and then jump back between the rocks; all he needed was a few gulps from the small puddle. Joey was getting weaker and weaker by the minute; this was his only chance. With what little strength he had left, he plunged out from the small rocks and jumped as far as his legs could take him.

It took one more leap, and Joey reached the puddle. His tongue flicked in and out, slurping up water. He lapped up more than half the puddle in no time, feeling so relieved to get his energy back. Now he felt that he could jump a marathon. He decided to drink the remainder to have something in reserve.

After Joey had finished the last drop of water, he noticed a small yellow stone at the bottom of the dried-up puddle. It was the size of a pebble not much smaller than Joey in his frog form. The pebble began to move; then it started to slowly spin around until it spun faster and faster, and as it did it, it looked as if it was growing. It spun faster and faster and grew bigger and bigger. Joey had to jump quickly out of its way.

When he turned back, the pebble had transformed into a huge yellow rock. All of a sudden, the rock burst into a bright-yellow light, and all that was left was a cloud of yellow dust.

CHAPTER 20

Coming across Chuckup

As the dust cleared, there, standing in front of Joey, was a fat, funny-looking yellow creature. Its neck was long and thick; its arms were thin like sticks, but its hands and feet were enormous. It had huge round black eyes and a wide mouth. A few strands of yellow hair stuck up from its head.

Joey was afraid the creature was one of the druggon's servants. He quickly jumped backwards. "Hey, wait, please don't go," the yellow creature pleaded in a high-pitched voice. "I won't hurt you, please come back." Joey peered inside its mouth, which looked like that of a big fish with a big gullet.

Joey stayed where he was, not sure if this was a plot. But the yellow creature did not try to come near him, and Joey thought that he did seem friendly.

"Who are you?" asked Joey. He was a little startled that he could talk. It was the first time he had spoken since he had turned into a frog.

"My name is Chuckup," he said as his mouth opened wider and out came about twenty yellow-spotted toads. The toads were quite big compared to Joey, who was only a little frog. However, Joey stood out amongst them because of his blue fluorescent colour. The toads scattered throughout the cave, and soon they were all gone.

"Sorry about that, the toads only come out from my mouth when I say my name," said Chuckup.

"Does it hurt when they come out?" Joey queried.

"Yeah, it feels like my stomach turns inside out. But I'm used to it now." He patted his big stomach with both of his wide hands.

"So why don't you change your name?" asked Joey.

"I've tried that, I still . . . well . . . you know . . . I can't say it."

"Oh, you mean chuck up?"

"Yes."

"Is it a curse?"

"No, I've always had it. They say I'm a rare species. I'm one of a kind. Anyway, I want to thank you for drinking that water."

"Why?"

"Because that was a curse on me from the druggons, or should I say Villazian, the so-called master."

"You know Villazian?" Joey asked in amazement.

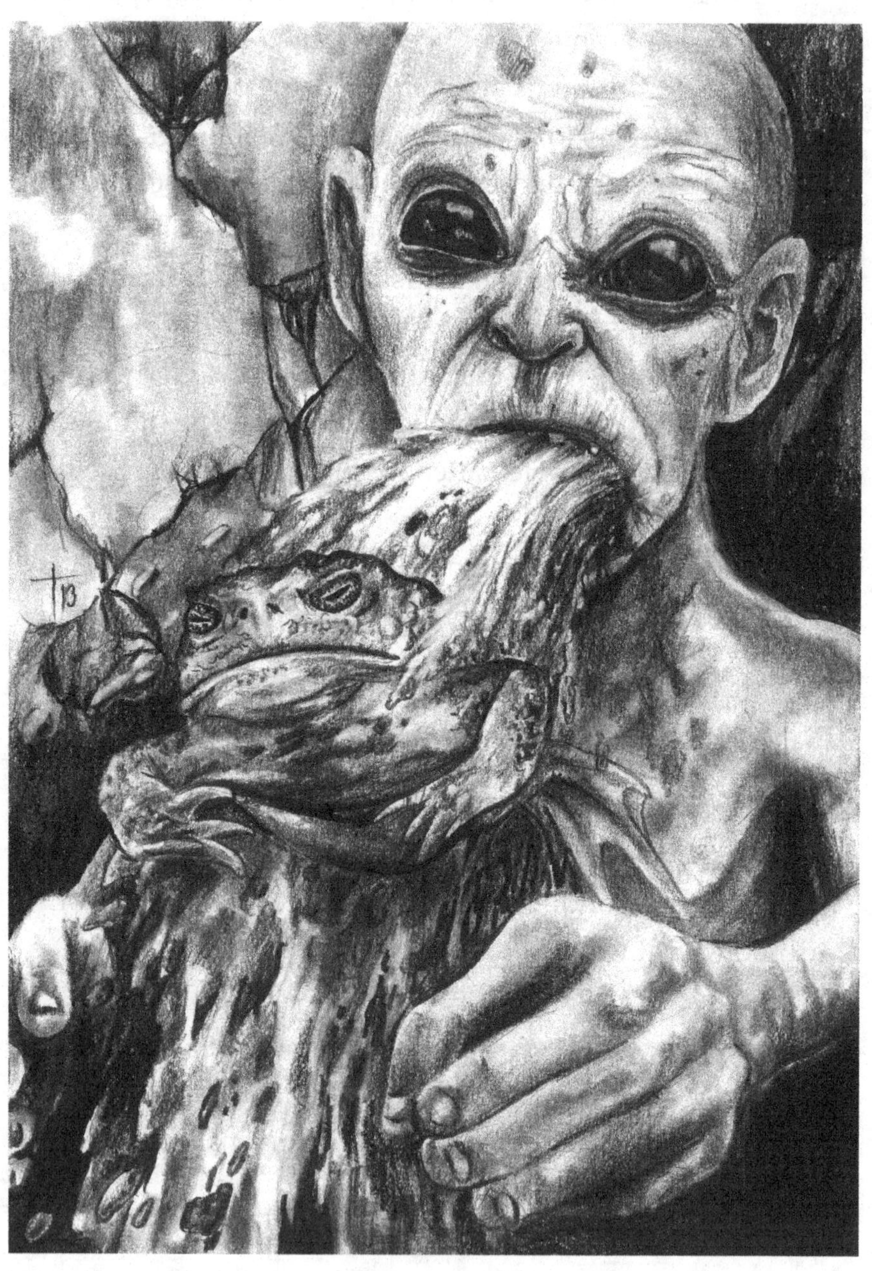

"Do I know him? Who doesn't around here? He's evil. I was one of his slaves longer than I can remember, and I got fed up with it. I stood up to him and told him I was not going to stand the slavery anymore. Just as I was about to walk through that black stone, he turned me into a pebble and placed a puddle over me. He said if no creature drinks the water before it evaporates from the fire balls, I'd be destined to be a pebble for all eternity. It was so lucky you turned up. How can I ever repay you?"

"Actually, I should be thanking you. If that water wasn't there when I needed it, I would have died of thirst. I hadn't realized how much frogs need water. By the way, I'm not really a frog. I'm really a human boy in disguise. My name is Joey Willis."

Chuckup suddenly looked around and placed his pointer finger across his lips.

"Did I say something wrong? What are you looking for?" asked Joey.

"I was checking if anyone was listening to our conversation. I know you." Chuckup bent down closer to Joey and quietly whispered, "You're the Chosen One. If the druggons find out you're here, they'll fry you. And it wouldn't be hard for them to fry a frog."

"Oh yes, you have a point there. Thank you. You're a very kind creature. There is so much I have to learn here in Magical World, especially about myself. I'm obviously a serious threat to those druggons, otherwise, they wouldn't be so intent on destroying me. Also I think it has something to do with the charmal stone. I wish I knew what I could do to them."

Chuckup nodded his head to agree with Joey. "Yes, they are very secretive about it. Nobody here knows what you could do to them. But we all thought you would know. Now that makes the situation a lot harder, hmmmmm."

"I'm sorry to disappoint you. But I promise somehow I'll figure it out. Like I said, it must have something to do with the stone. Once I get to it, maybe I'll know."

Chuckup put his hand over his mouth, his eyes widened, and he took a deep breath. "Do you have any idea where the stone is kept? This place is very dangerous, and you could die before you get to it."

"That's why I changed into a frog. My magic cape allowed me to. I can jump so freely, and I am small. Once I get to the stone and Astina, who is someone I must rescue, I can change back to myself, take the stone, and turn myself and Astina into frogs and get out of there. The only problem is, the druggons now have the rebs guarding the entrance of this cave with their snakes."

"Oh, well, I think I can help you there. I can, well, you know, say my name and use the toads to distract them."

"What a great idea. Thank you, Chuckup, you're a smart cookie."

"Did you say cookie? Where? I love cookies," Chuckup said, looking all around.

"No, no, there is no cookie—it's just my way of giving you a compliment." Joey smiled.

Chuckup looked quite disappointed, so Joey quickly reassured him. "I promise you, when this is all over, I'll get you plenty of cookies. You have my word." He thought about Budda's fettal and how he always organized plenty of food and how the good Magical World contained all sorts of trees and plants that consistently had delicious food.

Chuckup's long face immediately turned into a big, happy smile. Joey thought he looked cute with his large mouth that almost covered his entire face.

"Well, you're going to have to hide somewhere until I get the others," explained Joey.

Chuckup smiled even more. "Don't you worry about me, I can change into a cave wall if I want to. I'll be right here when you get back." With that, Chuckup's body changed colour and blended with the cave wall. All Joey could see were the outline of two open eyes and a big mouth.

"See, I'll be here waiting for you. The druggons don't know about me being able to do this," Chuckup said.

"Wow, you're amazing, Chuckup. I've never seen anything like this."

Chuckup's eyes and mouth made a reaction as though he was a little embarrassed. "I suppose it is amazing," said Chuckup, and then his eyes became serious. "You better get going now."

"Oh yes, I better go now. I should be back in an hour," Joey said confidently.

"I certainly hope so, if not, I'm coming to look for you," said Chuckup.

Joey hurriedly jumped farther into the cave, keeping safely to the sides in case the druggons or rebs came around the corner. He quickly passed each cave room without a chance to look inside any of them. It was very fortunate for Joey no one had seen him or come his way.

Finally, he stopped in front of his destination—the cave with the fallen rocks and bursting flares of fire. It felt like a sauna, and he was worried that he could dehydrate again, but time was of the essence, and he was not going to waste any more of it.

Joey took the plunge and jumped swiftly between rocks falling from the walls and dodging the flares. Although, sometimes, he was not able to determine where the next lot of fire would flare or where a rock might fall. So he used his instincts; he did not dare look back, only forward. He felt like a ping-pong ball.

He took a look up towards the two cages at the end of the cave. There inside the cage that held Astina were Budda and Ben. They all now sighted him, and they crowded to the front of their prison. Joey wondered if they sensed who he was. He could hear them calling out, "Come on, little frog, you can make it." But by calling him little frog, Joey realized they were not aware it was him.

Astina's arms were through the bars with her hands out, ready to catch Joey. She could see he was getting weaker by the minute as, once again, he was desperately in need of water. "Come on, little froggy, we'll get you some water. Come on, you can make it," Astina kept up the encouragement. Joey was so relieved she realized he needed water.

He was so near, yet so far. His weak legs could not move anymore, and he collapsed. Joey could vaguely see and hear his friends urging him on, but there was no energy left in him. Then everything around him went quiet and dark.

CHAPTER 21

The Charmal Stone

Joey woke up in a small bath of soda water with constant splashes on his face.

"That's a good little froggy," said Astina while she continued to splash water on his mouth.

Joey's tongue immediately flicked out and swallowed the soda water. Instantly, he felt alive again; it amazed him how frogs recovered so quickly. Joey was relieved his friends had such a caring nature for every living creature. He also wondered how they had rescued him or if he himself had somehow made it to their cage.

Astina, Budda, and Ben were staring at him very closely, which made him curious as to why. He was only an ordinary frog. Then he remembered his colour. He glanced at his feet and remembered that no ordinary frogs were bright fluorescent-blue or, better still, had a rainbow-coloured tongue. They must have realized he was a special frog.

"Guess who?" said Joey.

All three of them stood back with their mouths wide open, looking as if someone had risen from the dead. Then Astina smiled widely and squatted closer towards Joey.

"You can talk. Father, the little frog spoke." Astina frowned and glanced at her father. Budda could only keep staring at Joey.

"Yes, he spoke, and I recognize that voice. Joey, is that you?" Budda also squatted down closer and waited for his reply.

"You guessed it. It's me Joey."

"It's a trick, it's another trick from the druggons. Joey is not a frog," interrupted Ben; he almost looked like he was going to cry.

"It is me, Ben, I can turn back into a boy if I want to, but I don't want the druggons to see me. Come on, Ben, can't you recognize my voice?"

Ben went down on his knees between Astina and Budda and approached Joey at a close range. "Well, I suppose I can believe you because I don't think I have ever seen a blue frog with a rainbow-coloured tongue, and I don't think those mean druggons could create a frog as beautiful as you," said Ben, looking more relaxed. Then he glanced at Astina and Budda, who both nodded in agreement.

"I couldn't have put it better myself," said Budda, messing Ben's hair.

"Oh, Joey, I knew you'd be here to help us. How did you find us? And what are you going to do now?" asked Astina. She smiled and appeared happy and excited, especially compared to what Joey had seen from his pillow image.

"Never mind about that now, I'll explain it all later. I first need to get the charmal stone. And thanks for the water, I would have died out there."

"Budda used his magic bed. He slid it underneath you and carried you here," interrupted Ben.

"Thank you, Budda. I hadn't realized how easily frogs dehydrate, especially in a heated cave like this one."

Budda smiled and splashed more water on Joey's body. "I knew you were special the moment I saw you. But I would have helped any creature in a dangerous situation like yours."

"I knew you would, that's why you're all my best friends. You're good to everyone. I've missed you all so much, especially you, Astina."

They all smiled happily, and Astina carefully patted Joey's small head with her pointer finger. "I've missed you too, Joey, I am so glad you are here with us now."

"So could the stone be here somewhere?" asked Budda.

"How did you know?" asked Joey.

"Well, a little frog like you wouldn't have jumped all the way through rocks and fire just to tell us you need to get the stone first, now, would you?" said Budda with a big smile.

"Apparently, the stone is right above this cage," said Joey.

Budda quickly pointed his finger upwards, looking at Joey with surprise.

"Yes, in the cage above us all," agreed Joey.

"So we've been here all this time not knowing the stone was right above us," said Budda.

"That's right. The plan is, I'll be going up there to quickly change back into myself, grab the stone, hide it inside my cape, and quickly change back into a frog. Then I'm going to come back down here and change you all into frogs. Together we're all going to jump right out of here." Joey thought about the snakes near the front entrance but decided not to tell his friends. For the time being, this was the only plan he had.

"You're going to turn us into frogs? No way, I don't want to be a frog," argued Ben.

"Don't worry, Ben, all you have to do is croak eight times, and you can turn back into yourself. Anyway, it's fun being a frog, you'll love it. Don't you agree, Budda, Astina?"

Budda's eyes squinted, and then he moved his head from side to side. "I'm not sure that's such a good idea. I mean, you barely made it here yourself. Who's going to give us water? Being a frog is not the same as being human. I don't think you should turn us into frogs. It's too risky."

"I can't think of any other way to get us all out of here," said Joey, and then he sighed. "But I suppose you have a point." Once again, Joey reminded himself about the rebs and snakes, but he still thought it would be best not to tell them about that just in case that put them off altogether.

Astina glanced at Joey and then at Budda and Ben. "I think Joey's idea is great. He said we could turn back into ourselves by croaking eight times. If it ever comes to that, Father, you could croak eight times, turn back into yourself, and then use your fettal to make a pond of soda water for all of us," said Astina.

Budda frowned and gave Astina a stern look. "You're forgetting I can't turn myself back in front of that fire and all those falling rocks. And I think if I turned into a frog, I doubt I'd be as quick as Joey, and even he nearly didn't make it."

"I know I barely made it here, but I was already tired before I even attempted to enter this dangerous cave. But I suppose you're right, Budda, it's too risky," said Joey. He continued to paddle in the pond and slurped more water. He felt like he had failed; he had not realized how complicated it was being a frog.

Astina slowly walked towards her bed with her head down. "Now we're all trapped here in this cave," she said as she slowly sat on the corner of her bed with her back to everyone.

Budda squatted down close to Joey's small head and whispered, "You haven't failed, Chosen One. I've been thinking, the druggons desperately want to capture and kill you, and for some reason, they are trying to keep that precious stone away from you." Budda pointed his finger above his head. "I have a feeling once you get that stone, you'll know what to do. I believe it will have great powers only you can use."

Joey briskly leapt out of the water. It was as if something within him had sparked. "Do you think so?" he asked with enthusiasm. Without a word, Budda slowly nodded his head. Joey jumped towards the front of the cage. "Then I'm going to get it."

"Wait. There is just one thing I'd like to ask you once you get that stone. I know this is probably not the time or the place to ask, but there's a good chance that that stone could show you who Astina's earth-parents . . ."

"Say no more, I'll help you find her parents," interrupted Joey. Without another word, he jumped out of the cage again using his quick frog reflexes to avoid the fire and falling stones before he briskly made a huge final jump to the top cage where the charmal stone was located. The moment he stood in front of the stone, he was stunned. It was so glorious, and the nearer he was to it, the more strength he felt.

Previously, when Joey had seen the image through the pillow, the stone had not sparkled or shined quite as much. In fact, it appeared that Joey's presence made the stone light up more brightly. It was like looking at the morning sunshine. Joey carefully glanced around the cave; he was going to change back into a boy, but first he had to be sure none of the druggons could see him. There was nowhere for him to hide, so he was relieved that there was no sign of any druggons near the cave.

He closed his eyes. "Well, here I go. Croak, croak, croak, croak, croak, croak, croak, croak." When he opened his eyes, he found himself back to his usual self, and it had happened in a moment with no pain or discomfort. And there beside Joey sat Clipper.

"You're a good frog, Clipper. Thanks for letting me be you for a while. It really helped me get here. Now let me put you back inside my cape until I figure out what to do next. I don't want to lose you, my dear little friend."

Clipper made a small croak as if he understood what Joey had said to him, and then he jumped onto the palm of his hand. Joey carefully placed him back inside the small pocket. While he put Clipper back inside his cape, he noticed the ground had become white. He took a good look around and noticed the whole cave was brightly lit. It was as if someone had just turned on a fluorescent light switch throughout the entire cave. He turned back to the stone but quickly shut his eyes and turned away from it; it was like staring straight at the sun.

Joey peeped out of one eye, then slowly opened his other until he became accustomed to the brightness. The sight of the stone was beyond belief.

Joey recalled Budda explaining about everything having its own energy and how the universe was made up of different energies. Now he knew that the stone was energised by his presence. As he gazed at the stone, he felt pleasurable warmth and pure energy run through him. Without even touching the stone, the small scratch he had on his finger healed instantly.

Carefully, he reached out to touch the stone with both of his hands. It was the most precious gift. Gently he picked it up, feeling hypnotized but so strong. He knew that the stone had given him something new inside himself. Slowly the bright light became less and less until the stone went back to normal just as he had seen it in his book.

Joey thought of what Budda had asked him about finding Astina's earth-parents. He wondered how the stone could help him find out who her parents were. He kept gazing at the stone, constantly thinking about finding Astina's parents. The stone started to change. It became white, and then he noticed an image inside the stone. He heard familiar voices coming from the stone, and then he saw an image of his parents in a happy moment once on Earth.

It was the time his mother had organized a huge Christmas party. The image looked slightly different to what Joey had remembered at that Christmas party. The chairs and tables were set out exactly the same, but something was missing. Then Joey noticed that there were no other people at the party, just his mother and father laughing and talking between themselves. No one else was at the party.

Joey held the stone close to his heart. He stared at the falling rocks and fire blazes and tried to think of a way he could help his friends escape from their prison. At that moment, all he wanted to do was rescue his friends and take them somewhere safe. He quickly gazed at the rock that was so close to his heart and once again saw a different image inside the rock. The image was showing him how to use his hands to stop the fires and falling rocks.

Quickly, he put the stone inside one of his pockets and held both his hands out wide, one hand towards the ground and the other above. Instantly, a white light flashed and burst out from the end of his finger tips. It was so powerful that the bars of the cage Joey was standing blew out into the flames and rocks and smashed into tiny pieces. The ceiling of the cave slowly formed a thick layer of ice, turning the flames on the ground into steam and covering it in white snow. The cave was now like a winter wonderland.

Joey felt very proud, and he jumped down on to the snow to face his friends.

"What happened?" asked Budda. He and the others looked deathly pale, their mouths half open.

Joey smiled at his friends. "The stone has given me powers beyond my wildest dreams. Stand to the side, all of you. I'm going to get you all out of here!"

The three of them huddled together in the corner of the cage, away from the bars, Their heads were bent, and Budda put his arms around Astina and Ben. Joey lifted his hand and out came a white flash, which instantly shattered the bars, making a gap big enough for an escape.

The three of them remained huddled together. Joey asked, "Is everyone okay there?" They turned to face him and stared closely at the hole Joey had made through the bars. Joey waved his hand. "Come on, what are you all waiting for? Let's get out of here," he roared.

They trooped out of the cage and joined Joey in the snow. "It's wonderful the stone has given you such great powers, Joey," Budda said gratefully.

"Yes, it is, but I still have no idea how that power came from my fingers. This is confusing the hell out of me. I only hope I don't end up hurting someone with these powers by accident. I wish I could have more control or some instructions on how to use it," said Joey as he looked around him in wonder.

"I'm sure you'll figure it out. You're the Chosen One, remember?" Budda smiled. All of a sudden, their smiles froze. They looked as if they had seen a ghost.

CHAPTER 22

The Ice Wall

"What's wrong?" asked Joey.

Budda pointed directly behind Joey. He quickly turned around, and there, only metres away, were the druggons with Villazian, tall, fierce, and overpowering, in front of them. Before Joey had a chance to say or do anything, Villazian blew fire from his mouth.

Without hesitation, Joey lifted his hands to shield and protect his friends. Before the fire had a chance to burn them, the white power shot out of Joey's fingertips and slammed into the fire, leaving a ray of steam.

The druggons launched a full attack, blazing their fire at Joey and his friends. The white power that came from Joey's fingers repeatedly spurt ice like a fire brigade's hose. Although he fought hard to keep his friends and himself from the flames, the battle was at a stalemate. He was neither winning nor losing. All Joey's efforts were helping them to survive but not to escape.

"Quick, all of you, get behind me and stay together!" yelled Joey.

On and on went the barrage of fire. Again and again, Joey managed to extinguish the flames. As time passed, it was a question of who could keep all this up.

The druggons actually looked as though they were slowing down. Joey was also tiring. He felt like a fireman holding a hose, and his arms were heavy. He could not see his friends behind him, but he could feel their restlessness and fear. Even Budda was powerless.

Joey started to change his thoughts. He concentrated hard. His white power started to change, and his power doubled. Now he was throwing twice as much ice. The ice slowly started to push the druggons backwards.

Back, back, back they went. Until the ice pushed them right out of the big cave. The druggons, now exhausted, had hardly any firepower left. This helped Joey to trap them in a small cave, the white power still coming from his fingers.

All this power created an ice wall that blocked the entrance of the small cave. The druggons were now completely trapped. Joey could see through the ice; it was as clear as looking through a glass window. Joey imagined it would be like a freezer in that small cave with the ice being so thick and cold. In fact, the ice was so thick it would probably drown them if the druggons regained their strength and melted it with their fire. Now the druggons were Joey's prisoners.

Budda, Astina, and Ben were still huddled at the back of the cave, unaware of what he had done. Joey called back to them, "You can all come out now. The druggons can't hurt you now. See for yourselves." His hands felt cold, but otherwise, he felt unharmed after his long battle.

Budda, Astina, and Ben made their way through the rocks and stared at the cave where the druggons were trapped. Their mouths almost dropped while they stared at the ice. "Make sure you don't stare at that ice too long, you all might melt it. Come on, everyone, we should be celebrating. I've captured them all, they can't hurt us now," said Joey.

Budda looked at Joey with awe in his voice and said, "I never thought even the Chosen One would be that powerful. You're amazing, Joey."

"Honestly, I don't think you should compliment me for having so much power. I still don't know how I did it. Now, we'd better hurry up and get everyone out of here before that ice melts. I don't know if I'd be able to do that again." Joey lifted his arms out to his side and shrugged his shoulders. "It was a fluke. It wasn't me, it must have been the charmal stone."

"Surely you must have some idea how you used it," exclaimed Budda, looking disappointed Joey couldn't share a secret.

Joey glanced at his fingertips and slammed his hands to his side. "I wish I knew. But let's not waste any more time. Come on, let's get out of here."

They all quickly ran out of the cave, leaving the druggons behind them to freeze. "Let's split up. Ben, you go with Budda. Astina, come with me. We don't know how many people are treated like slaves around here. We have to search all the caves until we find them all," said Joey.

"Good idea," said Astina.

The cave had four different directions. The middle one headed towards the entrance. Behind them was where the druggons were captured. The other two directions were to their right and left, and Joey was not sure where they led to, and there was nothing Joey could recall from his pillow image. So he decided to take the right with Astina while Budda and Ben took the left.

They all decided that once they were finished their search, they would all meet back near the cave entrance. Joey was relieved to find there were not too many passages; otherwise, any one of them could have gotten lost. Joey and Budda wanted to make sure that every human and cowchee was found and saved. He worried about the ice melting. The cave outside the druggon's prison was still warm from the fires, and if the druggons regained their strength, it would not take them long to melt their way through the ice wall.

Joey pulled out his balon, and Astina used her wings. Together, side by side, they quickly flew through the unknown cave. Joey saw Budda carry Ben on his back, and he too used his balon to zip through the other unknown cave. He was relieved and happy to use his balon again; it was the quickest and most convenient way to find the humans and cowchees.

Joey looked at Astina and smiled. "It's great to have you back, Astina. Well, it's just you and me now." Astina returned his smile.

"I thought I'd never see you again, I'm so happy to be back with you," she said.

"Now that I have the charmal stone, you'll be safe and never be apart from Budda and all your friends," Joey assured her.

CHAPTER 23

Fairy Magic

Just as Astina was about to say something, they came to a sudden halt. They had reached a dead end. Joey pulled out a torch from his cape, and in its beam, he and Astina noticed a dark hole indicating another cave.

Strong iron bars crossed the entrance, and an awful smell came from the cave, a bit like the smell of an animal stable. Joey held the torch higher, and what they saw horrified them.

People and cowchees were scattered everywhere. They looked weak and ill. From the looks of their torn, ragged, stained clothes, they never showered or freshened up. Joey peered closer inside the bars and noticed most of them had their mouths sealed.

"Oh no! They must have the virus!" cried Astina, covering her mouth with her hand. "The problem is, they won't come with us. They think they need the druggons to survive, and anyone who doesn't have the virus won't come because they are afraid that if they try to escape, they will get the virus too. Joey, you've got to work on your stone and fix this so they will believe us." Astina looked at Joey with tears running down her cheeks.

Joey held her hand and pulled out the charmal stone from inside his cape. He stared at it, moving his head from side to side. "I wish I knew how to use this stone. I really wish," he sighed. At that moment, the stone showed him an image. "Hey, something is happening here. Look, Astina." Quickly he showed her the stone.

She stared and stared at the stone and looked at Joey, disappointed. "I can't see anything. The stone only allows you to see its images."

"The stone is showing me . . ." Joey did not say any more. He was stunned with what he saw. The stone was showing him the inside of his mind. At first, his thoughts were when he wandered about Astina's parents on Earth, then his memory of his parent's Christmas party.

"What is the stone showing you, Joey? Tell me!" demanded Astina.

"Shhhh," said Joey, holding his hand up. He could not take his eyes off the stone. It showed him trying to think of a way to rescue Astina, Budda, and Ben away from the cave with the fire and falling rocks. The stone then showed him the power he had with his hands. Again the stone showed Joey's thoughts on how he could get the druggons and rebs away from his friends and himself. The stone showed him how his power had increased and how he shoved the druggons and rebs right out of the cave with an ice wall. And finally, the stone showed him his thought on how to use it.

"That's it!" roared Joey.

"What is?"

"I think I know at last how to use the stone. All I have to do is think about any problem, and the power comes naturally. Back in the cave with the druggons, I hadn't realized I was thinking about protecting you all, and the white power came out of my hands. The stone has shown me all the problems I was thinking about and has given me the solution to every one of them." Joey jumped with excitement. "Astina, I know how to use my powers with this stone. I can do anything now."

Astina smiled happily at Joey. "Wow, that's wonderful. Now you can use all your great powers. Yippeeeee!" she cried as she flew around the cave with tremendous joy.

But Joey stayed still. He had remembered something the stone had shown him earlier. When he thought of Astina's parents, he saw his parents. That's impossible; they could not be her parents. Then he remembered Budda telling him he was going to reunite Astina with her earth-parents.

"What's wrong?" asked Astina, puzzled.

Joey pretended to smile. "Nothing, nothing, I was just thinking. That's all." There was no way Joey was going to tell Astina, Budda, or anyone that he had found her parents and that her earth-parents were his parents.

He was not going to lose his parents. As far as he was concerned, he liked Earth, and they were going to stay there with him and his sister once they returned home. But he could not help wondering what Astina would look like as a human on Earth.

"Were you thinking about curing these people so that the stone could show you how?"

"Ah . . . yes, yes, that's right, I'm just waiting for an image to appear." Joey was relieved that he had put the nonmind reading powder over him. Not that that would interfere with the stone reading his mind, but there was no way he was going to allow Astina to read his mind, especially now.

Joey searched through the bars for Olivia. He could not see her, but then again, maybe he would not be able to recognize her if she had caught the virus. There were so many, and neither the people nor the cowchees had noticed Astina and Joey.

Again Joey looked at the stone. He concentrated hard and thought of how he could break open the cage and then heal the virus and take away the curse that had been so bitterly wreaked upon these people and the cowchees.

An image appeared on the stone; it revealed Joey reaching inside his cape pockets to yank out a white ball about the size of a soccer ball. The ball was thrown hard against the cage, and the ball vanished immediately.

Joey could hardly wait for the stone to show him the rest, but he knew they were running out of time, so he quickly looked inside his cape and found the open pocket.

"I've got it, Astina, I know what to do to save these people and the cowchees. Stand back!" he roared.

Astina flew behind Joey who pulled out the ball and held it carefully. He took a closer look at it and noticed tiny white fairies carved around the ball. There were thousands of them, and he could also feel small movements. Joey's eyes almost popped out of his head; he could not believe what he was seeing.

"Look, Astina, this is no ordinary ball, this is a huge group of fairies all bunched up together."

Astina moved forward to get a closer look. "Oh goodness!" she shrieked. Then she gently touched the ball and said, "Oh, they are gorgeous. What do you have to do?"

"I have to throw the ball at the cage. But now I'm worried I'll hurt these little fairies, I thought it was just a ball."

"Oh no, I don't think you'll hurt them. Remember, Joey, they are magic," Astina assured him.

"Well, here goes." Joey gently held the ball with both hands and aimed it towards the cage. "You better stand back again, Astina. I'm not sure what will happen next." Joey held the ball high above his head and threw it as hard as he could at the cage. The cage vanished like a bolt of lightning, and the ball divided into thousands of small winged creatures.

The people and the cowchees looked both stunned and afraid. They tried to huddle in the corners of the cave. Joey did not blame them for being afraid; they probably thought this was another plot from the druggons.

"It's okay, everyone, we're here to save you all. The fairies want to cure you from the virus!" roared Joey with all his strength. But the people and cowchees were panicking, waving their arms and knocking the fairies away. Joey did not know how to calm them down.

Joey and Astina were bewildered. The humans and cowchees had been treated so badly by the druggons that they had lost faith in any goodness. They were so filled with terror and dread that Joey and Astina could not get through to them that they were trying to help. How could Joey calm them? Then he had an idea. He remembered his flute.

The flute pocket instantly opened, and he quickly seized it. In the middle of chaos, and without delay, he played his flute. The screams stopped. The people and cowchees gazed at Joey placidly, and even the fairies took pleasure in the music. One of the fairies sat on top of Joey's nose, smiling and gazing at him as though it had instantly fallen in love with him. Everyone stood motionless and lapped up the glorious tune until he finished playing.

With his pointer finger, Joey cautiously positioned the fairy that was sitting on his nose onto his finger. The fairy was so tiny that Joey had to be extra careful not to hurt or squash it. He grinned at the fairy and then looked around the cave. He was relieved he did not have to continue to play his flute to keep them all settled.

"Okay, now that I have everyone's attention, cowchees and people, I am here to save you all. I know you're not allowed to think of escaping because of the curse the druggons have placed upon you. I know you all fear you'll attract the virus, and for those of you who already have the virus, I realize you're livelihood solely depends on the druggons. But you all have to trust me. I have brought these fairies here to release the curse from you all. Please, everyone, let them cure you. I am the Chosen One. You must know I am much more powerful than the druggons. You must let the fairies heal you and come with me. I want to take you all to the real Magical World where there is plenty of food, love, and happiness. Trust me and please, everyone, have faith. The druggons were wrong to treat you all so badly."

Joey smiled, lifted his hand, and then clicked his thumb and fingers towards the fairies. "Come on, my fairy friends, heal these people and cowchees. We don't have much time."

All the cowchees and people stood peacefully and allowed the fairies to touch their faces. With every touch, a bright light flashed, and within seconds, those with their mouths sealed started talking. They touched their mouths, tongues, teeth, and lips. There was a lot of talk and excitement between them.

The moment had finally come. Joey felt proud and was so grateful he had found the charmal stone. For the first time since he had been in Magical World, he felt like he belonged there. Without him, the people and cowchees would not have been healed from the virus. Joey and Astina also saw that the fairies had not only cured the virus, but they had also refreshed them with clean clothes, and already they looked healthier. It was as though they had never lived in the cave with the druggons.

Once the fairies were finished their task, they all grouped back together, turned into the ball, and zapped back inside Joey's cape.

Astina grinned widely and jumped for joy. "You did it, Joey, you saved them!"

"Yes, I did it." But Joey's smile faded from his face as he searched the cave again.

"What's wrong?" asked Astina kindly.

Joey turned to Astina, struggling for the words, "I don't see Olivia."

Astina held his hand. "Maybe Father has found her. Come on, let's go and see. Remember, we're running out of time. We've got to get these people and cowchees out of here."

Joey nodded and pretended to smile. "You're right, we better get everyone out of here." He held his hands up in the air. *"Can I have everyone's attention, please!"* he roared. Everyone slowly became quiet and waited for Joey to continue.

"Good, now that I have everyone's attention, I want you all to quickly follow Astina and myself. We'll lead you out of these caves. Come on, let's go." Joey motioned his hand for them to follow him and turned towards the entrance of the cave where the fairies had previously made the bars disappear. They all quickly trooped out of the cave. Joey could feel the air was getting warmer, and he worried that the ice would melt.

"We've got to move faster, everyone!" yelled Joey.

He could not use his balon, and Astina could not fly because they wanted to make sure nobody was left behind. Joey pulled out a few floating beds from his cape for the little children. Astina kept pacing up and down the cave passage, making sure nobody was left behind.

CHAPTER 24

Deceived by a Friend

At last they reached the entrance of the cave. Joey was searching the cave walls for Chuckup when he felt a splash on his boots. He noticed a stream of water trickling down from the cave where he had trapped the druggons and rebs. The ice had started to melt, and Joey was filled with fear.

"Chuckup, Chuckup, Come out, it's me, Joey! Joey called, feeling most agitated. *Chuckup, come out!"*

Astina rushed to Joey's side. "Who's Chuckup?" she asked.

"He's a friend I met when I first got here. He's supposed to be disguised in these cave walls somewhere, but I can't remember exactly where I last saw him. Just look at this water, the ice is melting. We have to get everyone out of here."

"Don't worry, I'll help get these people and cowchees out of here as quickly as possible. You just keep looking for your friend," Astina assured Joey.

"Chuckup, it's me, Joey, come out. I'm not a frog anymore, I've changed myself back into a boy."

In a flash, Joey saw eyes open farther down the cave wall. He ran up to the spot and met up with Chuckup's eyes. Chuckup smiled, and Joey saw his fantastic disguise. If it was not for Chuckup's eyes and his obvious smile, Joey would have walked right pass him. Slowly Chuckup emerged from the wall and gave Joey a big hug that almost completely smothered Joey.

"Oh, Joey, you made it, and you look so much better as a boy—and a blue boy too, oh my." Chuckup giggled.

"Yes, I made it, and I have the stone with me. I've also captured the druggons, but we must hurry and get out of here. You see, the charmal stone gave me powers through my hands, a white force came out and trapped the druggons and rebs in the far cave with ice surrounding them." Joey pointed in the direction. "I mean really thick ice. It's given us some time to save these people and cowchees, and now all we have to do is get everyone out of here."

"Oh, so you don't need me to chuck up frogs?" asked Chuckup.

Joey shook his head from side to side. "No, I'm afraid not."

Chuckup grinned. "Hey, are you going to show me the stone? It really amazes me how much power a stone could give someone."

Joey shook his head again and placed his hand inside his cape. "Oh no, not just anyone can have power from the stone. It only gives me the power. And believe me, this stone is very powerful." Joey pulled out the stone and held it in the palm of his hand.

"Oh my, Joey, that is a beautiful stone," Chuckup said admiringly.

"I was amazed when I first saw it. Its bright light was dazzling, and it was the light that gave me my powers."

"Does that mean that the stone gave you powers that you can use without actually being present?"

"No, I don't think so. I mean, I don't know. So far, I haven't been without the stone, and as far as I'm concerned, I'm not going to lose this stone. It's mine for keeps," said Joey awkwardly.

"Do you mind if I hold it to get a closer look?" asked Chuckup eagerly.

Joey hesitated for a minute, and then he nodded. "Yeah, why not?" He did not know why he hesitated. Chuckup was a good friend, and there was no reason why Joey could not trust him. Maybe it was because Chuckup was the only one who had asked Joey to hold the stone. He carefully handed it to Chuckup. Chuckup smiled and stared at the stone.

Suddenly, the people and cowchees screamed in terror. Joey quickly turned around and saw the druggons and rebs coming towards them. They had obviously escaped from the ice prison, and with the ice melting, water was running through the caves.

"Oh no!" yelled Joey. He turned back to Chuckup to take back the stone. But not only had Chuckup vanished, so had the charmal stone.

Joey slammed his fist on the cave wall. *"Chuckup, where are you? Bring me back the stone. I know you're afraid of the druggons, but I need that stone to save us all!"* screeched Joey. He was flushed with anger.

In no time, the druggons and rebs had Joey and his friends surrounded. Now there was no escape and little chance to fight them, at least, not without the charmal stone.

Joey wondered if he did still have the powers even without the stone in his possession. He raised his hand towards the druggons and rebs and thought about his white power. He waited and waited for the power to come. But nothing came. Joey thought about his wet blanket, but the pocket would not open. Joey suddenly realized that the stone had combined all his powers; without it, he was totally powerless. How could he have been so careless and allow Chuckup to hold the stone? Now he knew why he hesitated earlier. It was his instincts telling him not to show Chuckup the stone. If only he had listened.

"Chuckup, Where are you? I promise I'll protect you. Please bring me back the stone!" Joey called out desperately.

In the next instant, the druggons gave a huge roar, which was followed by a blast of fire. They had created a circle of fire right around all the people and cowchees, Joey and Astina included. They were in danger of being burnt, and there was terror in the air.

"Joey, why aren't you using your powers from the charmal stone?" asked Astina.

"I showed Chuckup the stone, and now he's gone with it. I'm completely powerless. I can't even use my wet blanket."

"What do you mean you can't use your wet blanket?"

"I think the charmal stone must have combined my powers. My pockets are all sealed. No matter how hard I think, my pockets won't open. You've got to help me find Chuckup, he has the stone." Joey was becoming very panicky.

"What does he look like?" Astina asked, gazing around.

"I'm not sure. He could be disguised as anything. He could be a frog, a puddle, or hidden in the walls."

"A puddle, hidden in the walls?" exclaimed Astina with a bewildered look on her face.

"I don't know. But if you see anything odd, it just might be him."

"Are you sure he's not with the druggons?" asked Astina.

Before Joey had a chance to answer, he noticed Chuckup. "*There he is!*" yelled Joey, pointing his finger at him. Then he saw who was standing next to him. It was Villazian.

"Oh no, Villazian has captured him. Just look at that Astina."

Together, Astina and Joey stared at Chuckup. But he was no prisoner; Villazian and Chuckup were laughing together.

"That dirty, rotten—"

"What are we going to do now, Joey? Where could Father be?" Astina cried.

Joey felt hopeless. He deeply regretted trusting Chuckup. He thought he was his friend and that Chuckup had told him the truth about having a curse. Joey now realized he had lied to him. It was a deception beyond belief.

Joey was now boiling with anger. He closed his eyes and deeply concentrated on the charmal stone. He could feel his heart beat rapidly; it felt as though it would jump out of his body.

CHAPTER 25

More Power to Joey

The flames continued to burn ferociously, and the air was filled with screams of fear. Slowly the fire was burning up whatever space was left. The heat was becoming overwhelming; sweat poured down Joey's face.

But Joey continued to concentrate harder and harder on the charmal stone. He visualized it. He thought about holding it in his hand, placing it beside his heart, then moving it down to his stomach, and finally, inside his belly button. Joey wanted to believe the stone was with him now. He believed with all his heart and soul that the stone had penetrated his belly button. He felt that the stone was inside him and that his powers would never leave him again.

With that, Joey felt something cold hit his belly button. He touched his belly button with his fingers and felt something smooth and cold just inside its surface.

Instantly Joey looked down at his stomach. He could not believe what he was seeing.

"Astina, look, I've got the stone. The power is inside me now. Look at the stone!" Joey said excitedly. "Nobody can ever take it from me now. Somehow I have been able to wish the stone back to me."

Astina's downcast face brightened straightaway. "How did you do that?" she asked.

"I concentrated really hard for the stone to come back to me, and I made sure that, this time, the stone would stay with me for good. No one can ever take my powers from me. Astina, I had it in me all the time. I just needed total belief."

"Oh, Joey, that's wonderful!" Astina declared.

The fire was now incredibly hot. The people and the cowchees were beginning to collapse with exhaustion and dehydration. Joey could see the druggons and rebs laughing and taking great pleasure in what would be the slow burning and killing of them all.

"Quickly, Joey, you've got to do something to help!" cried Astina.

Joey nodded at her. "Step aside, Astina, I've got work to do." He stood tall and proud, and then he lifted his hands. Once again Joey concentrated really hard. But this time, he did not think about the white power; this time he thought of something else.

Villazian gazed at Joey suspiciously. He looked a bit agitated, as if he sensed Joey was up to something. Villazian looked inside his huge claw, which was where Joey assumed he was keeping the charmal stone.

Quickly, Villazian stared back at Joey and blew out a blanket of fire that raged ferociously from his mouth. It was obvious he was so angry because he realised that the stone was not with him anymore. He whacked Chuckup across his head; the hit was so hard Chuckup flew across the cave.

Just as Villazian was about to attack, Joey's thoughts had made the power come through. The situation was now reversed. Instead of the fire surrounding Joey, Astina, the people, and the cowchees, it was surrounding Villazian and all the druggons and rebs. But the fire was not as slow; instead, it burned bigger and stronger. Joey's powers were far greater than those of any other person or creature in Magical World.

The fire caught hold of the rebs, the druggons, and Villazian, who all squealed in horrific pain. Joey had no sympathy for them. He had given them a chance when he had placed the ice wall around them. Instead, they were all too eager to see innocent people and cowchees burn to death. There was not an ounce of compassion in them, and who knows how long their torture had gone on.

"I gave you all a chance to leave us alone when I created an ice cage around you, but you all continued to try and kill us all. Villazian, you didn't listen to me. Now you can all burn in hell because that's exactly where you all belong!" The stone had intensified Joey's voice. He was amazed and shook his head in disbelief. It was as if he were

speaking through a microphone; his voice echoed loudly throughout the caves. "*Good always defeats evil!*"

Villazian was burning, but he was still very much alive; he roared and squealed in pain. Joey could smell Villazian's scaly flesh burn. He tried to fly to escape the flames, but Joey had created an invisible wall blocking them in. The more anyone tried to escape, the more the walls pushed them into the burning furnace. Eventually, every one of them vanished into ashes, and the fire instantly disappeared as if it had all become zapped clean.

It was as if nothing had happened. Joey walked to the spot where they had all been incinerated and crouched down, touching the ground with his hands. It was just warm, but with no sign of ash or any other trace of a fire. The druggons and rebs had completely disappeared. Joey realized this meant that the evil was gone.

The people and cowchees gathered around Joey. They all appeared stunned and unable to speak until a boy stood out from the crowd. He punched his fist into the air and yelled, "*Here, here for the Chosen One! Here, here, the Chosen One has save us!*"

As the boy continued to punch his fists in the air, the crowd followed. They too threw their arms in the air, praising and yelling, "*Here, here, the Chosen One. Hoorayyy!*"

They shouted and cheered with joy, grabbing Joey and holding him up high. Joey Willis was now famous. He was their hero and their saviour.

At that moment, Budda and Ben suddenly arrived with a group of children. Astina flew to Joey's side and whispered in his ear. From the pleased look on Budda's face, she must have told him Joey had destroyed the druggons and rebs. But the group of children that had come with Budda were dressed in rags and looked haggard and ill. Joey immediately raised his arms, opened out his hands, and closed his eyes.

A ray of white light filled the dull cave. Then rays of assorted colours illuminated the dullness. The glorious colours spilled into crystals, trees with plenty of food, and a stream of strawberry soda water. The children were instantly cured and cleansed.

With wide eyes and smiles, the children peered at their new clothes. They were dressed in many different outfits according to their personality and their inner desires. Some ballerina outfits, some were dressed as princes and princesses, there were cow girl and cow boy suits, a policeman, a fireman, and even a spider-man outfit.

All the children looked happy and refreshed as though they had never endured the hardship and cruelty the druggons had inflicted upon them. One of the boys yelled, *"It's magic!"* Then there were cheers and hoorays from the entire crowd. There was so much laughter and joy amongst them. All the fear and sadness was gone. Joey felt so happy and proud.

But Joey still had Olivia in his mind. Finding her was what he most wanted. She had to be somewhere.

He paced through the crowd and carefully observed every child until he grasped a child's shoulders and turned that child around, only to find a little redheaded boy wearing a cowboy hat. Joey had not noticed his hair until he turned him around. The boy smiled and stared at him. "So you're the Chosen One?" he asked.

Joey nodded and studied the boy. He had not let him go because he remembered the boy from somewhere, but he just could not place it. From the look on the boy's face, it was as if he was trying to remember Joey too.

"Have we met before?" they both asked together, and then they smiled at each other.

"Oh yes, I remember you. I saw you through the door," said Joey. "You're the boy through the glass door back at the cave where Budda and I left our friendly snake, Sess."

"Friendly snake . . . What door?" asked the boy, frowning hard.

"Oh, don't worry about that, you wouldn't have seen Sess or the door for that matter, but you were in some kind of hospital. You pointed your finger at us. You were trying to tell the nurse something. I presume it was us."

"Oh yes, I remember now. There was this hole through the wall showing your face and your fat friend beside you. I had no idea who you were until now. I mean, no one has a blue face for real. I thought you were wearing a mask or had your face painted and that you were one of those funny clowns that make kids laugh in hospital. But the nurse couldn't see you, so she made me go to bed. After she was gone, I snuck out of my room to see if you were still there, but you weren't. Then I thought it was probably my imagination or just a dream because when I checked the wall there was no hole."

"What's your name?" asked Joey gently.

"My name is Alex Baker."

"How old are you, Alex?"

"Nine."

Joey put out his right hand and seized Alex's hand and shook it gently. "Nice to meet you, Alex. Do you know how to get back to that hospital on Earth?" asked Joey curiously.

Alex shook his head. "No, if I knew, I certainly wouldn't be here with those horrible ugly creatures you just destroyed."

Joey nodded. "Yes, I suppose you're right." Joey stood taller than Alex, who was so much smaller than his age. In fact, it made Joey feel more protective of him. Joey patted Alex's shoulder and smiled. "Do you know where you are and how you got here?"

Once again, Alex slowly moved his head from side to side, a sad look on his face, and gazed towards his feet. "No, I wish I knew. The last thing I remember before I came here was lying in a hospital bed with machines and doctors and nurses around me and Mum crying near the doorway."

"So you've only experienced the druggons and rebs here in Magical World?"

"Magical World! Do you call this Magical World?"

"Yes, you're in Magical World. If you've only experienced the druggons, then you've missed out on a lot. There's a good side to this world. I'm sure you'll love it here. That's why I'm here, to make Magical World the way it should be. It was bad luck you met the druggons and not Budda or Astina at Riddells Withals, but you don't have to worry now. Just take a good look around yourself and see if you like it now." Joey held his arms out and gazed around. "This is the real Magical World, Alex. See those plants and trees over there?"

"Yes," Alex said, nodding.

"There are lollies and cakes on them. You can eat anything here. And that red river over there is strawberry soda water. Go and try some, it's really delicious, and the best thing about it all is that it's good for you. You'll never get sick eating the food here. Although I have to admit, I have every intention of finding my way back to Earth. If you still don't like it here by the time I find my sister, you're most welcome to come back to Earth with me."

"Thanks, I appreciate that," Alex said as he looked at the strawberry soda water and edible plants. He looked as though he was hesitating to try the food and drink. Joey reassured him with another pat, and after a few moments, Alex joined the crowd and carefully sipped a little soda water. He looked at Joey, licked his lips, and proceeded to drink more eagerly. Joey knew he would love the soda water because everything in Magical World tasted fantastic.

CHAPTER 26

Astina's Photo

Joey simply stood by and watched everyone eat and drink with sheer pleasure. There were many happy sounds and faces coming from the crowd now.

Budda quietly approached Joey. "You have done a great deed, Chosen One. Without you, everyone would have died. You are learning a great deal about your powers. Well done," he said gently as he held Joey's shoulder.

Joey glanced at Budda. "I am glad I've helped everyone here, but I still haven't found Olivia. She is the reason I came here in the first place. Where could those druggons have put her?" asked Joey anxiously.

Budda sighed. "I wish I could help you, Joey. I feel hopeless, just as I feel hopeless in not being able to find Astina's parents."

Joey swiftly turned his head away from Budda. He could not allow Budda to see his reaction, and he was grateful he had his nonmind reading powder over him.

Budda tapped Joey's shoulder. "Have you, by any chance, been able to find out where Astina's parents are on Earth with your stone?" he asked quietly.

Joey shook his head from side to side. "No, no . . . sorry, er, the stone couldn't help me on that. Like you said, it's the same situation with Olivia. The stone won't show me where she is." Joey felt guilty for lying to Budda, but there was no way he was going to lose his parents on Earth although he was deeply sorry for betraying Budda.

"I have a photo of Astina as an earth-child. This was all I could get from my resources. Maybe this might help you use the stone to find her parents."

Joey watched Budda pull out a flat stone from his cape. As he did, Alex pushed through the crowd and interrupted them both. "That food is so different, Joey. I mean, what is that food?"

Joey wasn't paying much attention to Alex. He was now more than ever anxious to find out who Astina looked like as an earth-child. Budda gently lowered the shiny white flat stone. Joey bent his head to have a closer view. Gradually, an image appeared. The figure looked very familiar to Joey, and then he saw something that almost blew his mind. He looked up at Budda and back at the stone. Alex pushed in between them again, and he too peered at the stone and stared at the figure. "Hey, I know who that girl is, that's—"

"*No!*" interrupted Joey coldly.

Alex and Budda both looked at Joey in total shock.

"I mean, I'll help you find her parents, but now isn't the time. We have to get these people and cowchees somewhere safe. Remember the Lexus." Joey stepped forward and put his hands on his waist. "Outside these caves it will soon be getting dark, and we've also got to help the sick people at the village," snapped Joey.

Budda nodded his head slowly. "Yes, yes, you're right, it was wrong for me to ask you now. I'm so sorry, I'll try and find Astina, and then we can work out what to do next."

Joey then placed his arm around Alex's shoulder. "Alex is staying with me, if you don't mind." Without another word, Joey quickly led him away from Budda and the rest of the crowd.

"What's wrong, Joey? Why did you want me to be with you?" asked Alex curiously.

"Shhhh," Joey placed his pointer finger over his lips. "You mustn't tell Budda who the girl in the rock is," he whispered.

"You mean the girl he showed us in the stone?"

"Shhhhhh, yes, you've got to promise me you won't tell him who she is."

Alex pulled his cowboy hat off his head and tilted his head innocently to one side. "But why, why don't you want me to tell him who—"

Joey quickly put his hand over Alex's mouth. "Don't say her name, you must never say her name," he whispered coldly.

Alex looked stunned and afraid. Without another word, he nodded his head slowly in agreement. Joey said, "Good, I promise I'll help us find a way to get back to Earth." Alex nodded again, and Joey pulled his hand away from his mouth.

"You know who that girl is, don't you?" asked Alex quietly.

"Yes, of course I do. She's my sister. I know she is here somewhere, that is why I came here in the first place. You see, the druggons kidnapped her from the beach where we were playing." Joey shook his head. "You see, I have no idea where they put her. You said you know her, Alex, have you seen her here? If only I could find her, I'd then be able to concentrate on finding a way back to Earth."

"I only remember her from the hospital on Earth."

Joey stared into Alex's eyes. "Do you mean she was in the hospital that time you saw Budda and me in the wall?"

Alex slowly nodded, "Yes."

"Then the druggons didn't kidnap her. She must still be on Earth. Why was she in the hospital Alex?"

"You don't know?"

"No. Was she hurt? Were Mum and Dad with her?" asked Joey.

"Well, she called them Mum and Dad, so they must have been her parents."

Joey grabbed Alex, shook him roughly, and shouted, "What happened to her?"

Alex scrunched his face up tightly. "Please stop, you're hurting me."

Joey realized he had lost control and quickly released Alex. "I'm sorry," he said sympathetically. Joey slammed his fists into the sides of his thighs. "It feels like it's been weeks since I've seen my little sister, but in all reality, earth-time hasn't changed at all. But I don't understand. I don't know why Olivia was at the hospital, she should have still been at the beach."

"Didn't your parents tell you anything about your sister's health? She was having chemotherapy. She has cancer."

"Chemotherapy! Cancer . . ." Joey stuttered shaking his head. "No, you must be mistaken. The picture Budda showed us . . . you must have the wrong girl." Joey was completely stunned.

"I was having chemo too. I'm telling you that picture was definitely Olivia Willis, she and I became buddies at the hospital. The only problem is, I didn't get to say good-bye to her. You see, when I had my chemotherapy, I woke up here in Magical World." Alex gently touched a small orange-coloured plant. "You see, I knew these plants were edible from before the druggons captured me. When I first came here, I experienced the good parts of Magical World, and thanks to you, I'm back in the real Magical World. Tell me, Joey, why don't you want

Budda to know about the girl in the picture? Who is your sister? Olivia?" Alex asked gently.

Joey went silent for a moment and anxiously paced up and down. He was hesitant to tell Alex, but he had to trust someone. He knew he could trust Alex because he was Olivia's friend, even if it was for a brief moment. "I know you probably think I'm wrong about not telling Budda. I didn't mean to lie to him but . . ." Joey quickly grabbed Alex's shoulders and stared deeply into his bright-blue eyes. "Alex, you have to promise me you won't tell Budda or anyone else here what I am about to tell you right now."

Alex slowly nodded his head. His face turned grim, and he furtively looked over his shoulder as if to check if anyone was near them, then he turned back to Joey. "Okay, I promise.

Joey released his shoulders and insisted they both sit on a large rock. He heaved a deep sigh. "Well, here it goes. Astina does not have her parents with her here. I mean, they were here, but the druggons sent her parents to Earth as humans. Budda has been searching for them ever since Astina was a baby. He's tried every power he could think of to bring them back, but nothing worked. Only the charmal stone works."

"Great, then you can use it to help Budda find her parents," interrupted Alex, looking very excited and smiling deeply from ear to ear.

"Let me finish. I have already used the stone. I know who her parents are."

Alex's smile faded from his face. "Then why don't you tell Budda?' he asked quietly.

Joey nodded. "I'm getting to that. You see, Alex . . ." Joey struggled for the words. "Astina's parents are my parents. I can't allow Budda to take my parents away from Earth, away from me and Olivia. I want to go back to Earth. I want to be able to grow up. Did you know we stay the same age here? We never get older."

Alex shook his head. "No, I had no idea."

"That photo Budda showed me was Astina as an earth-child. You see, the part that I don't understand is how could Astina be Olivia? If I tell Budda that's Olivia in the photo, he'll automatically know my parents are Astina's parents."

"I wish I could help you, but I don't understand this world either. Anyway, how did Budda get a photo of Astina as a human if she was born here? I think you could ask him that without him suspecting. I mean, it's a perfectly logical question seeing how he told you Astina was born here. It might give you some answers."

Joey smiled at Alex. "You know, Alex, you're right, and you're not just a pretty face. In fact, you're a very smart kid. I can see why Olivia wanted to be your friend." Alex smiled and blushed. Joey patted him on his shoulder. "Come on, let's go and find the others," said Joey.

CHAPTER 27

Joey's Secret

Alex and Joey set off side by side and then mingled amongst the crowd until Joey noticed Astina and Budda at the far end of the cave near the soda water stream. He also caught a glimpse of Ben only centimetres behind Budda and Astina, cupping up the soda water in the palms of his hands and placidly drinking it.

Astina and Budda looked as if they were deep in conversation. Joey wondered what they were discussing, and he thought about taking away the nonmind reading powder, but that was too risky. It might give them a quick opportunity to read his mind and find out what he didn't want them to know.

Joey bent down to Alex and pointed his finger in the direction of Astina and Budda. "Look, I've found them. They're over there near the soda stream, follow me," he whispered in Alex's ear. Alex nodded eagerly and followed Joey closely. Joey felt Alex grab his cape. Joey wondered if Astina and Budda's discussion was about him having the nonmind reading powder on.

There were times Joey knew Budda and Astina had their nonmind reading powder on, so maybe they were aware of him having it on all the time. Now that the druggons were gone, there was really no reason for him to have it on.

Joey thought of Alex not having nonmind reading powder, so quickly he placed the nonmind reading power over Alex. Luckily, Alex did not notice Joey put the powder over him as it only showed a slight trace of dust. But as Joey looked towards Budda and Astina, he saw that Budda had seen what he had just done. There was a serious look on his face. It was the same serious look as the time Joey wanted to know about the old lady in the bathroom. Joey sensed his suspicion and disappointment.

As they approached, Joey overheard Astina ask Budda, "What's wrong, Father?"

Then Astina noticed Joey. "Oh, Joey, I'm so proud of you," she said excitedly and quickly gave him a hug.

"I'm happy to be here too," said Joey, returning the hug.

"Astina, I want to introduce you to my new friend, Alex Baker. He says he knew Olivia back on Earth. They were friends for a while," said Joey calmly. He noticed Budda's eyes light up.

"Oh dear, I remember you now," interrupted Budda. "Yes, this was the boy we saw through the door in the caves back where we met Sess."

"That's right, and he's told me that Olivia was with him in hospital having chemotherapy," said Joey sadly.

"No, he must have the wrong Olivia. Anyway how does he know the girl in the hospital was your sister?" asked Budda suspiciously.

"Ah, umm, well, I told him, er, her full name when he asked me why I was here. There can't possibly be another Olivia Willis, and the description he gave me of her was very much Olivia," explained Joey as he looked towards Alex. Alex smiled back, but he did not say a word.

Budda just stared at them and then looked directly at Joey. "Of course, you're right, Joey," he said and then smiled.

Joey looked down guiltily. He hated lying to Budda, and he wondered if Budda had sensed his lie. Joey felt a pang of guilt as he watched Astina fix her lovely red cape and smooth her brightly coloured wings with her hands.

"Oh, Joey, you've made this cave look wonderful. It's great watching the people and cowchees eat and drink so sweetly. Father, why don't we bring Riddells here? I'm dying to see Erac and Alcon especially, and he'll only come back to us if it's safe for him."

"Yes, yes, all in good time, my dear. We've first got to come up with an idea to save these people and cowchees from the lexus and the snakes outside these caves." Budda stared directly at Joey. "I presume that's what you want too, Joey?" he asked in a sarcastic tone.

"Yes, of course," replied Joey firmly. He then peered at his belly button. He concentrated deeply, but nothing happened. Joey feared the stone was too good to be true. "I don't understand," he said disappointed.

"What don't you understand?" asked Budda. "And why are you looking at your belly button?"

Joey was getting annoyed with Budda's remarks. "Because the stone is inside me and nobody can take it away from me now. The time I showed my friend Chuckup the stone, he took it and gave it to Villazian. I thought he was on our side, but apparently not. I instantly lost all my powers, even my wet blanket wouldn't work."

"It's true, Father, we thought we were all going to die," interrupted Astina with a grim look on her face.

"Then how did you get it back?" asked Budda anxiously.

Joey rubbed his hand on his forehead. "I don't know, I just thought really hard about getting it back. I mean, all the people and cowchees were about to cook in the flames. I think, for the first time, I was really afraid. I kept thinking about getting it back then, somehow, my belly button felt cold and my powers came back."

Joey pulled his belt away from his belly and pointed his fingers to his belly button. "See, the stone is in me now."

Budda's eyes widened, and he shook his head as if he just had a fright. "You've done well, Joey. That is an almost impossible magic to do, but somehow, you've achieved it. You must have used the power within you to bring the stone back. You brought it back with the goodness of your heart—with love and kindness."

"Goodness of my heart? Love and kindness?" repeated Joey.

"Yes, the goodness within you somehow brought back your stone and powers. Once again, only the Chosen One can do this," Budda assured him as he lifted his head high with pride.

"I'm just glad I have it back. But right now, it's not helping us find a way to get these people out of here safely."

"Maybe the stone believes the people and cowchees are safe here at the moment. Also the stone won't give you all the answers, otherwise, it would affect your destiny," explained Budda.

"What do you mean affect my destiny?"

"I mean the stone might not show you how to do everything. Sometimes, you have to figure it out for yourself."

"So do you mean it won't help me all the time?"

"Sometimes our powers stagnate. And we need to figure out how to release the stagnation."

"Stagnate? What do you mean stagnate?"

"I mean, your good powers can get depressed. Sometime our powers can have too much evil mixed in them. Our powers need to be nurtured. Yours might be having a problem at the moment because you just had a battle with the druggons. I mean, you've recently used a lot of your good powers, I'm not surprised your powers won't work now." Budda looked away as he said this.

Joey realized Budda was not happy with him, and he felt it had nothing to do with him not being able to use his powers. In fact, he was concerned that Budda might have figured out he was keeping something from him, and he hoped he had no idea it was about Olivia and his parents.

"So how do I nurture my powers?" asked Joey while he stared at Budda's every move and eagerly waited for his answer.

At that question, Budda declared, "You can either give it time as it will nurture itself over time, or if you want to speed up the process, you can cleanse it. To cleanse your powers, you have to be good and honest at heart. Just like your goodness and honesty saved these people and cowchees from the fire. I find thinking about wonderful things, like plants and trees growing healthily and beautifully, can also cleanse your powers. Or imagine a mirror around yourself and reflecting the stagnation away from you. It's difficult, but it can be accomplished."

Joey knew what he meant about honesty. It confirmed his suspicion that Budda was not happy with him, but Joey decided to ignore this and pretended he did not sense his disappointment. He remembered that he had kept this from Budda before the druggons attacked them, and his powers had still worked.

Joey did not believe honesty was the reason why his powers were not working. "Well, I'll just do nothing for now. I'll let my power nurture itself, everyone here seems safe. Anyway, I don't think the lexus or snakes could come inside this paradise." Joey opened out his arms. "Otherwise, my stone would be helping me right now."

"Then I should bring Riddells Withals here," said Budda desperately. Joey could see the game he was playing and that he wanted to have it out with him. He didn't blame him, but he had to protect his parents. As far as he was concerned, Earth was where his parents were staying, with Olivia and him.

"I . . . I wouldn't rush into that yet. Couldn't you wait until we get the people back from the village?" asked Joey nervously.

"Oh, but didn't you say it seemed safe here now? I mean, you think you don't need to nurture your powers," insisted Budda with half a smile.

"Can't you just give it a rest? snapped Joey. I haven't had any sleep for hours. Just because you don't need any sleep, hey, I'm just a boy. You're the adult, why can't you figure something out yourself?"

"Oh, come on, Joey, I was merely suggesting . . . it's a quiet time now, and I thought the quicker you learn how to nurture your powers, the better off you'll be in any bad situation. I mean, you just never know. I urge you to try now while it's quiet and nothing is happening," insisted Budda, shrugging his shoulders.

Joey sighed as he reminded himself to be calm and kind. He did not want to be moody, especially towards his friends. "I'm sorry. I usually get cranky when I'm tired."

Budda tilted his head to one side. He then pulled out his fettal and waved it about. Instantly, a floating bed appeared in midair. Budda half smiled. "I'll take care of things here and make sure everyone is safe. Snuggle up, Joey, the bed's for you, now get some rest."

Joey gazed at the bed. As always, Budda made the bed look comfy and cosy. It looked just like a four-poster bed, and it had white silky curtains for privacy. Joey peeked inside the curtains. The bed was huge and covered with a beautiful gold blanket and rainbow-coloured pillows. From the inside, it turned into a little private room. Joey then looked back at Budda. He felt a tinge of guilt for being rude to him a moment ago. After all, he had been like a father to Joey.

"Thanks," smiled Joey. "Before I go to sleep, I'll try and nurture my powers. I like the idea with the plants. I'll imagine green plants growing all around me."

Budda smiled back. "You get some rest. I'll take care of things here. There's a blue cupboard full of your favourite food in there. I'm sure you'll be hungry too."

"You must have read my mind. I hadn't realized how hungry I am."

"Well, usually when I'm hungry, I get cranky. Anyway, I can't read your mind, you've got your nonmind reading powder on. Maybe you should take it off. I mean, we're not in any danger at the moment."

Joey climbed onto the bed and poked his head through the curtains. "I think I prefer to have my nonmind reading powder on. I mean, I'm not used to anyone reading my mind back on Earth. I also think there's a possibility we are not completely out of danger yet."

"But, Joey, it allows you to read other minds. It helps you sense danger if it comes," replied Budda, looking very concerned. "Anyway, it didn't bother you when you first came here. I thought you were fascinated with the idea of reading other minds."

"I am," grumbled Joey. "But I'm not fascinated with others reading my mind at the moment—besides, I have more powers now. I certainly don't want anyone knowing how to use them. Especially if we come across more enemies, you just never know." Without another word, Joey closed the curtains. Budda did not answer back.

Joey studied the little room Budda had prepared for him. It was very pleasing to the eye, and the bed was very comfortable. He sighed and once again felt guilty. He peeped out through curtains, but Budda was gone.

Then he noticed Budda floating high amongst the yellow puffy clouds in the red sky. He also observed many other floating beds. Budda had obviously made beds for everyone, and there they were all crowded in the red sky.

There was a particularly bright-red bed directly opposite him. Just as he was about to close his curtain, he noticed the red bed curtain was slightly open, and through the gap, he caught a glimpse of Astina inside her room.

"Astina," he called out.

She looked startled and paused for a moment before she opened her curtains wider. "Joey, I thought you'd be asleep by now."

"Yeah, I was about to. I wanted to see if Budda was okay, and then I found all these beds around me. Boy, was he fast."

Astina smiled and nodded. "Yes, that's my father. He wanted to make use of the safe time we have and get everyone rested."

"Hey, do you want to come and join me in my bedroom? There's plenty of room here."

"Umm, Father strictly told me to stay away from you so you could nurture your powers and get rested. I think he's right, I'd better stay here," Astina replied, grinning.

"I can still nurture my powers while you're here. I mean, I've got to eat first. I wouldn't mind having your company while I eat. Come on, I won't tell Budda," insisted Joey.

Astina looked down, around, and then back at Joey. "I really shouldn't. Oh, okay, but only for a little while," she said carefully.

Joey smiled at her and parted his curtains further. Astina checked to make sure nobody saw her, then in a flash, she jumped out, flapping her glittery wings. Joey noticed her throw some nonmind reading powder and seal her curtains shut. She quickly glided inside Joey's bedroom. Joey felt like he had been in this moment before; once again, Astina reminded him of Olivia. There were many nights he and his sister could not sleep, and he would persuade her to sneak into his room to talk and play games. He could not help but think about the similarity.

"What are you thinking about, Joey?" asked Astina gently.

Joey opened the cupboard in which Budda had provided the glorious food. He shrugged and said, "Oh, nothing really . . . well, it's like every time I spend time with you, it reminds me of Olivia."

Astina lowered her head looking deeply concerned. "Oh dear, you miss her, don't you?" She placed her hand on his arm. "Don't worry, we'll find her."

Joey closed his eyes for a few seconds. "I don't know if we'll ever find her. It's just that I miss my parents and my home. I only wish I could go back, but I don't even know how to do that." Joey offered Astina a plate of sausage rolls and a glass of soda water.

"I'm sure Olivia misses her parents and her home too." Astina said gently as she put down her glass and held Joey's shoulder. "We will find her, and once we do, Father will help you both go back to Earth. You've got to have faith."

"Are you saying Budda knows how I can get back to Earth permanently?" he asked, dumbfounded.

Astina slowly nodded her head. "Yes, of course. I thought you knew." She quickly covered her mouth. "Oh no, don't tell Father I told you. I just remembered I wasn't supposed to tell you. Please, Joey, promise me you won't tell him, he will be so disappointed with me."

Joey took her hands in his. "Don't worry, I won't tell him anything you tell me. Budda will not be disappointed in you, and thank you for telling me, Astina. He was trying to make me feel guilty for keeping a secret."

"What secret do you have from Father?" asked Astina in surprise.

"I, er, I meant that he is guilty from keeping that secret from me, but let's not worry about that now. I've got people and cowchees to save, and I haven't found Olivia yet, so I'm not in a rush to go back to Earth."

Astina hugged Joey. "You are wonderful," she declared.

Joey hugged her back and then slowly held her in front of him. "By the way, has Budda told you how I can get back to Earth?" he asked gently. "Please, Astina, you can tell me any secret you have with him. I promise I won't let him know that I know."

Astina hesitated for a while.

"Please, Astina, I just told you I won't go back until my work's finished here, you've got to trust me, please," Joey pleaded and waited anxiously for her to answer.

She gave Joey a serious look. "I'm not so sure myself. I mean, I confronted Father the very first time he was snappy with you and he wouldn't say much. That's all I'm going to tell you, you have to figure the rest out for yourself." Without warning, she hurriedly flew back to her bed.

"Wait, Astina, don't go!" yelled Joey. But it was too late; Astina waved and closed her curtains.

While Joey ate his food, he thought about what Astina had just told him. He realized her loyalty towards Budda was very honourable, and it was clear to him her father meant the world to her. He thought hard and tried to remember the first time Budda was snappy with him. Then he remembered his magic classes, the time he read about the old healing woman. That was the first time Budda was upset with him. He could now clearly recall the visualization from the book of the Chosen One. The old woman in Budda's mansion had a particular herb in her hand; it was orange with pink specks.

Budda told Joey that she had been banished from Magical World. Apparently, the healing woman looked like she lived on Earth but occasionally visited Magical World. Joey realized this because of her age and her looks. Therefore, she must know how to get back to Earth. Joey felt a wave of shock strike through him. Budda had tried to make him feel bad for keeping a secret, but he himself had kept this important information from Joey.

Joey felt hurt and angry. He had thought that he could completely trust Budda. It had never occurred to him that Budda would stoop to any level to keep him in Magical World. The more Joey thought about it, the more upset he felt. Budda only wanted him in Magical World for his own needs; he did not care about his sister. In fact, Olivia was not his priority. Of course not; she was just an earth-person to Budda and a good reason for Joey to stay in Magical World.

He tossed the last bit of his sausage roll inside his cupboard. He had lost his appetite. He wanted to confront Budda and have it out with him, but then he thought of Astina. He had promised her he would not tell Budda. He really appreciated her friendship and knew she was his only true friend in Magical World together with Alcon and Erac. If only he could find them again; he missed them and wished they were with him.

Joey lay on his bed, snuggled into his pillow, and closed his eyes. He had to nurture his powers. He thought about his mother's garden; she had always had a wonderful garden. It was filled with roses, daisies, lavenders, geraniums, and violets. His mother's garden was extra special; somehow, she had flowers all year round. He did not know how she did it, but for some reason, nothing ever died off. The plants would always have new flowers within a week after she pruned. She also grew sunflowers and nearly every fruit and nut tree you could imagine. In the winter, there would be plenty of oranges, mandarins, and lemons; and in the summer, there would be apricots, cherries, peaches, nectarines, and apples.

In the middle of the backyard, there was a huge walnut tree. By the time summer was over, his mother and father would have collected six or seven huge sacks full of walnuts, each sack the same size as a potato bag. Joey took pleasure in eating the fresh walnuts straight from the tree, and he relished the cool shade it provided during the hot summer. Joey imagined himself sitting under the tree with a slight breeze rattling the leaves.

While Joey thought about the lovely garden at home, he began to feel utterly relaxed and at ease. It was as if he were really in the middle of the garden lying on his mother's outdoor lounge. The smell and the breeze on his face felt real. At last Joey drifted into a deep and restful sleep.

CHAPTER 28

Trapped while floating

Joey could hardly have been asleep for long when he was awaken by a roaring noise. Quickly he sprang from his bed, feeling a wave of fear and panic rush through him. The noise sounded like some huge beast outside his bedroom, and it became louder and louder.

For some reason, Joey hesitated to take a peek outside the curtains. He did not know why, but his senses were stopping him from opening them. But he would have to have a peek, just a tiny peek. He had to find out what the noise was all about. Joey lightly touched the curtains with his pointer finger.

The curtain did not budge, and suddenly, it felt as hard as a rock. They still looked like curtains, but something was different. Joey slammed his fist into the curtains around him, but it was hopeless; the curtains had become a wall.

Joey presumed this must have been Budda's way of protecting him and all the other beds. He wondered if the roaring sounds came from the lexus. Had they found their way inside the cave? Joey needed some answers and wondered if there was some way for him to communicate with Budda. Not that he really wanted to talk to him; he was still furious with him, but now was not the time to be angry with him. From the sounds he could hear, this was definitely serious trouble.

Something sparked in Joey's mind. He remembered the suits Budda and he wore the first time they flew to Rockwell Mountain and how they had communicated to each other through them. He wondered if Budda had thought of it too. Joey did not wait a moment longer; he quickly pulled out his suit from his cape and put it on. It was worth a try. The thought had come to him, and his instincts were working. The nurturing must have worked to bring his powers back.

Once he had his suit on, he could hear nothing, so he called out, "Budda, can you hear me? Budda it's me, Joey." Eagerly he waited for a response, and waited and waited, but there was no answer. It seemed his powers needed more nurturing because nothing came from the stone through his thoughts. Or maybe this was a situation his powers could not help him with.

Sitting on his bed, Joey wondered if he was still asleep and this was another nightmare. What if the druggons' curse was still giving him nightmares? He blinked hard as he remembered this was what woke him up from his previous nightmare, but nothing happened; he was still in his suit on his bed.

Joey decided that thoughts of escaping were getting him nowhere. He kept looking at the curtain. The roaring outside was getting louder and louder; it was almost unbearable. If only he could see through the wall.

Suddenly, Joey felt the stone in his belly button move. He glanced down. A bright light pierced through his suit and beamed directly on the curtains. Joey was rather astounded at how the light went through his suit, but the stone was very powerful, and once again, he was relieved his powers had returned.

Joey's eyes stayed fixed on the spot where the white light radiated brightly. The light slowly transformed into a large square. It was almost the same size as the large television set at home on Earth. Slowly the rock curtain became invisible, and Joey could see through it. But he could not see any beds outside, and Astina's bed had also disappeared.

The light now radiated from the window in the curtain wall rather than from Joey's belly button. He was now able to move freely around. Quickly he approached the window; the view was so real. Joey tried to put his fist through the window, but to his disappointment, it was only an image, and there was no hole in the curtain wall. He shook his hand to try and ease the pain from slamming it into the wall.

The view outside his bedroom was very clear; at least, he hoped it was a view outside. He wondered if he was looking at an image that would show him his future and not the present. But there was nothing more to see than red sky and yellow clouds.

Suddenly, out of nowhere, a large vicious mouth appeared in the square image. Joey screamed and fell backwards. Fear rushed through him; his whole body felt hot, and his heart pounded. He was almost thankful to be trapped inside his bedroom. Joey realized the creature was a lexus. He remembered the last one he had seen from his invisible home back in the cave with Budda and Ben. It had been terrifying, but this particular one was even bigger and scarier.

The beast looked as though it could slam his bedroom into pieces, but Joey could not feel anything. It was as if he were invisible. That's what it was; Budda must have made all the beds invisible. "Oh, Budda, I wish you could talk to me right now," said Joey out loud.

"Of course I can talk to you, Joey," answered a voice inside his suit. Joey's eyes almost popped out of his head; he could hardly believe that it was Budda's voice. His anger and resentment instantly vanished.

"Is that you, Budda?" he asked, just to reassure himself that he was not imagining it.

"Sorry I took so long to answer you. I heard you the very first time, but I couldn't respond until I had all the other beds turned into rocks, and I had to make sure no one was left out," Budda replied.

"Wow, how did you do that? Don't tell me, I know it's your powers, Lord Budda," Joey said in wonder.

"Of course, you and I have many gifts, and the reason why we have our gifts is to use them to help others. What makes our powers stronger is if we do it from the goodness of our hearts and not because we want to have greater powers."

Joey nodded slowly. "Yes, it's all making sense now. Anyway, where are you? Do you have your own room?"

"No, I don't need sleep remember. I'm just outside your room in my suit."

"Then come near my window so I can see you. I can see you, can I?"

"Of course you can, only you and I can see each other," Budda reassured Joey.

"Well, that's a relief. Is there any chance you can also stop the roaring noise. It's very hard for me to hear you with this racket going on."

"That I'm afraid I cannot do that. And if I tried to stop the noise, we'd have no idea whether they were still here or not. Who knows how long they'll hang around. This isn't the village, and there is no night here. Normally they only come out during the night, but for some reason, they're here in Magical World daylight."

"So what are we going to do if they don't go away? We can't stay here forever," Joey said anxiously.

The fierce lexus moved away from Joey's window, so Joey stood up and peered through. A few metres away, he could see Budda in his suit. Joey waved. "Hey, I'm over here," Budda spotted him and waved back, and Joey waited for him to come closer. "Come on, come over here," he yelled.

Budda shook his head. "No, I can't right now. You have a huge lexus sitting in midair just above you."

"Oh, come on, Budda, they can't feel or hear us. We're like ghosts to them; they'd just go right through us."

"Yes, they would go right through the bedrooms, but they wouldn't be able to go through me. I'm only invisible to them, I'm not a ghost. If they bumped into me, they'd know I'm here."

"Then you'd better keep your distance," said Joey. "I was going to suggest I go out there with you on my balon in invisible suit, but I think I'll change my mind since you said they could feel us."

"Come on, Joey, this isn't the time for you to be a chicken. Who knows how long these creatures will be out there. The cowchees and people don't know what's going on, and I can't talk to all of them."

"What do you want me to do? We can't fight these creatures."

Budda paused for a moment. "I don't know. There must be something we can do. I mean, these beasts must sense there's something around here, otherwise, they wouldn't be hanging around. And believe me, Joey, they won't leave until they find us."

"Can't you come in here with me for a while? We can give ourselves time to think about what we can do. Maybe my stone could help us," Joey suggested.

"Did you get anything from the stone yet?" asked Budda with a concerned look.

"I tried, but all I got was this window. I'm sure my powers have been nurtured enough. I thought about my mother's garden and my powers returned."

"Yes, that's all well and good, but does the stone show you how to send these creatures away?"

Joey concentrated hard on how to remove the lexuses away. He waited for a good, long time, but nothing came from the stone, and no pockets opened in his cape. "No, nothing. I was so sure I had nurtured my powers."

Budda threw his arms in the air. "I thought this might happen," he said in frustration.

"What do you mean?" asked Joey.

"The stone will only help you if the creatures had tried to attack us or had seen us. You see, the stone thinks the creatures are harmless. The stone is only pure and good, it would only help if the lexus creatures attacked us. And it's too risky for us to show ourselves to them. These creatures are quick, and you won't have time to look at your stone to find the solution."

Joey gave himself a few moments to think through the situation again. "Then if the stone does not think these creatures are harmful, do you think there's a chance they could become friendly?

Budda shook his head from side to side. "I don't think that's worth the risk. Remember what Jack said? They love to eat humans."

"That's what Jack says. I mean, it's only his word. To be honest, I don't really believe what Jack says. I don't trust the guy, I mean, you've seen the way he treated Ben."

"Come on, Joey, just look at these beasts, do you honestly believe they'd be capable of being friendly?" Budda lifted his hands up as if to show Joey the beasts. Joey peered out and observed two of the lexus beasts fighting and roaring loudly at each other. They wrestled and flipped each other into the air; both of them were fast and had tremendous strength.

One lexus was slightly larger and quicker, and it seized the smaller lexus's long tail in its mouth. He spun it around and around like a helicopter propeller. On and on it went until, finally, the larger lexus released the smaller lexus's tail.

The smaller lexus travelled through the air at such speed it had no control, so it spread its wings out and slammed into the soft clouds to try and slow itself. Its speed reduced, and it managed to turn itself around, and it headed straight back up to the large lexus to continue the fight.

The larger lexus remained in midair, waiting. Without warning, it grabbed a leg from the smaller lexus and ripped it right off his body. Before the injured lexus had a chance to even roar with pain, the larger lexus leapt over him and took a huge bite from his head. He then continued to eat the rest of the smaller lexus as if it were a chicken drumstick. After it had finished, it roared like a lion and pounded his fists on his chest just like a gorilla. It was clear he was the leader.

All the other lexus creatures flew farther away from Joey's bedroom, and eventually, the roaring noise faded. "Now do you suppose they could be friends?" asked Budda, who appeared quite shaken by the incident.

Joey shrugged his shoulders. "I suppose you're right. Though I was so sure my instincts were right about them being friendly. I wonder why I felt like that."

"Maybe it's just wishful thinking on your behalf. There must be a way we can banish those creatures, just like you did with the druggons."

"I wish it were that easy, but it's not. My stone won't allow me to banish every creature. If I am the Chosen One, then I am the one who has to make the major decisions, not the stone. I realize now that the stone is only a tool. Maybe we both need to work something out together."

Budda nodded. "You're right, but forget about the idea of being friends with them. Now let's see." Budda placed his pointer finger in front of the head of his suit. It was a normal habit of his regardless of whether he had his suit on or not. Joey thought it looked awkward and a little funny though he knew it was Budda's way of thinking.

One of Joey's habits when he was thinking was to rock himself. So he rocked himself on his bed just as he did whenever he had to do his homework. It somehow relaxed him and helped him to think clearly. Joey rocked and thought for a good while, asking himself what he and Budda could do. But nothing came to mind.

The situation was starting to get to Joey, so he rocked himself harder and harder until he heard a small thump on his pillow. To his surprise, it was his flute. "My cape," he gasped and carefully searched inside it. With the commotion of the two lexuses, he had completely forgotten to check his cape. Once he looked inside, he noticed the open pocket where the flute was normally found. Without another thought, Joey grabbed the flute and hid it behind his back.

"Did you say something about your cape?" asked Budda.

"Er, um, I was just thinking about getting my balon out so I could join you, and I was just looking inside my cape."

Budda opened his arms out wide. "Well, it's about time you decided to join me."

Joey did not want to tell him about the flute yet. He now believed that his instincts about being friends with the lexus creatures were spot-on. But most of all, he was relieved his cape was again helping him to find solutions. Joey knew if he told Budda this, he would not agree and would not allow Joey to take any risks, but he now knew he had to take a chance.

Joey got ready to leave his bedroom. He stood tall, still with his suit on, his balon ready. and his flute hidden behind his back. "I'm ready now, can you tell me how to get out of this room?"

"Okay, now I want you to listen carefully and follow my instructions," Budda said. "Close your eyes. I want you to imagine you are standing in midair next to me and concentrate really hard, don't lose that thought. I want you to completely focus on standing right next to me and nothing else."

CHAPTER 29

The Magic Flute

Joey was in deep concentration when Budda interrupted. "You can open your eyes now."

Joey felt a bump and quickly opened his eyes. He was flabbergasted; he was out of his room and floating in midair beside Budda. Joey immediately turned to face Budda while bearing in mind he still had the flute behind his back.

Luckily, Budda had still not sensed that Joey was about to use his flute. Instead, Budda's eyes were focused in the direction of the lexus creatures. They did not ever seem to keep still, and Joey knew that Budda was worried they might bump into them. The lexus creatures could not see them, but they might accidentally touch them and ruin their disguise. Budda seemed a lot more terrified of them than Joey, but as far as Joey was concerned, time was running out and he must play his flute.

Joey searched the red sky for a clear area to give himself time to play and a chance for the lexus creatures to listen to his music. He also had to think of an excuse to keep Budda safe and away from him. He did not want to draw them near Budda. It was bad enough for him to risk his own life let alone that of his friend, and Joey still thought of Budda as his friend even though he felt he had betrayed him. It had always been Joey's nature to forgive and to pretend bad times had never happened. Joey felt that it was a waste of time and energy to be angry at anyone for very long.

"How about we split up?" suggested Joey.

Budda looked at him seriously. "What for? I mean, are you crazy? It's very dangerous around here. These creatures are all over the place, and we all might accidentally bump into each other."

Joey rolled his eyes. "We've got to do something, standing here isn't going to get us anywhere."

"No matter what happens, we are not splitting up. It's too dangerous, got that?" growled Budda.

Joey shrugged. "Oh, all right then." He must think of another idea and fast. With his flute still tightly clenched in his hand behind his back, he tilted his head high and gazed at the clouds, quietly asking himself over and over how he was going to get Budda away from him.

Suddenly, he had an idea. He carefully observed where the lexus creatures stood in the red sky. They were still all over the place, but getting closer and closer to Joey and Budda. He had to act, so he dashed into the one empty space he had seen.

"Nooooo, what are you doing, Joey?" shouted Budda.

Joey was alone in the empty space, away from Budda and the lexus creatures. Now was his chance to take his helmet off and play his flute.

"Come back here this instance!" Budda ordered as he streaked through the air towards Joey. But Joey zoomed around continuously, only just avoiding Budda and the lexus creatures. He came to a halt and quickly yanked off his helmet.

"Noooooooooo!" roared Budda, looking shocked and horrified and just as Joey had pulled out his flute and played only a few notes, Budda grabbed him and shook him like a rag doll. "What are you doing, Joey, put your helmet back on before they see you!" he yelled, continuing to shake Joey with rage. The flute was accidentally knocked from his hand and started to fall.

Budda and Joey wrestled one another. Budda tried to force Joey's helmet back on his head, but Joey resisted and pushed Budda away, and at the same time, he flipped back and completely lost balance on his balon. He powered down through the red sky, trying to spread his arms and legs out as if to land on a yellow cloud or at least grab on to one, but he kept missing them. His flute plunged down ahead of him.

The ground was getting closer and closer. "Where is Alcon now to save me this time?" thought Joey. While he continued to power down, he caught up with his flute and managed to grasp hold of it although he didn't think it was much help to him now. Once he landed on those purple rocks, he was going to die.

"*Arrrrrrrrggggghhhhhh!*" he screamed and closed his eyes as tightly, thinking all the time of Alcon.

"*Help!*" he roared, and just as he was about to splatter on the purple rocks, something swooped underneath him. He opened his eyes and saw familiar scaly red skin. "Alcon, you're back. Oh, it's so good to see you again."

Alcon flapped his wings hard, continuing to swoop through the air, and he turned his huge head around to gaze at Joey and said, "It's good to see you too, Joey, but I don't know how I got here. Did you put a spell on me or something?"

Alcon turned his head back only to instantly stop in midair. "*Aarrggh!* Where are we? And what are those ugly dangerous-looking creatures?" he shrieked.

Because of the sudden halt, Joey almost fell off his back. "*Wait!*" he yelled. He saw that the lexus creatures had surrounded Budda like a group of lions ready to pounce on their prey. Without another word, Joey started to play his flute. The whole time Joey played, he hoped like nothing he had ever hoped for in his entire life that they would respond to the music and become friendly. Joey noticed that Alcon was enjoying the tune while he rested casually on one of the yellow clouds.

So far though the lexus creatures had not responded to the tune, but neither had they attacked. Nevertheless, Joey continued to watch his fingers play and play and play. He thought he would run out of breath, and finally, he stopped with exhaustion. When he looked up again, he couldn't see anything. There was no sign of the creatures, but Joey was relieved to see Budda floating in midair with his eyes closed. Joey realised that this was his meditating mode, and there was Alcon snoring on a yellow cloud fast asleep.

Although the whole ordeal was completely exhausting for Joey, he felt totally relaxed and at ease. It was as if he had not had a worry in the world. Maybe it was because his instincts were telling him the battle was finally over. It certainly looked as if everything was well.

Carefully, Joey slid off Alcon and stood on the fluffy yellow cloud. Since Alcon was sleeping and Budda was meditating, Joey decided to rest. His eyes felt heavy, and he felt like he had not slept in days. The cloud was extremely comfortable, not even an earth-bed could have been as comfortable as this. It was as if the cloud was made for him; it moulded into his body and seemed to massage it. After all the struggle with Budda and the hard landing on Alcon's back, his body had hurt, but the cloud had taken away the soreness. Joey allowed himself to drift off into a deep and peaceful sleep.

CHAPTER 30

A Transformation

Joey felt as though he had barely slept when he was woken up by the noise of children, small cowchees, and unicorns flying, laughing, and playing around him. He noticed he was no longer on the yellow cloud; instead, he was resting on one of Lena's banana lounge chairs outside the milkshake shop. He sat up quickly and realized he was back at Riddells Withals.

Erac and Astina were only a metre away from him. Astina was cuddling Erac and whispering something into his ear. She had not noticed Joey was awake, but Erac saw him, and he made a neighing sound and tapped his front right foot towards Joey. Astina quickly turned and screamed with joy. "Joey, you're awake!" She ran towards Budda's mansion calling, "Father, Father, Joey is awake."

Budda came bolting out of his front door towards Joey with a huge smile that almost covered his whole face. "Joey, you did it! Those lexus creatures completely disappeared. I'm so sorry I tried to stop you."

"Where did they go? How do you know they won't come back?" Joey asked.

"That's the point, they didn't go anywhere—they just vanished," explained Budda, holding his arms up in the air.

"Vanished?"

"Yes, vanished, disappeared," Budda nodded.

"But how? I mean, my flute was supposed to make them become friendly, not make them disappear."

"That was impossible. Those creatures couldn't be our friends. They are no different to the druggons. And they are ugly," said Budda convincingly.

"Maybe so, but I was so sure my instincts told me they'd be our friends."

"Well, your instincts must have been mixed up. The flute is supposed to take away anything bad because it is pure and good. Remember, Joey, when good appears, only wonder and joy can come from it. The flute didn't harm them, it only played beautiful music. Only good comes from good, and if bad comes along, then bad and evil becomes more bad and evil to itself. But eventually, good will overpower it. It either dies or disappears. Nothing good can come from bad and evil. You must always remember that, Joey, especially when you return to Earth."

From the entrance of the banana milkshake shop out came the blond lady, whom Joey remembered as Lena, carrying a tray of milk shakes. As she approached them, she half smiled and then placed the milk shakes on a strawberry table next to Joey. "Here are the milk shakes you ordered," she said, glancing towards Astina.

"Thank you, Lena, you're so kind," Astina said as she handed Joey a glass. "Here, you must be so hungry and thirsty."

"You must have read my mind, thanks," smiled Joey as he took the glass and looked at Lena. "And thank you, Lena, it's nice to see you again."

Lena bowed her head. "I'm so sorry, Chosen One, that I didn't believe you at first about those druggons."

"No need to apologize, the past is the past, what's done is done. The main thing is we're all safe now," he said kindly.

Lena planted a quick kiss on Joey's cheek. He blushed; Lena was very attractive. She giggled a little and, without another word, ran back inside her shop. Joey glanced around at his friends. Erac smooched beside him, bumping him every now and then with the side of his head, though he was careful not to poke Joey with his horn. Joey grabbed him and cuddled him; he could not resist cuddling him.

Once again, Joey noticed the blue colour on his arms brighten into a brighter blue. "Oh, I love you so much," he said and squeezed him tighter. "I've missed you, my friend. I am so grateful to you. If it wasn't for you, I would never have been aware of my powers. Thank you so much."

"Neeeeeeigh," answered Erac, who then started to lick Joey's face like a puppy, which was very unusual for a horse. But then, Joey knew Erac was no ordinary horse. In fact, he was not a horse; he was quite a unique unicorn.

Joey slowly released Erac and continued to pat the soft fur on the side of his head while looking at Budda. "What about the people in the village and Jack, are they here with us in Riddells?"

Budda moved his head from side to side, "No, they are not here. We have to convince them they are living in Magical World before we can allow them in Riddells Withals. We're going to have to go to them, but I do have Ben. He's in one of the classes at our school, and he looks like he fits in well here."

Joey smiled. "That's great, now we'll have to convince the rest of the people in the village. Let's go now," he said impatiently. He quickly leapt off the banana chair and placed his half-emptied milkshake onto a strawberry table.

"Wait a minute, can I come too?" asked Astina.

Budda shook his head. "No, dear, you must stay here with Erac."

"Come on, Father, if I come along, they'd have to believe more in Magical World. I bet they haven't seen a cowchee before or, better still, a unicorn."

Budda raised his eyebrows. "All the more reason why you can't come along," he snapped. "You know what happened to those lexus creatures while Joey made magical music without warning them—they disappeared. If these people see anything about Magical World without understanding our world, they may disappear too. We have to bring magic to them slowly."

Astina looked so disappointed that Joey felt sorry for her. It reminded him of Olivia, of the time his parents would not let her go out with him and his mates to watch them at the go-kart racing. "Hey, can't we disguise Astina and Erac? There must be some magic that could make Astina look human and Erac like a horse. Maybe we could disguise Alcon into an owl or eagle and he could come along too. They could be our backup in case we get into any trouble. It would be an easy transformation."

"Well, I—"

"Oh please, Father, let us come with you, please," interrupted Astina with both her hands clasped in a prayer position, waiting for his reply.

Budda did his usual frown and then half smiled. "Well, all right then." Before Budda could say another word, Astina leapt and screamed with sheer delight, and then she flew around with Erac and Alcon.

"Thank you, Father, thank you!" she yelled. Budda waved, nodded his head, raised his left eye brow and smiled and looked at Joey.

"You've made the right decision. Astina will love the children and the people at the village. Anyway, we're going to need her to convince them to believe the stone will cure the sick and that Magical World can be real for them too," said Joey.

"Well, I'm still not thrilled about letting her come with us. I just don't want anything to happen to her."

"I think you're more afraid of losing her," said Joey quietly.

Budda had a grim look on his face, and his head moved from side to side. "Of course not, why would I be afraid of losing her?"

"You've practically raised her, and she's eager to make new friends. Maybe you're afraid she won't spend much time with you. I don't know, but you sure do sound like the way my dad was with Olivia."

"Well, you're wrong," snapped Budda. "Astina is free to choose whomever she wants to be friends with and whatever time she wants to spend with them is entirely her choice."

"Okay, whatever you say." He realized it was a subject Budda would not discuss, and no matter how much he tried to convince Joey or himself, it was clear he was afraid of losing her.

Budda sighed heavily. "Now, do you want something to eat before we head off? You know the village doesn't have much to eat, and we can't just throw them our magic."

"Why not?" asked Joey.

"Because they may reject it, and there goes our chance of them believing in Magical World."

"Oh, I see. You think they might be a bit like Jack and not believe in magic?"

"Yes, I'm afraid so. We have to be very careful. We can't allow anything to discourage them from believing," said Budda firmly as he waved to Astina and Erac to come down.

Joey watched them fly down with Alcon following behind. "Hey, we're bringing Alcon too, aren't we?" asked Joey eagerly.

Budda sighed. "Yes, I suppose he could come too, but I doubt he'd want to come along, he might be afraid of the earth-world."

"Oh, come on, give him some credit. He might be afraid of the druggons but surely not earth-humans. You saw how he carried me on his back when you bumped me off my balon with all the lexus creatures surrounding us."

"Please stop making up stories—that must be your imagination. Alcon was nowhere near the lexus creatures."

"Well it just goes to show how observant you really are. Who do you think saved me?" asked Joey sarcastically.

"The cloud saved you, Joey," answered Budda who was annoyed now.

"You're wrong, Alcon did. Anyway I'm going to ask him to come with us, and I bet he'll come. *Hey, Alcon!*" yelled Joey, waving in his direction. Alcon stumbled towards Joey with his tongue hanging out as usual.

"Did you call me, Chosen One?" Alcon asked.

"Yes," said Joey. "Are you coming to the village with us?"

"Village!"

"Yes, the earth-village. Astina and Erac are coming in disguise. I thought maybe we could disguise you as an owl or eagle, and you could come along with us."

"An eagle, earth-village, ahh, I . . ."

"Oh, come on, you're going to love these people. You've got to meet Suellen, and especially Lucy. They're great little girls. Okay, maybe we could change you into a human instead of a bird so you could talk to them."

"*Human!*" roared Alcon, looking grief stricken.

"All right, you can stay as an owl."

"An owl, what's an owl?" asked Alcon, dumbfounded.

"An owl is a bird that stays awake during the night and sleeps during the day," explained Joey.

"Owl, night, day?" repeated Alcon.

"Trust me, Alcon, you're going to love it, and maybe we could make you a special owl that doesn't have to sleep during the day."

"Does this owl fly?"

"Of course owls fly—I wouldn't have suggested it otherwise."

Alcon paced around for a few minutes and then a huge smile came over his face. "Okay, then I'll be glad to come with you." He joined Astina and Erac, and then they flew in the air, singing with excitement. Budda's eyes nearly popped out of his head; he looked as if he could not believe what he had just heard and seen.

Joey smiled at Budda. "You see, I told you he'd come with us."

Budda shook his head. "Joey Willis, you never cease to amaze me. You must have a magic influence on him." Budda smiled back at Joey and pulled out his fettal, which he waved in the air a few times. A flash of light appeared and then a splash of confetti glitter twinkled like a blanket in the air. Within a few moments, the glitter cleared, and Joey could see an owl flying in the red sky, and on the purple ground, a human girl and a white pony stood side by side. The transformation had gone very smoothly.

Joey almost fainted when he saw the girl. He could not believe his eyes, and just as he was about to say something, Budda put his arm around Joey's shoulder. "Don't be alarmed, Joey, this little girl and pony are the human and animal versions of Astina and Erac."

"Father is right, Joey, it's me, Astina." She pointed her hands towards her chest as if to show herself to Joey.

"I-I-I-I-I see," said Joey, lost for words. The little girl he was staring at looked identical to Olivia. Joey was relieved he did not call out her name. He still wanted to keep Olivia's identity a secret, and he was determined not to let Budda know who her earth-parents were. Joey was thankful he had kept the nonmind reading powder on himself. He needed to protect his family; it was hard enough losing Olivia, let alone allowing Budda to take his parents from Earth.

Joey wondered how Budda could have possibly known Olivia's looks for Astina to borrow as an earth-child, or could this be a coincidence? Joey could not understand, and he wondered if Budda really knew how his sister looked like and if all this was some sort of a plot. But then again, it was not Budda's idea to bring Astina to the village. It must have been a coincidence.

"Are you okay, Joey?" asked Budda with a concerned look on his face.

Joey quickly nodded. "Mmmm, yes, I'm fine. It's just so strange to see Astina, Erac, and Alcon looking so different."

Joey tried to look normal, but he could not help but continue to stare at Astina. His first thought was that he had found Olivia. But in all reality, it was Astina; his real sister was still lost. Anyway, Astina still wore her lovely red dress. This was how Joey really knew the difference between Astina and Olivia. Olivia would never wear such clothes. Shorts or jeans and a T-shirt were more to his sister's taste.

Just as they were about to leave Ben ran to Budda's side and hugged him.

"Ben will have to come with us, he can come as himself." said Joey smiling at Ben.

"No, I do not need to worry about another child being safe, you stay here Ben," demanded Budda.

"No, Come with you," cried Ben.

"We'll have to bring him with us, you know what happened last time we left Ben behind," reminded Joey.

"Okay, very well, but you'll have to stay close to me." Budda hugged Ben.

"Come on, everyone, we've got a lot of work to do," said Joey. He waved his hand for everyone to follow him, and they all trooped towards the entrance of Riddells Withals. They were ready to face whatever challenge they had to face.

CHAPTER 31

Nothing but White

"What's wrong with you guys?" Joey asked as they reached the village. None of them answered; they just stared ahead. So Joey turned to look at what they were staring at. His heart sank as he tried to take in what was in front of him. It was the village all right, but everything looked in a far worse state than previously.

"Oh no, the village. Where are all the people and the houses, the hospital, Suellen and Lucy. Oh my god. Come on, everyone, they need our help!" yelled Joey. He was near to tears.

Budda had not said a word, but he ran with Joey ahead of the others. They all ran to where most of the people lay sick and almost dying on the ground. "We have no time left, we've got to start saving them. I've got to use the stone's powers now," Joey stated.

Budda nodded his head in agreement. He too looked like he was in total shock, and he did not dare try to argue or stop Joey though it was not Budda whom Joey had to worry about. From behind them appeared Jack.

"What's this I hear about the stone's powers?" roared Jack angrily.

Joey and Budda almost pulled out their weapons from their capes. Jack had startled them and made them think they were being attacked. Maybe they really were under attack; Jack had a riffle in his hands, and he pointed it towards Joey and Budda.

"Don't point that gun at us, Jack. We're not here to cause anyone any harm. We're here to help," said Joey firmly. At the same time, he had his wet blanket and stone ready just in case.

"Here to help, sure! After you two left for Rockwell Mountain, everything here got worse. Victor and Max disappeared, and our homes instantly burned. Many healthy people died in the fires, and more people died from the virus. You see, Victor and Max weren't here to save the people that died, so what have you done to them?"

"Victor and Max were Villazian and Megram disguised as humans. They were druggons," Joey replied immediately.

"*Druggons?* What are you talking about? This isn't any more magic stuff, is it?" snapped Jack. He put his finger on the trigger of his gun as if preparing to shoot them. "Now where are they?" he demanded.

The people around them appeared to become terrified with Jack's anger. But Joey was not afraid of Jack; he stood straight and tall. The gun was nothing to Joey. Not even Budda, Astina, Alcon, and Erac were frightened of him.

"Your friends are gone. I've banished them. They were the reason why nearly all the people were sick and dying. Victor and Max created the virus and caused the fire that burned your homes down. Think about it, that's why they were the only ones who could cure some of the people. They were not your friends, they were your enemies. Now if you don't mind, we've got people to save, so put that gun away. We are your only hope. We are not your enemies, Jack, we are here to help you all."

"So you think you can save us. Well, I don't believe you, and neither do these people. You're lying. If Victor and Max were the cause of this virus, then why are more people dying from it? Didn't you say you had banished them?" Jack's voice was full of mistrust.

Joey could not answer Jack as he realized he had a point, but then again, viruses are like curses. Even though the druggons were banished, the curse was still there, and Joey hoped his stone could take the curse away.

"I am not going to let you get away with whatever you've done with Victor and Max," said Jack as he aimed his gun directly at Joey.

Before Joey had a chance to say anything or take cover, Jack fired his gun. The bullet hit Joey on his chest, and he fell straight to the ground.

"Joeyyy!" cried Astina, running to his side. "Oh no, Joey, please don't die. Father, quick you've got to help him."

Budda cradled Joey's head in his arms. "Joey, Joey, can you hear me? I want you to stay awake. Don't close your eyes. Joey, Joey, can you hear me?" pleaded Budda.

Joey could not talk. He glanced at his hand where he held his chest and noticed his blood was bright blue and was pouring out from him. His wound felt numb, and he did not feel any pain.

Budda looked at Jack angrily. "Don't you think there are enough people dying? As Joey said, we're here to help you, not harm you. Why don't you just put that gun away, Jack, and let us save everyone."

"If only you and your friends would get the hell out of here. We don't need your help, Bud," said Jack sarcastically as he spat on the ground near Budda and Joey. "Now get out of here, you scumbags, before I shoot the rest of you."

Budda placed Joey on Erac's back and called to the others, "Let's get out of here."

Budda, Astina, and Erac fled the village, with Alcon flying high above them. They moved as quickly as they could out of sight.

"This will do. Let's stop. I've got to see Joey's injury," said Budda. He pulled out a floating bed from his cape and held it near Erac. Budda carefully picked Joey up and placed him on the bed. "Joey, can you hear me? Please wake up."

Joey slowly opened his eyes. "Yes, I can hear you," he whispered. "I don't feel any pain, I just feel numb all over."

"Yes, yes, I know, Joey, don't talk right now, you're getting weak. You're losing too much blood. I had to wait until we were away from Jack and the people to help save you. We have to be very careful not to use magic in front of the people, remember?" Joey nodded his head slightly.

"This is why you have to stay awake. Only you can save yourself now. This wound is too big for my healing stones to cure, and the bullet is still inside you. Joey, you must concentrate on getting the bullet out of you. You must heal yourself. Can you do that?" Budda urged Joey as gently as he could.

"I'll try," Joey said as he closed his eyes and thought about the charmal stone inside his belly button. He deeply concentrated on the bullet, but he appeared to drift off to sleep.

"Joey, stay awake," insisted Budda, giving Joey a slight tug. "I'm going to put some healing stones around your wound. It may stop the bleeding."

Joey gazed down at his chest and noticed that the stones were partly healing his wound. But it looked as though the stones were not strong enough to allow his wound to completely heal. It had bought him some time to gain some strength to finish healing the wound himself.

The sound of more gunshots came from the village. Joey turned his head towards the sound and saw Alcon dodging the shots. Barely able to raise his arm, Joey pointed towards Alcon. "Gunshots, Alcon. Save Alcon," he said weakly.

Budda looked in the direction Joey pointed and then turned quickly to face Joey again. "Alcon will be fine, he's got quick reflexes. You've got to concentrate on healing yourself. Please focus, don't change your thoughts. Think about healing yourself. Alcon is okay, he can take care of himself. Anyway, if you heal yourself, you can then use the stone to heal anyone of us. Please, Joey, you're running out of time." Budda cradled Joey like a baby. "Come on, Chosen One, you can't leave us now. Concentrate."

Joey took a deep breath and did as Budda told him. Although it was difficult for him not to think of what was going on around him, he closed his eyes and thought about the stone. He thought about its powers pulling out the bullet from his chest. He was still numb, but then he felt a slight movement inside his chest near his heart. It amazed him that he did not feel any pain, but he knew the stone was helping him. Even though his eyes were closed, Budda kept quiet, and Joey realized that the stone must have glowed and that Budda would have seen it. He continued to concentrate hard.

A wave of power ran through Joey. It was much stronger than the very first time he had received powers from Erac. This was like an amazing force. As the force lifted him off the floating bed, it was as if something was pulled at his chest. His body was like jelly in the air, and his back was shaped like an arched bridge. Slowly Joey opened his eyes.

Everything was quiet around him as a white light sliced through the sky and completely surrounded him. It was as if he was in a world of his own. The light carried him higher and higher into the sky, and still all Joey could see was the white light. He wondered if he was dying or whether the stone was healing him. He remembered Budda saying something about communicating with the white light and its special powers.

After a few moments, Joey felt strong enough to try and stand. But it was so strange; he was doing an air walk in the sky. He looked down to his wound. His chest was dry, and the wound had completely disappeared. There was not one trace of blue blood on his cape.

"The stone worked, I'm healed. Budda, Astina, Alcon, Erac, Ben, where are you all? Buddaaa!" he cried and frantically looked around. His friends did not answer his calls, and he could not hear or see anyone. He was in complete whiteness and silence. Joey touched his body all over just to be sure that he was not a ghost and was still a real human. His body felt real. But if he was a spirit, he would probably still be able to feel his own body. What if this was what death was like?

"Where am I? Is anybody here?" he cried out as he tried to run through the white nothing. He ran and ran and ran, but he could not emerge from the whiteness. Joey felt very alone, lost, and afraid.

CHAPTER 32

Understanding the Truth

Out of nowhere, Joey heard a familiar voice. "White light, bring Joey back to us, guide the Chosen One to us," the voice echoed softly.

"Budda, Budda, I heard you. Can you hear me? Where are you?" cried Joey. He was so relieved to hear Budda's voice. In front of him appeared a tinge of blue amongst the whiteness. The blue formed into an earth-sky, and he saw two white doves fly towards him. The closer they came, the more the blue covered the whiteness until finally the white disappeared and Joey was left standing on a cloud in the middle of a bright sunlit earth-sky.

It was a perfect day. The white doves continued to fly around him until they settled on a cloud right next to Joey. The birds stood still and watched him. They looked peaceful and did not appear afraid of him like ordinary birds would on Earth. Joey held out his arm as if to touch one of the doves, but just as he was about to touch the bird, it opened its mouth. Out came a force of white light. Joey looked at his hand and noticed it changing shape. He tried to pull his arm back, but it was like a force sucking him in. "What are you doing?" he cried out.

The white light continued to pull on his arm, and his whole body turned soft like jelly. Horrified, he saw and felt his body being sucked inside the bird's mouth; he had no control at all. Within seconds, the white light was gone, and Joey could see the blue sky again. He turned to see where the doves were, but he could only see one of them. It looked huge. Joey tried to say something. "Chirrrpppp" was all that came out of his mouth. He stuck his arm out and saw that it was a blue wing. "Chirp, chirp, chirp," he squeaked.

Joey decided to stop chirping and turned and stared at the other dove.

"You're not going to be like a dove for very long," said a voice in his head.

"What do you mean? And why am I a blue bird?" said Joey in his head. He felt weird; it was like he was talking to himself, but he was really communicating with the other dove. The other dove was another voice communicating in his mind.

"You won't always be a blue bird. Fountain and I are only here to help you find your way," said the voice.

Joey continued to stare at the bird beside him. "Are you mind-talking to me?" The bird nodded. "So is this how birds communicate with each other?" asked Joey.

"Yep, I'm afraid so. We never talk out loud. We just chirp. It's a bird's special gift to be able to talk with our minds. It's great when you want to find a certain place. All I have to do is ask my mind how I get to the North Pole."

"Fly straight ahead for several morning suns," answered a different mind voice.

"Whoops, no, no, just practising. We don't need to go to the North Pole."

"Oh, then why did you ask?" queried the other voice.

"I was just explaining to the Chosen One how we mind-talk and find our way to a certain place. Sorry to trouble you."

"Oh, okay, that's fine, carry on."

"Thanks anyway."

"So because Fountain swallowed me, does that mean I'm Fountain for the time being?" asked Joey, studying his feet and wings carefully.

"Yes, I'm afraid so. He specifically asked me to ask you to be careful with his body. Don't ruffle his feathers, it's only for a loan."

"I can't believe I'm a bird. Not long ago in Magical World I was a frog, and now I'm a bird. Wow, this is amazing. By the way, what's your name?"

"Guidy."

"As in you're supposed to guide me?"

"I don't know. The white light decided to call me Guidy for its own reasons, but I'm here to help you find your way."

"So how are you going to do that?" asked Joey as he flapped his wings slightly up and down, slowly lifting himself above the cloud.

"I was told to show you your earth-home. That's why we're here back on Earth. I'm supposed to take you to your future." Joey landed back on the cloud and looked at Guidy in disbelief.

"Wow, you can do that?" asked Joey, dumbfounded.

"Yes, I can do anything the white light asks of me."

"Gee, thanks. Hey, could you show me the future lottery numbers? So we can win the big one. Dad's so into playing the lottery. Mum and Dad always argue about how many tickets Dad buys every week. It would be great to let Dad win the big one. I'm sure that would stop their arguments."

"No, I'm afraid I can't show you anything that could materialistically change your destiny. I'm only here to help you find your sister. At the moment, her life is entirely in your hands," Guidy stated in a matter-of-fact manner.

"Where is she? I mean, forget about the lottery ticket, Olivia is so much more important. How can I save her?" asked Joey anxiously.

"Follow me, Chosen One." Guidy flew off the cloud and into the sky. Joey flapped his wings and followed him; he was amazed that he instantly knew how to fly.

"I'm so glad you're here to help me. Thanks, Guidy."

"No problem. It's my job to help you. Nevertheless, you'll be doing the work, not me. I'm just here to show you your future. Take care, Chosen One, we're going to be in for a bumpy ride."

Guidy dived into the air, and Joey followed closely behind. They flew so fast around the Earth, it was like they were rockets travelling into the future. Joey had no idea where they were headed; he just followed Guidy's tail and did his best to keep up with him.

They travelled at such a speed that the earth just became a spinning mixture of colours. Joey felt dizzy, and there was an enormous amount of pressure on his tiny feathered body, but he did not yet feel tired. At this speed, they must have flown for thousands of miles.

At last they came to a stop. Joey found that he and Guidy were hidden inside a flowering tree by a path that led to a familiar house in a familiar street. It was Joey's home, though he almost did not recognize it. It was different—a big green metal fence was built around it with a single gate and a padlock attached to it. All the windows were secured with red shutters.

The other houses in the street were also slightly different; they appeared to have been renovated. Only one house looked as Joey had remembered it.

Guidy and Joey flew into his parents' backyard and rested on a branch in the walnut tree from where they had a view into the living room. Joey thought that the tree had grown even larger, and it was full of walnuts. They must be in the middle of summer; after all, the sun was scorching hot.

Quite unnoticed, Guidy and Joey stared into the living room. Joey could see himself as a human sitting next to his mother on the floor. They were both looking through the family photo albums. His mother was crying; she looked very thin and pale. As she cried, he heard her say, "Why Olivia? Why Olivia? Why did she have to get so sick? I can't watch her go through so much pain. Oh, Joey, I wish there was a miracle. I wish there was a cure for cancer." Joey held his mother tightly and cried with her.

While he held his mother, he gazed out of the window toward the walnut tree, directly where he, as a blue dove, rested. The real Joey stared and stared, and then he smiled.

"I wish there was a miracle too. I wish there was some sort of magic, real magic, to take the cancer away from Olivia."

Guidy turned to face Joey the dove. "Let's go, I've shown you enough here," he said.

The future he saw depressed Joey. In fact, almost everything about Earth depressed him. Suddenly, he felt like taking Budda's advice to not return to Earth but to stay in Magical World. Then the moment when he last saw his family would always be the same, and Olivia would be alive and healthy. As Budda had said, time would stay the same on Earth until he returned. But he would still miss his family, and he could only see them if he travelled through space and was invisible to them. And that would only be in the past, not the present or the future.

In an instant, Guidy and Joey were back on their cloud. This time, they did not need to travel around the earth to get back. "Why did you show me that future?" asked Joey sadly. "What is the use of me finding Olivia only to lose her again when I get back to Earth? That didn't look like it was too far into the future. Mum still looked the same, only a little thinner, and I only looked about a year or two older."

"As I told you earlier, her life is entirely in your hands. Only the Chosen One can save her. That is what the future would look like if you do not help Olivia."

"How can I help her if I can't find her? I can't cure cancer or any kind of illness on Earth. I'm just an ordinary boy on Earth," Joey said hopelessly.

"It's not about what you can do for Olivia on Earth—it's what you must do in Magical World to save her on Earth. Think about it, Joey. This is all I can tell you. I've already told you too much."

"What do you mean this is all you can tell me? Guidy, if you know what I must do, please tell me, please!" he pleaded. He was almost on his bird-knees, begging for Guidy's help.

"I'm sorry, Chosen One, I wish I could tell you, but I can't. It's time for me to go now. My only advice to you is to be honest with yourself and others. Always speak the truth, and you'll find your answer."

"What do you mean? I have been honest, I haven't lied to anyone," said Joey defensively.

Guidy did not answer, but flew into the whiteness. "No, wait, don't go, Guidy. I need you, please." Joey tried to fly after him, but when he flapped his wings, he realized they were no longer there. He was back to his normal self. The blue sky had disappeared, and Joey found himself swamped again by the whiteness.

"Great, how am I supposed to help Olivia here in this whiteness?" yelled Joey. He was pleased to have his voice back, but once again, he felt lost and hopeless. He thought about what Guidy had just told him, about being honest and always telling the truth. Then he remembered how he was not honest with Budda about Astina's earth-parents. But then Budda was not honest with Joey about the old woman with the herbs.

All of a sudden, Joey felt really tired. This was all too much for him. As he floated in the white space, his eyes became heavy, and he drifted into a deep sleep.

CHAPTER 33

The Original Cave

All of a sudden, Joey opened his eyes. He had no feeling of tiredness. He quickly sat up, only to see leaves and branches all over him. It looked like he was in a cave of some sort, with only a small hint of light in the distance. Directly in front of him, he caught a glimpse of Olivia. "Olivia," he called.

Budda appeared in front of him and covered his mouth gently but firmly and said, "*Ssshhh*." Budda motioned to Olivia to come forward. She tiptoed quickly towards them.

"Oh, Joey, it's me Astina. You must be hallucinating, you probably dreamed of Olivia," whispered Astina. Joey remembered then that Astina was disguised as a human and that her disguise looked exactly like Olivia. He was back with his friends.

"I did not sleep. I was somewhere else. It was completely white, and then I heard Budda's voice say, 'Guide the Chosen One.'"

"*Sssshhhh*, not now, Joey, you can explain later. We're hiding because Jack's outside this cave, and he is trying to kill us. Keep quiet, both of you," said Budda firmly.

Joey did as he was told and kept quiet. He touched his chest where the wound had been and looked around the cave, which seemed rather familiar. Deep in the cave was a floating fireball whose flame was bright blue. Joey knew it must have been one of Budda's magical lights.

Something caught Joey's attention behind the flame. On the wall, he saw something he had seen before. It was footprints and handprints painted yellow, red, and purple. He spotted the yellow left hand and the red right hand and remembered they felt like real hands wedged into the cave wall. This was his cave; the cave on his beach.

At last he had found his way back to Earth. But how could he be on Earth if Budda and Astina were there too? Slowly he stood up. "Jack is not outside this cave," he said.

Budda's face whitened, and he put his hand over Joey's mouth again. "*Ssshhh*, keep quiet," he hissed.

Joey tried to move away, but Budda was too strong for him. "Joey, please, we can avoid conflict if we keep quiet. Jack will never find us here. You see, from the outside of this cave, you can't see an entrance, there's a huge rock in front of it."

Arguing with Budda was not going to get Joey anywhere. In fact, at that moment, he felt a little frightened of Budda. He knew he was powerful too, and he certainly did not want to get on the wrong side of him. So he calmed himself down and obeyed Budda, who slowly released him.

"I don't believe Jack is outside. We are not near the village anymore," whispered Joey.

Budda frowned. "Of course he's out there. You heard the gunshots. Goodness, Joey, we thought we were going to lose you." Budda touched Joey's chest where the bullet had entered his body. "You've healed yourself quite nicely. Where did you go, Chosen One? You were out of it for some time," asked Budda gently.

"How long was I gone?"

Budda rolled his eyes and gazed up towards the cave ceiling. "Oh, I'd say probably four earth-time hours."

"Oh no, that means a lot of hours have already passed on Earth," Joey replied.

Budda frowned. "What are you talking about? We're in Magical World. The time will remain the same on Earth. We've been through this before, Joey, you know that."

Joey shook his head. "I'm afraid I don't think we are in Magical World. This is the same cave I was in when I went looking for Olivia before I came to Magical World." He pointed towards the foot—and handprints on the cave wall. "Look over there on the wall, I remember those prints. We are at the beach. Jack is not outside this cave."

"Are you saying people use guns at the beach on Earth?" asked Budda.

Again Joey shook his head. "Of course not, it's against the law." Before Joey could say any more, he heard the shots himself. The shots became so loud and continuous that he covered his head with his arms. *Bang! Bang! Bang!*

Budda and Astina huddled close to the ground with Joey. Joey had never seen them so afraid before, but then he realized that they would have been terrified when he was shot.

"Who ever invented guns?" muttered Budda.

Listening to the constant gunfire, Joey became absolutely convinced it was not Jack. This had to be a group of men and was now more than ever determined to find out. He stood up. "You two wait here, I'm going to take a peek outside the cave. That can't be just Jack firing, or maybe it isn't Jack at all. That noise is more than one gun firing."

Budda grabbed Joey's arm and pulled him down. "Oh no, you don't, you're going to stay right here and wait until the firing stops."

"But—"

"No buts," retorted Budda.

It annoyed Joey every time someone tried to tell him what to do although he made exceptions for Budda because he was special and he understood he was only being protective of him. But this time, Joey was determined to have his own way. He waited for Budda to release his arm and planned how to make his way to the cave entrance.

Just as he was about to make a run for it, he stopped. An idea had come to him. He remembered Clipper the Frog; he could disguise himself as Clipper again. It was the best disguise and a good way to find out who was shooting out there. Joey also knew this would probably get Budda off his back. He was in no mood for an argument, and it was senseless hiding in the cave waiting for the shooting to go away. Even if it did, he wanted to know who was firing those shots out there.

Joey lifted his cape and smiled. The pocket where he had found Clipper the first time was already open. Gently he held Clipper in his palm. He was relieved to see his powers still worked in the cave on Earth, but then again, he needed to prove he really was on Earth. The only way he could do that was to see what was going on outside.

Joey glared around at Budda and saw his serious eyes fixed on him. He had his fettal out. Joey smiled and slowly opened his palm so that tiny Clipper was in full view.

Budda frowned so Joey pointed his finger at Clipper and then at himself. Immediately, Budda understood what Joey wanted to do. It surprised Joey that for once Budda accepted one of his ideas. Maybe he realized that he could not stop him anyway. Maybe he was getting fed up with not being able to do anything and had to surrender to Joey's idea.

To become Clipper was the only thought on Joey's mind, and within a few seconds, he was converted into a beautiful bright-blue frog.

"Be careful, Joey," whispered Budda loudly.

Joey faced him and flickered out his bright rainbow-coloured tongue. Budda nodded in appreciation.

Once again, Joey was overwhelmed to be Clipper. He felt so good and as light as a feather. The cave entrance was quite a few jumps away, but he had the patience, and there was plenty of water running down the cave walls.

Joey was convinced that outside the cave, he would find himself on his beach.

CHAPTER 34

A Strange Celebration

Finally, Joey jumped his way to the end of the cave's entrance. This was the moment he had been waiting for, and this time, no one was around to stop him. The entrance was awfully large compared to the first time he had walked in, but now of course, he was a frog, and everything around him was naturally huge.

Joey stayed hidden among the small rocks. He knew children played all along the beach and enjoyed collecting small crabs, turtles, and other living creatures. If any of the children saw him as a blue frog, they would catch him, and Joey would never be free; they could even accidentally kill him. One time, when he went with his school friends to the bush, they had found lots of frogs, and they kept them in plastic containers in the sun all day. The following day, the frogs died. He had to make sure no one could see him.

Outside the cave, Joey was overwhelmed with what he saw. There was certainly no one shooting guns and no sign of Jack. What he did see were lots of people scattered around enjoying themselves. And it was the very same beach Olivia and he had played on before he entered Magical World. This confirmed what he suspected; they were definitely back on Earth.

Suddenly, some firecrackers went off in the warm night air. It slowly dawned on Joey that this was a New Year's Eve celebration. Joey realized time was passing on Earth. The day after Christmas was the day Olivia and he were last at the beach.

The firecrackers were loud and glorious. They made Joey feel so much at home that he almost forgot why he was there until he accidentally let out his long tongue.

A short distance away, Joey could see a group of children with torches heading in his direction. It was too dark for him to see exactly how many children there were, but it sounded like a group of six or seven. He quickly hid inside the bushes. Now that he knew there was no shooting, he decided it was safe enough for him to turn back into a boy. All he had to do was croak eight times, and he had to do this very quietly so the children would not hear him.

"Croak, croak, croak, croak, croak," Joey stopped and went silent. The children were very close now. All he needed was another three croaks, but it was just too risky now. Instead, he kept still and hoped they would not come near him.

The children were looking for something. They shined the torch around and rustled the bushes. He feared they would soon spot him; it was difficult for him to conceal himself with his bright-blue skin.

"There has got to be lizards around here somewhere, Mum said she saw some blue tongues around here last week," said a thin blond boy holding the torch not far from Joey. It was lucky the boy could not see him, but Joey could see him clearly. In fact, the boy looked very familiar. He was from the same school as Joey, and he was a bully and troublemaker. Allan Potter was his name.

Joey knew he was as good as dead if Allan found him. He decided that if Allan found him, rather than be caught, he would quickly croak his last three, although Joey did not want anyone from school to know about his powers and Magical World. For some reason, he felt very protective of his magical powers and Magical World. Magical World was not a place for Allan Potter or his schoolmates to see or hear about.

The bush above him parted. Allan had finally found him. The torchlight almost blinded him, but he kept still. He knew if he tried to jump away, Allan might hurt him. Joey remembered the time he caught frogs with his friends; a few frogs tried to jump away, and they were accidentally squashed. Some of them were even caught by the legs and ended up amputated into pieces. He also remembered his friends had laughed about that experience.

While Joey stayed frozen to the spot, he thought about his life and how it could all be over. He felt like something had stopped him from croaking his last three times. Was it his instincts that made him determined not to allow Allan or his friends know about his magic? Would he rather die than let them know about Magical World? That was the fate he could be facing.

The torch continued to shine on him for what seemed like ages, but nothing happened. Allan stared down at him and said nothing. It was as if Joey was invisible. "Nah, there's nothing here. They must have all gone. We'll come back in the morning, maybe we'll have a better chance in the day," said Allan casually.

"Yeah, come on, let's go, these torches are not helping us much," answered another boy from the group.

Joey was left alone. He wondered how they could not have seen him. He must be invisible on Earth.

"Croak, croak, croak."

Immediately, Joey was converted back into a boy. He could see his schoolmates still walking away. "Hey, Allan, wait!" yelled Joey. But he did not answer. No one could hear him. Joey was more than ever determined to talk to them even though Allan was bad to him at school. At that moment, Joey was happy to see him and did not care what he did at school. He missed Earth and all the people in it, good or bad. There and then, he just wanted to go home.

With all his energy and determination he ran away from the cave.

Bang!

"Ooouch!" Joey screamed.

Joey flew backwards onto the rough stony ground and knocked his head against something hard. He was in a lot of pain. He touched his head and felt a huge bump. He was dumbstruck as to what had happened. Something hard had hit him before he hit the ground.

He lifted himself up slowly and almost fell again. It was difficult for him to keep his balance, and his head throbbed with the pain. His vision became blurred, and he threw up without warning. Joey knew from the blow on his head that something was wrong.

Joey placed his hand on the stone in his belly button and thought of healing his head. It was difficult for him to concentrate, but he knew what he had to do before he passed out. He closed his eyes and then opened them again, and instantly, his vision became clear, and there was no more throbbing from his head. He touched it only to find that the lump had disappeared. "Wow, this is cool," he said out loud.

He walked slowly back until he came across what had almost knocked him out. It was an invisible wall, like clear glass, and it felt as if it blocked his way to the real earth.

Joey sighed heavily, and his head drooped. He felt overcome with disappointment and sadness. The clear glass surrounded the cave. Joey slammed his fists on the invisible wall in fury. *"Noooo!"* he cried and threw himself to the ground, weeping like a baby. He was so convinced he was back on Earth. He wished that Astina, who looked like his sister, was really Olivia and that they could go home.

The firecrackers had ended, and eventually, the celebrating crowd disappeared. Joey felt like a ghost, like a person who had died and turned into a spirit mixed with the living. Once again, he wondered if he really did die. Was this what death was like? Tears dripped down his cheeks, and when he went to wipe them away, he noticed his hands were smeared with blue blood mixed with bits of brown dirt.

Joey slowly slid his hands against the invisible wall; it felt rough, with funny-shaped bumps. It must be an invisible crystal of some sort. Joey was losing patience; he was getting fed up with Magical World. Olivia or no Olivia, he was angry; all he wanted was to go home. At that moment, he felt like a prisoner.

Suddenly, something from behind him gently touched his shoulder. "Joey."

Joey gasped and swiftly turned around. It was Astina. "What are you doing here?" he asked angrily.

Astina stepped back, looking as if she was about to cry. "I'm sorry, the noise stopped, and I thought something had happened to you. Oh, please don't be angry with me," she cried. Joey gently reached for her hand. "Oh no, Joey, your hands are bleeding," said Astina sympathetically.

"Astina, Astina, Come back inside!" shouted Budda. Abruptly, he appeared and stood dumbfounded at the cave entrance, gazing wide-eyed in every direction.

"Goodness, Joey, what happened? Oh my, this doesn't look like the village."

Joey walked towards Budda and stood directly in front of him. Budda looked down at his hands and then his face. "What happened? Are you all right?" he asked with the usual concerned look on his face.

Joey nodded lightly. "This is the beach where Olivia and I played before I came to your Magical World. The gunshot noise did not come from guns—the noise came from firecrackers, lots and lots of firecrackers. My people were celebrating New Year's Eve. So you see, now I know that earth-time is moving on without me, and I want to go back right now. I want you to tell me how to get back to Earth," Joey demanded.

Budda raised his arms as if to show Joey what was in front of him. "Well, you're here. Off you go. You don't have to worry about the suffering in Magical World. I guess they don't just call me Lord Budda for nothing. I think I can manage from here on. It's not your problem anymore," Budda said with a disappointed expression on his face.

Joey looked away. "Haven't you been listening to me? I would love to go, but there's this invisible crystal wall all around this cave. How do you think I hurt my fists? Look . . ." Joey walked to where he last stood and placed his hand, gently this time, against the invisible crystal wall.

Budda frowned. "I'm sorry, Joey, I don't understand. But I know that if you finish what you're meant to do in Magical World, then you'll be able to go back home to Earth. There's a reason why you are still here," he said sympathetically.

Joey calmed down and thought of Olivia. He gazed at Astina and pretended she was Olivia. Pointing his finger at Astina, Joey gave Budda a serious look. "Tell me why you made Astina look like that?"

Budda shook his head. "I didn't make her look like that, my fettal did. You see, my fettal is always true and correct. The fettal knew how Astina would have looked if she were human."

"But that's impossible, I know someone who looks exactly like that on Earth. That look is already taken, and that person does not have a twin." Joey made sure he did not reveal it was his sister who looked identical to Astina's image.

Budda's face lit up as if he had just won the lottery. "You do? Where is this person on Earth, Joey? This is wonderful news. If I could find the person who looks like Astina's earth-person, then I can find her true parents and unite them. Or you could unite them, Joey. Oh my goodness, this is wonderful news. Thank you, Joey." Budda grabbed Joey's hands and held them with gratitude.

"Oh, Joey, that's wonderful," Astina interrupted them both.

"I-I, er, I don't think that's a good idea. I mean, I'm not going to tell you where she is on Earth."

Budda's smile faded, and he dropped Joey's hand. His usual frown slowly appeared across his forehead. "Why not? And why did you not tell me from the beginning when we changed Astina into a human?" he asked very slowly.

Just as Joey was about to answer, a single gunshot came from the cave.

"Come out and face me. I'm not letting you all get away!" roared a familiar voice.

"Oh no, Jack's found us. Where's Ben?" asked Astina while she glanced at Budda.

Without another word, Budda ran back towards the cave entrance with Joey and Astina behind him. *"Wait,"* whispered Joey loudly. Budda and Astina stopped and stared at Joey. "Let me go in first, I'm living proof of magic. I can show Jack my healed wound. He's got to believe us now. He knows I'm supposed to be dead. Please, both of you, wait here."

"What about Ben? I'm more concerned about Ben than myself right now," said Budda.

At that moment, Joey realized Budda had become very close to little Ben. It was very similar to his relationship with Astina. Although Joey knew Budda loved and cared for all the cowchees and people equally, he sensed he had built a fatherlike closeness with Ben.

"You know Ben, he'll hide, he's good at that. Don't worry, I'll protect him with my life," answered Joey. Budda stepped aside with Astina close by, and he nodded slightly as he watched Joey go past him.

Joey cautiously entered the cave entrance. But everything had changed; it was no longer a cave. In fact, he was standing directly in front of the hospital in the village. Joey frantically turned around, but all he could see were trees and mountains. The cave had disappeared.

CHAPTER 35

How to Believe in Magic

How was he going to find his friends now? What if this was a trick to keep him away from them? What if Jack had done something to Ben, Budda, and Astina? Hurriedly he searched all around the village. He was very worried about Ben because he had promised Budda and Astina he would make sure nothing happened to him. But for all his efforts, the village was totally empty.

"Ben! Jack!" he yelled. He no longer tried to hide. He was so afraid something had happened to Ben that he did not care about risking his own life.

"Anyone here? Where is everyone?" Joey ran up the steps of the hospital, opened the two front doors, and found it was completely empty. He was not surprised, but he had hoped that at least one person would have been left behind to tell him something. Not a single sound came from the village.

Normally birds could be heard singing or seen flying around, but there was no sign of them either. It was as if something evil was lurking, and Joey could feel it in the pit of his stomach. This feeling was becoming very familiar to him. Joey wished Guidy was with him; he knew he would feel a whole lot safer.

Bang! Bang! Bang!

Joey gasped. The shots had returned. For safety, he ran back inside the hospital and positioned himself underneath a window making sure he kept as low as possible.

From his vantage point, Joey saw Jack appear in the village square right outside the hospital.

"Bud, I know you and your friends are hiding out there somewhere. Now come out and fight." With that, Jack fired his rifle again.

Bang! Bang! Bang!

Jack fired shots everywhere, and one of the shots hit the window above where Joey hid. Glass shattered everywhere. Luckily, Joey had covered himself with his cape, but he hadn't realized how much it would act as a shield. There was not one cut or scratch on him. His cape was as thin as silk, but it did not have a single tear. Joey completely wrapped his cape around him like a cloak, with only two slits for his eyes.

This was the moment he had been waiting for; it was time for him to face Jack. He walked to the entrance, pushed the doors open, and stepped outside. "*Jack, where are all the people?*" yelled Joey. He slowly walked down the steps towards Jack as he watched him with a deep anger.

Jack aimed his rifle at Joey. His face had become pale, and his eyes were wide with shock. *"Who are you? Don't move or I'll shoot you,"* he growled.

It was clear to Joey that Jack did not recognize him. He was eager to reveal himself there and then, simply to prove to Jack he was alive and completely recovered and that his magic was real. Instead, he decided to keep himself covered; he could not risk getting shot again.

"Jack, please don't shoot. I want to be your friend," Joey said very calmly.

Jack frowned, and his wrinkled face looked quite ugly. Obviously, Magical World could not make Jack look handsome. "Your voice sounds familiar. Take that sheet away from your face and reveal yourself," he demanded.

"I'll only reveal myself if you promise not to shoot me and let me talk to you. I only want to make peace with you."

Jack rolled his eyes and nodded his head. "How do you know me, and how do I know you don't have a weapon inside that sheet? I'm going to count to ten for you to take that sheet away from your face, and if you don't I'll shoot you anyway." Jack steered the gun directly towards Joey's chest.

Jack had given Joey an idea. Until then, he had been too honest and innocent to think of hiding a weapon, but it was obvious Jack did not want to be reasonable so he decided to prepare his wet blanket. Joey did not want to fight him, but he needed protection. Jack would have no idea his wet blanket was a weapon; he would only think it was a sheet like his cape.

"One, two, three—"

"All right, all right!" yelled Joey.

"Four, five—"

Joey flung his cape open and held his wet blanket by his side. Jack turned as white as a ghost and appeared stunned for a good few minutes.

"Didn't I shoot you? I did, I shot you in the chest. You're supposed to be dead."

"Yes, you killed me, and now I've come back to haunt you." said Joey with a mischievous smile.

Jack's eyes nearly popped out of his head, and before he had the chance to shoot, Joey slapped his wet blanket across Jack's arms. The rifle flew in the air and landed a few metres away from them. Jack landed on his knees, moaning in pain.

"Where are all the people?" demanded Joey.

Jack's pain was obvious. The wet blanket was a powerful weapon, and the burns on his arms were horrendous. For a small moment, Joey felt sorry for him. But he was not going to let Jack know that; instead, he held his blanket up high ready to strike him again.

"Jack, where are the people? What have you done with them? I'm going to count to ten—you'd better tell me by then, or I'll burn your face." Sweat poured down Jack's face, but Joey had to have some answers.

"One, two, three, four—"

"Wait, please don't hurt me. I don't know where the people are. Please, you've got to believe me. I've been trying to find them too. I thought you had something to do with them gone. How did you come back? You're supposed to be dead. Who are you? Are you a ghost or something?" Jack asked desperately.

"I'm not a ghost. I'm a human boy. They say I'm the Chosen One, but back on Earth, I'm just an ordinary boy. You see, Jack, after you shot me, my magic healed me. I know it's hard for you to believe this, but as you can see, I'm living proof."

Joey pointed towards his heart. "Look here, remember? This is where you shot me, not a scar, not a single scratch was left on me. This is the power of my magic. Even my cape protected me from the window you shot. None of this could have saved me on Earth.

"What are you talking about? Back on Earth . . . we are on Earth. You were just lucky the glass missed you. Why can't you get it through your head, young boy, there is no such thing as magic," snapped Jack. Joey watched him guardedly. Jack looked like he was becoming angry again; his face had turned red.

"Why don't you let me prove it to you? I'll take those burns off your arms," insisted Joey. And before Jack could say another word, Joey concentrated deeply and thought about healing Jack's wounds. The stone shined brightly on his belly button, and within a few seconds,

Jack's burns were healed. Jack stared at his hands and arms in disbelief, touching them to make sure the skin was clear.

"How could this be?" asked Jack in complete awe.

Joey smiled. He could see Jack's attitude begin to change. Joey wondered if his stone could turn Jack into a good person as well as healed his burns. But deep down, Joey knew that that was one thing the stone could not do.

"Now do you believe in magic?" asked Joey, still holding his wet blanket.

Jack looked first at the blanket and then at Joey. "Is that thing you're holding magic too? Or do you just hit hard with it?" Jack still looked flabbergasted.

"Oh, you mean this?" Joey lifted up the hand that held the blanket.

Jack pulled himself back. "Keep that thing away from me. I have my reasons for not believing in magic."

"And what reasons would they be?" asked Joey.

Jack hesitated for a while. He looked disorientated and lost in his own thoughts. "Five years ago, my wife and child caught the virus. Back then, the virus had just started, and I didn't know much about it. I was desperate, I wanted to save them. They were so sick I didn't know what to do." Jack stopped for a while and looked as if he was going to break down.

"Go on, Jack, tell me what happened."

"This ugly-looking man came into our village. He said he had a magical plant that could save my wife and child. But he said the magic would only work if they slept under the moon. At that time, there was snow. I didn't think it was a good idea for a sick woman and child to be left outside in the cold all night. But he told me if I were to come out of my hut to check on them, they'd die. If only I didn't listen to that wretched man." Jack shook his head helplessly and tears spilled down his cheeks.

"I believed him. Silly me, I believed him. My wife and child died of hypothermia—the virus didn't even kill them, the cold did. All because I believed this man's idea of magic. Stupid me, everyone thought I was evil. But I loved them so much I would have given my whole life for them. The people in the village were angry at me for a long time. They treated me like an outcast. But I didn't really blame them. They had every right to treat me like that. After that, I made sure all the people in the village never spoke a word of magic until you and your friends came along. I was angry for a very long time. I decided not to show anyone that I could love or care again."

"You had every reason to be angry, Jack. I'm so sorry you went through that. You must have come across an evil source that probably had something to do with the druggons. You see, Jack, sometimes bad things come to us only to test us. I mean, it's like the devil dancing around you. You have to believe in good no matter what, otherwise, the evil will win and make you unhappy. Once again you were tricked. After what happened with your wife and child, you carried this anger in your heart, and you attracted the evil. The whole village then carried the virus. Your situation went from bad to worse. What did you do with the ugly man that did this to you?"

"He left the village as soon as he gave me the herbs." Jack was still on his knees, and he looked up with remorse in his eyes. "What should I do to stop this evil?"

"Find the goodness inside your heart. Find a way to forgive the evil and let it go. I know it's hard, Jack, but this is Magical World, not Earth. All I know is that if you have a pure heart and goodness in you, everything will turn out better. Budda told me to imagine the white light."

Joey put his wet blanket away and kneeled down in front of Jack. He placed his hands gently on each of Jack's shoulders. "Come on, Jack, I'll help you. We can do this together. Now I want you to close your eyes with me and concentrate hard on the white light coming down on you and surrounding your entire body."

"Okay," Jack whispered softly.

"Don't worry if you think you're not doing it right. I'll help you, that's why I'm holding your shoulders," explained Joey.

Jack said nothing but nodded and kept his eyes tightly shut. Joey also closed his eyes again and concentrated deeply on the white light. He had no idea what was going to happen next, but he trusted his instincts and placed all his faith in what Budda had taught him about the white light. For now, this was their only chance.

Joey was really happy to have finally convinced Jack to believe in magic and that he really was living in Magical World. He could feel an amazing pull of energy around Jack and himself.

Suddenly, the force of the energy calmed, and Joey decided to open his eyes. He was so proud of what he could see in front of him. The sky had become red, the trees were many-coloured, and the red river flowed between the purple mountains. In the not-too-far distance, Joey could hear children laughing. "You can now open your eyes, Jack. This is the real Magical World."

Jack slowly opened his eyes. He gazed around wide-eyed in every direction. He stood up, looking confused. "What is this? How can this be? Am I really alive? Is this heaven or something?" he asked.

"This is where you've been the whole time. The village you and your people lived in became an illusion based on your bad beliefs. I mean, you believed you were still on Earth and suffering. If you had believed in real magic, and I mean really believed with all your heart, you would have been living in this. You're not dead, trust me—you're very much alive. Nobody dies in Magical World. Death here is only an illusion. You don't really die on Earth either, just go somewhere else. Only the people who stay on Earth miss their loved ones when they pass on." Joey could not believe he just said that to Jack. It was as if something had given him instant knowledge without him realizing it.

"So if we were in Magical World the whole time, does that mean my wife and child never really died?" asked Jack cautiously.

Without Joey realizing what he was saying or doing, he nodded his head as if to say yes. "Yes, yes, Jack, your family is very much alive." Once again, Joey could not believe he had said that too.

The look on Jack's face was incredulous. He stared right past Joey. His mind seemed to be a million miles away.

"Helena, Jacob," called Jack.

Joey turned and saw a woman and child playing just a few metres away from them. The woman stopped playing with the boy and looked in their direction. She held on to her little boy's hand.

"Helena, Jacob!" Jack called a little louder. The woman picked up the little boy and ran towards Jack.

"Jack!" she cried as she stumbled.

Jack ran to her, and within seconds, they were in each other's arms. Jack grabbed both Helena and Jacob and swirled them in the air, crying with joy. He then turned around to Joey with the biggest smile. Joey returned his smile. *What a reunion,* he thought.

Joey then focused his attention farther away. There standing in the middle of Magical World and clearly out in the open was Riddells Withals. He was glad to be back inside the true Magical World with Jack, but he still feared for the people in the village. He could not help but wonder if they too were in the true Magical World. And if they were here, how did they get here? And why was Riddells Withals out in the open?

Quickly he pulled out his balon and flew high into the red sky. He loved his balon; he was really going to miss it and his other gifts when he returned to Earth. Joey peered down to the ground and looked at all the wonderful trees full of delicious treats. He was going to miss that too. Magical World was certainly any child's dream. But even though all the things in Magical World overwhelmed and excited Joey, he still wanted to go back to Earth and one day grow up to be a man. He did not want to stay a boy forever. The more he thought about it, the more he felt good about going home. He smiled to himself.

CHAPTER 36

The Village People

Joey parked his balon in front of Budda's mansion. He jumped off and quickly placed it back inside his cape. Looking around, he saw all the people and cowchees happily doing their usual things. Certainly, Riddells Withals had been repaired magnificently. There was no sign of the enormous damage the druggons had inflicted on it.

Joey just stood and enjoyed watching it all. Lena was busy serving her milk shakes, but suddenly, she looked up in Joey's direction, and with a surprised expression on her face, she ran back inside her shop. Within a minute, Budda, Astina, Ben, Erac, and Alcon stood beside Joey.

"Joey!" they all yelled at him at once.

"Wow, how did you guys get here? And why is Riddells Withals shown openly in Magical World?" asked Joey.

Together they said, "You put us here." Then one by one, they all gave him a hug. Joey was confused, but he allowed himself to enjoy the moment as they all crowded together.

Budda was the first to pull away. "You got us here with your white light. Riddells Withals is still hidden, it can only be seen by the good and pure of heart, and everyone is welcome to live here," he explained.

Joey remembered that when he had used the white light on Jack and himself, he had also thought of being with his friends at Riddells Withals. "What about the people from the village?" Joey looked down at Ben and patted his head. "I'm so happy to see Ben here and safe with us." He smiled.

Budda placed his hand on Joey's shoulder, "Come with me, I have something to show you."

Joey and his friends followed Budda. He directed them inside his mansion towards his classrooms, which were filled with people and cowchees. Joey noticed that there were a lot more people than the first time he had been at Riddells Withals. Budda stopped in front of classroom number 4 and waved to Joey to enter. "Come, Joey, come," he said. Budda was smiling, so Joey knew it must be something good.

There in the front row was a person he thought he recognized—a very pretty small blond girl. He tried to focus and remember who she was, and then it came to him. It was Lucy. She looked so different; she was clean and healthy, with two arms and two legs. As she stared at Joey, he looked into her beautiful bright-blue eyes and realized she was no longer blind. "How? How did this happen?" Joey asked, absolutely stunned.

Budda smiled at Lucy and said, "Lucy, why don't you show Joey how this happened?"

Lucy put her hand inside her pocket and pulled out the pink crystal stone Joey had given her. "This stone is what brought us all here. You were right, it is magic. After you gave it to me, I held it all the time. Then one night, it became really warm. My hand and I felt really good. I felt like I had a wave of energy."

Joey remembered that was how he had felt when he used his stone powers.

Lucy continued her story. "I believed it was magic like you told me, and I kept thinking about the magic curing my virus. Straightaway my vision came back. Oh, Joey, it was the most exciting thing that had ever happened to me. And then a few seconds later, my whole body went back to normal, and I didn't feel sick anymore. I felt wonderful. Many people witnessed my miracle and then word got around the village, and everyone started to believe in magic. I'm sorry, Joey, I know you wanted me to keep the stone a secret . . ."

"It's fine, you don't have to apologize. I'm so glad you didn't keep it a secret," Joey replied.

"I don't know where Jack was at the time, but the whole village crowded around me wanting to know how I had been cured. I told them that I simply held the stone and constantly thought about being better. People wanted to try it, so I gave everyone a hold of the stone and asked them to believe in magic and to think of it healing them. Everyone in the village that had the virus was healed, and when we got to the last person, everything went white and then colours appeared around us. The sky went red, the ground went purple and smelt so yummy, and the trees had delicious treats on them. Then we all saw Riddells Withals, and that's how we came here, Joey."

Joey smiled and gave Lucy a big hug, and then he turned to Budda. "The stone must have worked straight after we destroyed the druggons," he said proudly.

"You mean you, not we," Budda corrected him with a broad smile.

"Let's just say it was the gift, the gift that I have inside me. Honestly, I really don't know why I am the Chosen One. I guess I'm just lucky. And it sure is a relief to see all the people from the village here enjoying the real Magical World. Hey, I have even brought Jack here with me," said Joey excitedly.

Budda's eyebrows shot up, and he looked worried. "Jack? Where?" he exclaimed as he gazed around, nervously scratching his bald head.

"Jack's fine now," Joey assured Budda. "He also now believes in magic and the real Magical World. He was only angry at magic because someone tricked him, and

I'm pretty sure it had been a druggon plot. You see, a stranger told him his wife and child would be cured with magic if he left them outside in the snow for the night. Well, it didn't turn out that way."

"A wife and child?" interrupted Budda with a surprised expression on his face.

"Yes, Jack has a wife and child. I know it's hard to believe, but he is a good man. Now as I was saying, he believed the stranger, but the stranger tricked him. His wife and child froze to death, and Jack thought they died only because he believed he was in the real earth-world, so he stayed angry all that time. But now he realizes we are in Magical World, and as we speak, he and his wife and child are right outside Riddells Withals. As you yourself said, only the pure of heart can see Riddells Withals."

"Yes, yes, you're right, Joey. Oh dear, no wonder Jack hated magic. My instincts told me he wasn't a bad person, so I'm glad you helped him, Joey," Budda said with a relieved expression on his face.

"Yeah, but I almost didn't help him. I mean, it was a challenge. I had my wet blanket ready just in case, but he came to his senses when I showed him the magic." Joey touched Lucy's hand again and said, "It's so good to see the village people here."

"I'm so glad you came to our village, Joey," Lucy declared, and she turned to the rest of the people in the classroom. "Three cheers for Joey."

Everyone held their arms up and shouted out, "*Hooray! Hooray! Hooray!*" There was so much joy and excitement, even all the other classes crowded outside number 4 joining in. Joey raised his arms in the air and cheered along with them all.

CHAPTER 37

Olivia's True Destination

After everyone had settled down, Joey moved over to Budda. "I'm happy to be here too," he said.

Somehow Budda knew that Joey was not completely happy. "You want to go home, don't you, Joey?" he asked sympathetically.

Joey nodded slowly. "I miss my family and my home. I miss . . ." The words almost choked him, but Budda knew exactly who he missed most.

Budda placed his hand on Joey's shoulder. "I know you miss Olivia." Joey looked miserable. "Then we must find her, and we will find her," said Budda with determination. "But there is something I want to ask you. I don't mean to be selfish, Joey, but do you remember the conversation we had before Jack came to the cave? I can't get this out of my mind. You said you knew Astina's earth-person. Please, Joey, you must tell me who she is."

"Why?" protested Joey.

"What do you mean why? I told you, Astina must be reunited with her real earth-parents."

Joey was becoming agitated though he knew he should stay calm. "I won't let you interfere with this earth-person's parents. I know this earth-person has a brother, and he needs his parents too. I'm not going to let you take that away from him."

"What are you talking about? I am rather offended by what you are saying, Joey. I have no intention of causing anyone any grief on Earth, I merely want to reunite Astina with her real parents."

"And exactly how are you going to do that?" asked Joey.

"Oh, Joey, are you thinking that I'd make Astina's earth-parents die on Earth just so I can reunite their daughter here? You have totally mistaken me, I mean to send Astina to Earth."

"*No*, Father!" Astina cried out.

Budda held Astina close to him. "Oh, Astina, dear, I didn't mean for you to hear that. I was going to tell you. Please don't be afraid, I think it's time for you to leave Magical World."

"But, Father, I don't want to leave Magical World," she pleaded.

"There, there, now. Please don't cry, my darling. Once you return to Earth, your memory of Magical World will be gone, and you'll be able to grow up and one day have your own children," explained Budda.

Joey thought about what Guidy, the white dove, had told him. That he had the power to prevent Olivia from getting sick. He realized that Astina must be part of Olivia; that she must be her spirit guide, and the only way that Olivia could stay on Earth would be if her spirit guide was with her. Guidy was right; Joey should have been honest with Budda. How could he have kept the truth from Budda?

"Olivia," Joey said as he grabbed Astina's hand and looked into her eyes. "I know it's you. Astina, you look exactly like Olivia. My parents are your earth-parents. I'm so glad I've found you at last. I'm sorry, Budda, I should have been honest with you. I should have told you the truth when I realized it," Joey confessed.

"Then you are very lucky, Joey, because some cowchees in Magical World are spirit guides for some of the earth-people. Not all, only some, it just depends on how well their souls can cope in the earth-world. So you see, Astina must be Olivia's earth-guide. And if that's the case, they must be reunited. Either Astina goes down to Earth or Olivia will end up here."

"I realize that now," beamed Joey. "Guidy showed me the future. He said to always be honest and I'd find the answer. He showed me Olivia was sick and dying of cancer, so that means that if Astina is reunited with Olivia, she won't get sick and die. I was very selfish to keep my thoughts from you."

Budda frowned and shook his head with disappointment. "You knew when I showed you the photo of Astina as an earth-person, didn't you?"

"I'm so sorry, Budda. Please try not to be angry with me."

Budda kept nodding his head, but slowly a smile came to his face. "It's fine, Joey, you're forgiven. Besides, if you had told me earlier, you probably would have left Magical World, and the people from the village wouldn't have been saved."

"I would never have left without getting rid of the druggons and saving the people," Joey declared.

"I'm still puzzled, Joey. You said Guidy showed you the future. Who is Guidy?" asked Budda, frowning again.

"Oh, Guidy was the white dove I met when I was trying to heal after I got shot. He showed me the future. You see, I turned into Fountain, another white dove, and we flew to my house on Earth where we could see the future. Only I failed to save Olivia."

"I see," answered Budda.

Joey looked at Astina. "But I'm so happy now. Astina, you've got to come with me, I promise I'll always be a good brother to you. You'll love Earth, I promise," he assured her.

Astina hesitated. She wanted to be happy and was very pleased at the idea of Joey being her brother. Even the idea of going to Earth was appealing. She looked at

Budda uncertainly, and he smiled gently at her. It was as if he could read her mind. Joey too could sense her thoughts.

"Now I don't want you to worry about me Astina. You are free to go with Joey. In fact, you must go. It is your destiny, and you have so much to learn on Earth. You must not worry about me, my child, we'll be together again once your time on Earth is finished. Just think of it as a holiday."

Astina approached Joey, and they both hugged. "Joey, I want to go with you, but I don't think I can leave Father. I'm going to miss him so much, and I know he needs me too."

"Nonsense! It's just like you to be thinking of others more than yourself, Astina. You must go with Joey and continue your destiny on Earth." Then Budda looked at Ben and smiled. "I have Ben now. Anyway, you won't miss me, my dear, because once you both go to Earth, you'll have no memory of your time here. You must not feel bad about this," Budda stated.

Astina ran to Budda, hugged him, and cried, "Oh, Father, I don't want to forget you."

Budda held her tightly. "My dear daughter, your memory will come back once you return to Magical World. I want you to meet your real parents and make Joey's family happy. You know what will happen to Olivia if you don't go to Earth with Joey. You will be doing the greatest of deeds. Now stop crying, my dear."

Astina wiped her tears away and bravely said to Joey, "Okay, I'm ready to go now."

Joey held her hand. "You won't regret this Astina, thank you so much. I knew you were my sister the moment you changed to her earth-looks. And come to think of it, your bedroom in Budda's mansion reminded me of Olivia. I promise Olivia—I mean, Astina—I'll take good care of you. Anything you want will be yours." Joey looked at Budda happily. "How do we get back to Earth? And don't tell me you don't know. I know you know."

"Before I show you how to get back to Earth, do you mind if we have a private word. We'll step outside the classroom, shall we?" Budda signalled towards the door.

Once they were outside, Budda held Joey's shoulders and gave him his usual serious look. "Are you sure you want to go back to Earth, Chosen One?"

Joey could not believe what he had just heard and for Budda to stipulate Chosen One as if he had a duty to stay. "Of course I want to go back, you know that," he said hoarsely.

Budda looked slightly upset. "Once you go back with Astina, you must not tell her about Magical World, nor anyone else for that matter."

"Do you honestly think I'd be that crazy? I mean, everyone would think I was mad. They'd probably put me in a mental hospital. And I thought you said once

Olivia—I mean, Astina and I go back to Earth, we won't have any memory of this."

"This is why I wanted to speak with you alone. Astina won't have any memory, but you most definitely will because you, my friend, are the Chosen One, and there may even be opportunities for you to come back," explained Budda.

Joey was most surprised to hear what Budda had just told him. He was also a little relieved because he had really enjoyed the time he had spent in Magical World. It had been such an adventure. But it had not occurred to him that he could have both sides of the world—to be able to enjoy growing up with his family and to sometimes visit Magical World. Smiling, he looked at Budda. "You mean I can visit Magical World whenever I want and still be with my family on Earth?"

Budda nodded at Joey and asked nervously, "Will you really want to visit Magical World again?"

"Of course, I would be honoured to. Just look at this place, it's any kid's dream. I know my main purpose was to find Olivia, but I feel so good now that I've been able to help you and everyone else. And I really appreciate your generosity. You are all so friendly and have made me feel very welcome in Riddells Withals. On Earth, at home, we hardly know our neighbours." Joey sighed and looked down. "I honestly wish Earth could be like Magical World."

"Then why don't you stay here, if Earth is so bad?"

Joey shook his head. "It's my destiny to go back, just like Astina. I want to grow up, and I want to be with my family. If I don't go back, it would be like they had died. The thought of them never being able to speak to me again . . . that terrifies me."

Joey knew if he did not go back to Earth, it would be as if he had died to his family. Earth-time at some point would have to move on. Time had only stood still for a brief moment while Joey stayed in Magical World.

"After Guidy showed me what the future might have been, I could never put my mother through that. My family needs me as much as I need them. I know that won't last forever, but for the time my family is on Earth, I must be there. But I promise if anything evil happens again in Magical World, I'll be right back to help out. But for now, everything is just the way it should be."

Budda patted Joey's shoulder. "I understand you now, and you're right. Your parents must be good people to have two children who put others first." He glanced at Astina through the classroom window and then focused back on Joey. "Anyway, I have no right to interfere with your destiny on Earth. But always know that you are welcome to come back for a visit or even dinner. My home is your home, Chosen One."

CHAPTER 38

The Blue Pendant

Joey gave Budda a heartfelt hug. "Thank you, I'll come and visit from time to time. But first, you've got to show me how to get home and how to get back here. Once I'm back on Earth, I won't have these powers."

"You'll know how to come back, just think about returning and follow your instincts," Budda assured Joey.

"But—"

Budda placed his finger over Joey's mouth. "Without you even realizing it, there'll be odd things that don't normally happen on Earth, similar to the footprints and handprints in the cave. From those signs, you'll know how and when to get back here."

"You mean I won't be able to come back here from the cave next time?"

Budda shook his head. "Those footprints and handprints won't be there anymore, and maybe even the cave itself won't be there. But something new will always show itself. All you have to do is think about coming back, and something odd will appear."

"But I won't have my powers once I return to Earth. My thinking about anything won't work down there. I won't be blue, I mean, I can't be blue—the kids would make fun of me, and I'd stand out too much."

"You'll have nothing to worry about, and you won't be blue." Budda pulled out something from his cape. It looked like one of his special books. "I want you to take this with you," he said as he handed the book to Joey. The book felt warm and cuddly, as if it were alive. On the front cover was a blue eye, which blinked at Joey. It also had a huge *T* on the side. It was the same book that Joey had read to learn more about his powers when he first came to Riddells Withals. "This book will show you how to use your powers on Earth."

"You really mean I will still have powers on Earth?" Joey exclaimed.

"Yes, you will still have some powers on Earth. It's just that they won't be obvious." Budda pointed to the *T* on the side of the book. "This *T* here is for 'The Chosen One,' it is really only for you."

"Wow, can I really take this back with me?"

"Of course, but you must take good care of it and never let anyone on Earth see it."

Joey held the book closely to him. "No way, I'll keep it hidden, and I'll treasure it forever."

"And when you come back here, you must bring the book with you," insisted Budda.

Joey nodded. "I will, I promise."

"I have a much better idea for you to hide the book. You can shrink it. That way, you can carry it with you at all times, and it won't fall into the wrong hands."

Budda pulled out a gold chain with a rectangular locket. He opened the locket. "Now I want you to concentrate and think about shrinking this book to fit inside this locket."

Joey closed his eyes and thought hard about making the book small enough to fit inside the locket. When he opened his eyes, he saw the book slowly shrink in his hand until it was just the right size to fit inside the locket. He placed it inside and closed it. The locket turned into a blue stone in the shape of a rectangle.

Budda took the stone and chain from Joey and secured it around his neck. Joey gazed down at the pendant hanging around his neck and touched it. "You're the best," he grinned. Then he held out his cape. "Can I take this with me too?" Budda frowned at him. "Just joking," laughed Joey. "Now will you help me get home?"

"All in good time. I just want to make sure you know how to get your book out and come back here. You know now don't you?"

"Yes, yes, all I have to do is concentrate and think about it."

"You've got it, son. And remember, now that you are aware of your powers, you'll never lose them. But you must be very careful how you use your powers.

We don't want earth-people to find out about Magical World. You must never use your powers on Earth."

"I already know that, and don't worry, I promise I'll just be a normal boy on Earth. And that is exactly how I want it to be," Joey said with a grin.

"Come on, let me take you to a special room to get you and Astina back to Earth."

The mansion that had been Astina's home all her life was enormous, yet it actually felt cosy and very welcoming. Every detail felt perfect to Joey, and it was like a museum full of colour and excitement.

Budda called to Astina to join them and then led the way to his special room. Joey felt a sense of loss rush through him. He had had such a magical time here, and he didn't know when he would return. Joey was going to miss this place so much, and he wondered how Astina felt.

Finally, they entered a room painted in yellow. Joey remembered something about it from his book. In a corner sat a large crystal bowl, and inside were small replicas of red and yellow feet and hands. They were very similar to the prints in the cave on the beach.

"Well, this is it. This is the way you can go home, Joey. I suspect this is very familiar to you," Budda said.

"Yes, I remember seeing this in my book," Joey answered.

"Of course you would remember. The book keeps this memory in your head. I suppose you know what is going to happen next?"

Joey nodded. "There's an old lady behind that wall in a washroom. You told me she was banished from Magical World."

"Er, well . . . That was not completely true. I'm sorry, Joey, I wasn't truthful about that because I knew you were not ready to go back to Earth then."

Joey crossed his arms, and Budda frowned. "Now don't get upset with me, you were not truthful about Astina's earth-person identity, and I have forgiven you for that."

Slowly Joey grinned. "I suppose you're right. Anyway, I'm glad I didn't go back straight away. If I had left, then I wouldn't have found the charmal stone and been able to use my full powers to save the cowchees and people or save my sister by not taking Astina back with me. No, I'm grateful you lied about that. I'm glad I was able to make so many new friends, especially Astina. If you had found her earth-parents without me, she probably would have refused to leave you."

"You're right, Joey, I would have stayed here with Father. You have convinced me to go with you. I could never have done it alone. You came here to truly save your sister, and you have accomplished that," Astina responded.

Joey walked with Astina up to the bowl of hands and feet. He picked up a small hand and touched the yellow wall with it. The hand marked the wall and slowly opened the wall; once it was completely open, there in front of them stood the old lady. Her hair was grey and long and almost covered her face. In the palm of her hand, she held an orange herb with pink specks. Joey had never seen such a plant before. The old lady did not say a word; she simply waited for Joey to take the herb. He picked it up and looked at Budda.

"You and Astina have to eat that herb," he explained.

Joey handed a piece of the herb to Astina, and they both smelt it. It smelt like an orange, a strong sweet smell. Joey's mouth watered, and he felt like eating it straightaway.

"Mmm, this smells yummy," said Astina. But then, she looked at Budda and became sad. "Oh, Father, are you really sure you want me to go. I'm going to miss you so much." Clenching the herb in her hand, she wrapped her arms around Budda.

Budda hugged her back. "My darling, you will not miss me when you go to Earth. I will miss you, but it will not be long before we will meet again. You must enjoy your life on Earth, you must never feel guilty. Even if someone close to you dies on Earth, you must not waste your time grieving. You must appreciate everything you have because everything you have comes from the great white light."

"Budda is so right, Astina. Let's go, it's time now." Joey said as he took Astina's hand, and together they put the herb into their mouths.

Instantly, Joey felt like he was spinning around in circles. Colours swirled around him, and he was getting dizzy. Astina was right behind him. Joey's eyes became heavy; he felt breathless and extremely tired. The force of the swirl was so powerful that, within seconds, Joey blanked as if in a deep sleep.

CHAPTER 39

The Sand Castle

The cold waves from the sea splashed against Joey's feet. He was half awake, but before he opened his eyes, he tried to remember his dream.

Very slowly he opened his eyes and saw the white sand of the beach in front of him. A few metres away was the sand castle he had made. It was spectacular, but he knew he could not have made it by himself. He sat up and saw Olivia touching up the bridge part of the castle.

The sand castle looked oddly familiar to Joey. Then he remembered the castle at Riddells Withals. He remembered Magical World, Alcon, Budda, Astina, Ben, and all his friends. He wondered if it was all a dream. He looked at his hands and noticed they were their normal colour. He shook his head and told himself he must have been dreaming about the castle and Magical World. Joey was glad the nightmare about Olivia being missing was over. He watched her work with eagerness and determination to finish the castle they had started to build together. Then Joey knew this was not the real

Olivia; she never had that much determination about anything.

Joey noticed the blue pendant hanging around his neck. He touched it, and though he was relieved to be back on Earth and safe with his sister, Olivia, he knew he had not been dreaming. He looked around the beach for Astina.

"Oh, Joey, you're awake now, I've been finishing off our castle. What do you think?" asked Olivia with a smile.

"Fantastic, wow, did you do all this? I mean, this is great—this is the best sand castle I've ever seen. We've got to take a photo of this," said Joey.

Olivia's smile was different. It was not like her to be so happy. She normally found something to pick on, even if it was something good. It was not like her to appreciate Joey's compliments. Joey thought of Astina disguised as Olivia in Magical World, and he wondered if she had come back as Olivia.

Suddenly, he was worried about the real Olivia. Was she still missing? Just before he started to panic, Olivia kicked the sand castle and crushed it. "Olivia, what are you doing?"

"You'll only tell everyone you built this castle all by yourself when I did most of the work. I'm not letting you get all the credit for my masterpiece."

Joey smiled, relieved to know this cheeky girl was definitely the real Olivia. But then there was still something slightly different about her; he could definitely see a little bit of Astina. And in that moment, he realized that Astina was always Olivia. She was the part missing in Olivia's life. Budda was right in saying every earth-person needed a spirit guide. Astina was Olivia's spirit guide; without her, Olivia would not survive on Earth. Now he knew he would always have both of them in his life.

"Come on, let's go home," said Joey, and he gave his sister a big hug, and together they headed home.

The End